READ IT AND WEEP

Center Point
Large Print

Also by Jenn McKinlay and available from Center Point Large Print:

Library Lover's Mysteries
Books Can Be Deceiving
Due or Die

Hat Shop Mysteries
Cloche and Dagger

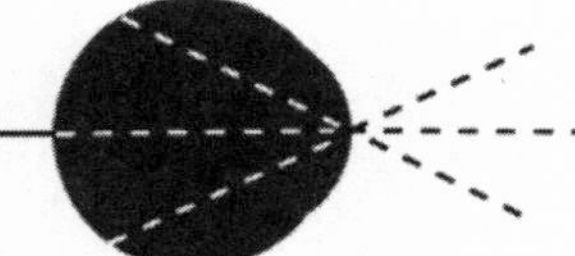

This Large Print Book carries the Seal of Approval of N.A.V.H.

READ IT AND WEEP

Jenn McKinlay

CENTER POINT LARGE PRINT
THORNDIKE, MAINE

This Center Point Large Print edition is published in the year 2014 by arrangement with The Berkley Publishing Group, a member of Penguin Group (USA) LLC, a Penguin Random House Company.

The text of this Large Print edition is unabridged.
In other aspects, this book may vary from the original edition.
Printed in the United States of America on permanent paper.
Set in 16-point Times New Roman type.

ISBN: 978-1-61173-960-2

Library of Congress Cataloging-in-Publication Data

McKinlay, Jenn.
Read It and Weep : A Library Lover's Mystery / Jenn McKinlay. — Center Point Large Print edition.
pages cm
ISBN 978-1-61173-960-2 (Library binding : alk. paper)
1. Libraries—Fiction. 2. Large type books. I. Title.
PS3612.A948R425 2014
813′.6—dc23

2013036165

For my pop, Donald K. McKinlay,
an artist who taught me by example to be
tenacious about my craft.
Thanks, Dad! Love you lots!

Acknowledgments

Knuckle bumps to my editor, Kate Seaver; her assistant, Katherine Pelz; and my agent, Jessica Faust. They make up the best team a writer could ever hope to have. Also, a special thank-you to my cover artist, Julia Green, whose gorgeous covers make me step up my writing game to make sure my words are worthy of her brilliance. Hopefully, I'm getting there.

As always, I have to give a shout-out to the Hub and the Hooligans, Chris, Wyatt and Beckett. Your patience, support and willingness to listen are invaluable and I can never thank you enough. I love you forever.

Finally, I have to thank my favorite librarian—my mom, Susan N. McKinlay, for instilling in me a love of books and reading. Second to loving me unconditionally, you gave me the greatest gift a child like me could ever have.

CHAPTER 1

Of course you're all going to audition for the play," Violet La Rue said. "It's the kickoff to our community theater season."

Lindsey Norris put down her scissors and glanced across the table at Violet. Violet's warm-brown eyes sparkled and her brown skin glowed. She was flushed with excitement for the upcoming production, which would be her directorial debut.

Lindsey knew it was going to dampen Violet's enthusiasm to learn that the rest of the crafternooners, with the exception of her daughter, Charlene La Rue, and the children's librarian, Beth Stanley, were not as enamored with being on stage as she was. Violet was a former Broadway actress, and her daughter was a local news anchor. They lived for being in front of an audience. As for Beth, she had been instilling the love of reading in children for ten years with her dynamic story times. She lit up in front of an audience. The rest of the crafternooners, well, it wasn't really their thing.

This theory was confirmed when Lindsey glanced around the table and noted that both Mary Murphy and Nancy Peyton had their heads down, completely engrossed with their card-making project.

The group had decided to get a jump on the holidays by making greeting cards. It was only September but judging by the mess Lindsey was making, she was going to need the next three months just to crank out a few decent cards.

The crafternooners met every Thursday at the Briar Creek Public Library, of which Lindsey was the director, to work on a craft while they discussed the latest book that they had read.

This week they were discussing *A Midsummer Night's Dream* by William Shakespeare. It wasn't their standard fare, but since Violet was directing the play in the Briar Creek Community Theater, they had all agreed to read it and give her their input as she was gearing up for auditions in the coming week.

"I think I have a crush on Puck. He's so charming. He carries the whole play," Beth Stanley said. Story time had just gotten out and she entered the room with a monkey puppet on one hand and wearing a banana suit.

It was no surprise that she liked Puck; with her diminutive stature and her black hair styled in a pixie cut, Beth reminded Lindsey of a sprite herself.

"Who in town would make a good Puck?" Nancy Peyton asked. Her blue eyes twinkled when her gaze met Lindsey's. "I'd offer up my nephew, Charlie, but he's too busy with the latest incarnation of his rock band."

Lindsey winced. Nancy wasn't kidding. Lindsey rented the third-floor apartment of Nancy's three-story captain's house, and her nephew, Charlie, lived on the floor between them. Usually, he only practiced once a week, but with the new band learning his material, practices had been more frequent, and both Lindsey and Nancy had taken to wearing earplugs while at home. The only one who didn't seem to mind the noise was Lindsey's dog, Heathcliff. As soon as he heard the bass beat of the drums, he began to wag and howl as if he were the lead singer.

"How about my brother, Sully?" Mary Murphy asked. She'd brought the food for today's crafternoon from her restaurant the Blue Anchor, so it was a feast of crab salad sandwiches and sweet tea. Lindsey turned and scowled at her. She knew Mary had been just looking for an opportunity to bring up Sully in the conversation. Lindsey had been dating Captain Mike Sullivan, known to his friends and family as Sully, up until a few months ago, when he'd decided to give her some space—space she had not requested. And so, they had spent the summer apart.

"Did you know the earliest reference to *A Midsummer Night's Dream* is from 1598?" she asked. "No one knows exactly when it was written."

"Nice segue . . . not," Charlene La Rue said. "Are you telling us you don't even want to picture Sully in tights?"

As soon as she said it, Lindsey's brain flashed on a mental picture of Sully in tights and tunic with a wreath of flowers on his mahogany curls. It did not help that the man had a sailor's muscular build and that tights on him would not be a hardship on the eyes.

"I am so not answering that question," she said, at which the others all laughed. When they quieted down, she couldn't help but ask, "How is he, anyway?"

"Pitiful," Mary said. "He worked like a dog all summer, almost as if he was trying to keep his mind off something or someone."

"Humph," Lindsey snorted. "Well, he wouldn't have had to if he hadn't dumped me just because he wrongly thought I still had feelings for my ex."

"Lindsey, I know I shouldn't butt in," Mary said. Her blue eyes, so like her brother Sully's, were full of anxiety. "But if you knew the things in Sully's past that make him—"

"No," Lindsey interrupted. "Don't tell me. If there is something Sully needs to share with me, he has to do it himself."

The crafternooners all made noises of agreement, but Mary looked as if she desperately wanted to say more. Lindsey shook her head.

"Don't worry," she said. "It's fine. I'm fine. Everything is fine."

"Fine? My experience with the fairer sex has proven that when a woman says she's fine, she is anything but," a male voice with a charming British accent said from the door.

The crafternooners all turned as one. Standing in the doorway was a man with reddish-blond hair, twinkling green eyes, a square jaw and a build that could easily carry off a pair of tights or anything else he wanted to dress it in.

"Robbie!" Violet leapt up from her seat and crossed the room to enfold the man in a warm embrace.

"Violet, my love," he said. "You're more beautiful than ever."

Charlene followed her mother and hugged the man, too.

Obviously he was a friend of the La Rue family. Beth, who was sitting beside Lindsey, nudged her arm repeatedly until Lindsey turned toward her.

"Do you know who that is?" she hissed.

"No, no idea."

"It's Robbie Vine," Nancy whispered from across the table. "The famous British actor."

"Oh my," Mary breathed.

Lindsey glanced at her friends. All three of them looked utterly starstruck. She glanced back at the man. He was incredibly handsome, and when he smiled at her, his mouth was bracketed by dimples that seemed to appear just for her, making it a very personal sort of smile.

He looked familiar, and then she remembered the movie she had just seen him in. There had been a shirtless scene that had been, for lack of a better word, revealing.

"Let me introduce you to my friends," Violet said and she tucked her hand around Robbie's elbow and brought him to the table. "Ladies, I'd like for you to meet—"

"Hello, Violet!" a voice interrupted her and they all turned to the door. "Oh, and Robbie's here, too. How perfect."

"Harvey?" Violet asked as if she couldn't believe what she was seeing. "Harvey Wargus?"

She looked down her elegant nose at the stubby little man who entered the room. His dark-brown hair was parted in the middle and flopped down over the sides of his head in a sag that was repeated by the brown mustache over his upper lip. He had a long torso and short legs and a large bottom, which added to his overall droopy appearance.

"Well, if I didn't know better, I'd think we were having a reunion," Robbie said. Then he turned and glared at the little man. "But of course I do know better because there is no way in hell you'd ever be invited to any reunion of ours."

“What are you doing here, Harvey?” Violet asked.

Lindsey glanced at the man. Now she remembered him. He had, at one time, been a theater critic in New York City. He’d been on staff at one of the larger entertainment papers when word got out that he was bribable, particularly by up-and-coming young actresses looking for some positive ink. His career was ruined when the boyfriend of a fourteen-year-old actress, who had been set up with Wargus by her very own mother, turned him in to the police.

Harvey pushed up his glasses with the ring finger of his right hand and fixed a perturbed gaze on Violet and Robbie.

“When I heard through the grapevine that Violet La Rue and Robbie Vine were teaming up again, I got myself assigned to review the show. I must say I am really looking forward to it.”

“Who on earth would hire a pervert like you?” Violet demanded.

“Oh, haven’t you heard?” he asked. “I’m working for Sterling Buchanan—you know, the multimedia mogul? I believe *you* know him quite well, Violet.”

Violet reared back as if he’d slapped her, and Charlene gasped. She took her mother’s hand in hers and squeezed it tight.

Beth looked confused, and asked, “Who is Sterling Buchanan?”

Violet closed her eyes, and Charlene and Robbie exchanged a glance over her head. He glared at Harvey and then gave Charlene a small nod.

"He's my father," Charlene said.

CHAPTER 2

Stunned silence greeted this announcement, and then Violet let out a sob and dashed from the room. Nancy hopped up from her seat immediately.

"You should be ashamed of yourself," she snapped at Harvey and then she kicked him in the shin. She dashed after Violet.

Harvey let out a yelp and began to hop on one foot while cradling his shin with the other.

"She kicked me!" he cried. "That's assault! I'm going to sue."

"Really?" Robbie asked. "It looked to me like she tripped when she tried to get around your big fat ar—"

"Agreed!" Charlene interrupted. "And if I were you, I'd leave before the rest of us trip over you as well."

She stomped her foot on the ground right in front of his toes, and Harvey scampered away from her.

"You can't intimidate me!" he cried right before he fled from the room, with the tail of his suit coat flapping behind him.

"What a baboon!" Mary Murphy cried, looking like she'd like to take her paper scissors to Harvey's unfortunate mustache.

"Now, don't be insulting our primate brethren," Beth said. "I think he's quite a bit lower on the food chain than them."

"You're right, what was I thinking?" Mary said. "Charlene, are you all right?"

"I'm fine," she said.

"Didn't we just have that conversation?" Robbie asked with a smile. "It's okay not to be fine, you know."

Charlene heaved a sigh and leaned against him as he wrapped an arm around her.

"You're right," she said. "I'm not fine. What the heck is my father thinking, turning Harvey loose on Mom like that?"

"Maybe you should ask him," Lindsey suggested.

"I would," Charlene said. "But I've never actually met him."

"Oh," Lindsey said. She felt like an idiot, but in her usual generous way, Charlene smiled at her friend and shook her head.

"No, don't feel bad, you couldn't have known," Charlene said.

"Still, I feel like a dork," Lindsey said. "I just can't imagine having a daughter as fabulous as you and never knowing you. It's tragic—for him."

"Thank you," Charlene said. "But I don't suppose you miss what you've never had."

"Well, then he's an even bigger moron than we supposed," Beth said.

"Isn't he like one of the richest men in the world?" Mary asked.

"I don't know," Charlene said. "I don't pay any attention to him."

"Well, I do," Robbie said. "The bastard is one of the top ten most disgustingly wealthy people in the world—if you count wealth only in a dollar sum. If, however, you count it by having a daughter who is as intelligent as she is beautiful, who has gorgeous children of her own and is one of the most respected news anchors in the country, well, then sadly, he is the poorest bugger I know because he never claimed such a prize as his own."

Charlene beamed at Robbie and hugged him tight. "And that is why I love you. You've always been the big brother I never had. I bet that's better than a father. Honestly, I think I traded up."

Robbie planted a kiss on Charlene's head. "It was a lucky day for me when your mum came to be a guest teacher at my acting school. You girls are my family."

Lindsey glanced at Mary and Beth. They looked as choked up as she felt, and she wondered if they should leave Robbie and Charlene alone to catch up.

Beth must have been thinking the same thing, because she half rose out of her seat and said, "I'll just go check on Violet."

"Me, too," Mary said.

"Me, three," Lindsey agreed.

"Was it something I said?" Robbie asked, and gave them his charmingly dimpled smile.

The three of them glanced at one another.

"We just thought you two might want to talk," Lindsey said.

"No, we're good." Charlene let go of Robbie and sat back down. She gestured for him to do the same. "Have something to eat."

"Don't mind if I do," he said, and tucked into the crab salad with gusto.

"Will Violet be okay?" Beth asked.

"Oh yeah," Charlene said. She grinned at Robbie. "She'll be fine. It's not the first time my dad has popped up in her life."

"So, he has tried to make contact with you?" Mary asked.

"Only after my career was on the rise," Charlene said. "I happened to take my first newscaster job at a station that he owned. I was there for a year before he figured it out, and that was only because I won an award for investigative journalism. When I got word that he wanted to set up a meeting with me, I quickly took another job at a station in another city, one that he didn't own. I haven't worked for any of his stations since."

"I'm trying not to be nosy," Mary said. "And I'm failing miserably. So I have to ask: Weren't you curious to meet him?"

"When I was younger, sure," Charlene said. "But by the time I finished college, I was so over it. You see, when Mom got pregnant with me, my father told her that his life plan did not include parenting. She was heartbroken, but she didn't want to tie him to a life he didn't want, so she chose to have me on her own. My mother is a remarkable woman."

"Here, here," Robbie agreed, causing them all to laugh.

"So, why do you suppose your father sent that toad here?" Lindsey asked. "It seems he must have an ulterior motive."

"I have no idea," Charlene said. "It could be that he doesn't know Harvey is reviewing Mom's show. There is some history there as well."

Mary, Lindsey and Beth gave her a horrified look.

"No, not that kind of history," Charlene said.

Robbie choked down a bite of salad. "Ugh, please, just the thought of Violet in a relationship with that wart puts me off my food."

"No, theirs is an old grudge from their Broadway days, which includes you as well, Robbie," Charlene said.

"Yes, Harvey has hated both Charlene and I since he trashed our show and then we both went on to win Tony Awards for it," he said. "It's as if he took it personally that we were good and he was wrong about the show. And they say actors are narcissists; I'd say critics are far worse."

"So you don't think your father sent Harvey?" Beth asked.

"I don't know. He's pretty high up to be concerned with what his minions are doing. Then again . . ."

"It does seem odd, doesn't it?" Lindsey asked.

"I'm going to check on my mom," Charlene said. "Come with me, Robbie?"

"Of course," he said. He polished off his food and gave the crafternooners a charming half bow. "The pleasure was mine, ladies."

Lindsey had to squash the urge to stand up and curtsey in return.

Mary, Beth and Lindsey watched as they left and then emitted a collective sigh of appreciation for the handsome and debonair Robbie Vine.

"I am *so* helping on that play," Mary said.

"I'm auditioning," Beth said.

"Count me in," Lindsey said. "Not for auditioning but anything else. If this Wargus fellow is as nasty as he seems, I have a feeling Violet is going to need all of us."

CHAPTER 3

Read it again, hon," Violet directed from in front of the stage. "And this time try it with a little less emotion."

Lindsey glanced up from where she and Nancy were meeting with the other people who had agreed to work backstage for the Briar Creek Community Theater's production of *A Midsummer Night's Dream*. Nancy was in charge, mostly because she could bribe people as needed with cookies.

Beth was on stage with Robbie Vine, and she was reading for the part of one of the faeries. She had really sunk her teeth into the part, and Robbie had his lips pressed together as if trying not to show his amusement.

"I think Beth might be better suited to finger plays," Nancy said fretfully.

"I think she's nervous because she is on stage with Robbie Vine," Lindsey said.

"Hmm," Nancy said. "Maybe you should go where she can see you and it will calm her down."

"On it," Lindsey said.

She went down the narrow aisle toward the

stage. The seats up front were empty, so she moved into one where she knew Beth could see her.

"From the top," Violet instructed.

Lindsey watched as Beth clutched the pages in her hand and nodded at Violet. Beth then glanced out at the audience and saw Lindsey, who gave her a thumbs-up signal. Beth gave her a small smile and then stiffened her spine. When Lindsey glanced back at the stage, she saw that Robbie was watching her.

She met his green gaze and then he gave her a slow wink that she had no doubt was meant to charm her. It probably would have worked if her heart wasn't completely out at sea with a handsome boat captain.

She didn't want to encourage Robbie so she gave him her best aloof look and turned her attention back to Beth. She heard Robbie chuckle in response but she didn't look at him to see if he was laughing at her or not.

Beth and Robbie read their scene; this time Beth reined in her overacting and nailed the part. Lindsey clapped when they were finished, and Beth flushed with pleasure.

As Lindsey walked up the aisle to return to the back of the theater, where the different crews were meeting, she was stopped by a diminutive woman with a curvy figure, which was accentuated by tight, low-cut clothes. She had a head of fiery red hair, a heavy hand with the eyeliner, and a very mean look on her face.

"Excuse me," Lindsey said as she turned sideways to navigate her way around the bombshell.

"Sure," the woman said. Instead, she moved in front of Lindsey, blocking her. "But here's a word to the wise: stay away from Robbie Vine."

Lindsey frowned. She was quite certain she didn't like the woman's tone. It had an underlying threat in it, which she found more than a little off-putting.

"I'm sorry?" she asked, thinking she must have misheard.

"He collects women like other boys collect trading cards," the woman said. "You may have caught his eye for the moment, but that's all it will be, a moment."

Lindsey opened her mouth to respond, but a voice from behind her spoke first. "Your claws are out again, Kitty."

Lindsey whipped around to find Robbie standing behind her. She felt her cheeks heat at the thought that he might have heard this woman speaking and think that she had any interest in him, which she didn't. She'd had her fill of difficult men for the time being and certainly had no intention of adding an actor to the short list of men who'd left her boggled and bewildered. No, she would much rather be single than be stepped on again, thank you very much.

"I'm just protecting what is mine," the woman said. She tossed her long, red hair over her shoulder and looked at him from beneath long, dark lashes.

"I haven't been yours for a very long time," Robbie said. "Our marriage has been over longer than it lasted."

His voice sounded weary, and Lindsey felt trapped in the middle of their uncomfortable conversation.

"And yet we're still not divorced," Kitty said.

Okay, now they were getting awkwardly personal. Lindsey started looking for an escape hatch or an ejector seat.

"Lindsey! There you are."

She glanced over Kitty's head to see Sully walking down the aisle toward her. Her heart gave a lurch at the sight of him. With his brawny sailor's build and thick head of mahogany curls, he was just as handsome as Lindsey remembered.

He stopped a few feet from their group and held out his hand to her. "Come on, Nancy is looking for you."

Lindsey didn't take his hand but she did latch onto the excuse to leave the awkward conversation.

"Excuse me," she said and stepped forward, forcing the woman to move aside. Lindsey moved around Sully as well, ignoring the way her arm tingled as she brushed past him.

"Until later, my dear," Robbie called after her.

Lindsey felt Sully's scrutiny as he fell into step beside her. She didn't turn to look at him; in fact, she studiously ignored him. What she did was none of his business, a fact that he'd made perfectly clear when he dumped her a few months earlier.

"So," he said. He was fishing, but Lindsey was not falling for it.

"What are you doing here?" she asked. She knew she sounded rude, but she could live with that.

"Oh, Nancy didn't tell you?" he asked. He looked amused. Lindsey was not.

"Tell me what?"

"I'm working on the set design crew," he said.

Lindsey stopped walking and turned to face him. "You're joking."

"Nope," he said. "Nancy said they had plenty of artsy types but that they were lacking muscle, so Ian and I agreed to help."

"You've never worked on the plays before, have you?"

"Nope, I'm a newbie," he said. His blue eyes studied her as if trying to gauge her reaction. "She made us butterscotch bars."

"So, you were bribed with cookies?" Lindsey asked. She tried not to smile and failed. She tipped her head down so he wouldn't see her amusement.

"You could say that," Sully admitted. "And I

heard there was going to be this really pretty girl working on the costumes, so I figured since I'm single . . ."

Lindsey's smile vanished. Who was working on costumes? She glanced over at the table with a narrowed gaze. The only other woman under the age of fifty working on wardrobe with her was Mary, who was not only Sully's sister but also Ian's wife. So it couldn't be her. Then it hit her that Sully might be talking about her.

She turned back to face him, trying to figure it out. He had a small smile playing on his lips and he gave her a small nod. She felt her eyes widen in surprise. He did mean her!

"I have to go check back in," she muttered and hurried over to her seat.

"How did it go?" Nancy asked as she slipped into her chair.

Lindsey blinked at her.

"With Beth?" Nancy asked. "Did she give a better reading with you there?"

"Oh . . . uh . . . yeah, it was great," Lindsey said.

Sully took the seat across the table from her, and Lindsey tried to pretend she didn't notice him. It was like trying to ignore an electromagnetic field. She could almost feel her hair standing on end due to his close proximity.

She shook her head, trying to shake off the feeling. She and Sully had run into each other a few times since they'd broken up—or more accurately, since he had broken up with her—and they'd always been very polite and courteous. Of course, they also hadn't lingered to talk to one another for very long.

She usually made sure to stay in motion when he came into the library so that she didn't have to do more than give him a cheery see-I'm-fine-since-you-dumped-me smile. Working with him on the play, however, was going to make it a little more difficult to avoid him, but she would just make sure she stayed busy.

"For the sets and the costumes, I want to go with a very pastoral look," Nancy said. "I talked to Violet, and together we sketched out a few of her ideas for the set and the costumes. Given that she has already blocked out the actors' movements, we need to make her vision work."

Nancy put several sketches on the table and turned them so that everyone could see. The sets looked to be convertible: when the scene changed from ancient Athens to a forest, the same structure would be there but the backdrop and smaller set pieces would change.

The forest set was definitely pastoral with loads of hanging vines and staircases that looked as if they were made of stone, while the costumes were mostly made of earth-tone fabrics with garlands of vines for the men and garlands of flowers for the women worked into the clothes.

"Impressive," Mary said. She turned and looked

at her husband. "What do you think? Can you manage that?"

"Of course I can," Ian said. He gestured between him and Sully. "With our brawn and your girls' sense of aesthetic, we'll build the best sets and costumes this theater has ever seen."

Lindsey couldn't help but grin at his confidence.

"Exactly," Nancy said. She looked delighted with her crew, and Lindsey noticed that she was glancing between Lindsey and Sully with a wicked twinkle in her eye.

She might have known. Butterscotch bars, her foot. Nancy was matchmaking and not even trying to be a little subtle about it. She glanced around the table and noted that Mary and Ian were looking pretty delighted as well. Great, it was a conspiracy.

She decided the best offense was going to have to be a solid defense.

"Fabulous," she said. "Since it's brawn versus aesthetics, how about we split up? Wardrobe can meet in one room while the set builders meet in another."

Lindsey glanced around the table to see Mary's, Ian's and Nancy's faces fall, while Sully gave her a blinding grin. It was as if he knew exactly what she was doing and he was amused by it.

"Whatever works for you," he said.

CHAPTER 4

Lindsey met Sully's glance and felt her insides go all fluttery. How did he do that with just a look?

"Oh, wow, is that the lemon?" Mary asked.

She was looking at the stage, and Lindsey dragged her gaze away to see Ms. Cole, one of her more dour employees, on stage. She had the script clutched in her hand and was standing with Milton Duffy, who was also reading for a part.

"I think they are reading for the parts of Oberon and Titania, the faerie king and queen," Ian said. "I could see Milton carrying it off with his Sean Connery good looks, but the lemon?"

Lindsey got an uncomfortable feeling in her belly. Ms. Cole, nicknamed "the lemon" by Beth because of her sour disposition, was an old-school librarian who believed in shushing and the prompt payment of fines.

Lindsey was pretty sure Ms. Cole would be delighted to use thumbscrews in order to encourage their patrons to pay their fines if Lindsey would only let her. As crazy as Ms. Cole made her, however, Lindsey really didn't want to see the woman humiliate herself. Lindsey had never been one to take joy in the misery of others.

She had never thought of Ms. Cole as a theater type, but then again, Ms. Cole kept to herself. Who knew what went on under her monochromatic clothing? Each day, she dressed in a variety of shades of one color. Today it was head-to-toe blue, from her navy shoes to her pale blue blouse. Until she met Ms. Cole, it had never occurred to Lindsey that not all shades of blue complement one another. On the upside, it was infinitely more cheerful than her usual all-gray or all-brown outfits.

"I didn't really think of Ms. Cole as one to get the acting bug," Nancy said. "She seems too buttoned down to cut loose into a character."

"From the top," Violet instructed.

Lindsey rose from her seat to watch the performance as did the others.

Milton read Oberon's lines in a deep and resonant voice. Without even looking at the pages in her hand, Ms. Cole spoke Titania's part. Her voice was clear and projected throughout the theater.

Lindsey stared in wonder. Ms. Cole, with her stout build and head full of gray sausage curls, was not how she would have envisioned the faerie queen, but her voice was musical as it wrapped around the bard's words, making them dance on the air and in the ears of the listeners.

Nancy and Mary were gaping at the stage as

well. Lindsey knew they were thinking the same thing she was: that if Ms. Cole lost the monochromatic clothes and wore a flowing gown with a wreath of flowers in her hair, um, perhaps with a wig of flowing hair, well, it was possible she'd make a lovely Titania.

"Is it just me?" Mary whispered in Lindsey's ear, "or is the lemon blowing the doors off of the place?"

"It's not you," Lindsey confirmed. "And if Violet is willing to cast an older Oberon and Titania, I think the two of them just nailed it."

When the reading was over, Violet thanked both Milton and Ms. Cole. Milton smiled and put his sheets on the edge of the stage for the next audition, but Ms. Cole strode to the front and center of the stage and gave a deep curtsey as if she were practicing for her curtain call on opening night. Lindsey couldn't help but smile.

Ms. Cole then handed in her script and strode up the aisle. As she passed by Lindsey and the others, Lindsey said, "That was excellent, Ms. Cole."

Ms. Cole inclined her head just a smidgen and kept walking. Lindsey sighed. After two years, Ms. Cole still just barely tolerated her.

"She actually slowed down," Sully said. "For her that's almost affection."

Lindsey chuckled and turned to find him grinning at her. "Thanks. I'll cling to that life raft."

"Do," he said.

He was standing closer than he'd been in months, and it was all Lindsey could do not to lean into him. She took a step back just in case the impulse overrode her common sense.

It wasn't that she was still mad at Sully for breaking up with her; okay, maybe she was a little mad. It was more self-preservation after the realization that the man was the original big, strong, silent type, which was lovely in the sense that he didn't talk her ears off, but it was annoying in that she had no idea what was going on inside of him because he didn't tell her.

She could be as book smart as all get out, but she wasn't a mind reader. And unless Sully started opening up and talking to her, any relationship between them was doomed because instead of telling her his feelings he just made decisions, like dumping her, which had blindsided her. She was not going to go through that again.

"Well, I'd better be going," she said. "Heathcliff will wonder what's become of me."

"I'll be happy to give you a ride," Sully offered.

"Thanks, but I have my bike," she said. She turned back to Mary and Nancy, and said, "So, I'm assuming we wait for the cast to be announced, because we can't make the costumes until we have the proper measurements."

"All except for me," a voice said from behind her.

Lindsey turned to find Robbie Vine there.

"That's right," Lindsey said. "You're Violet's special guest brought in specifically to play Puck."

He gave her a slight bow. Then he held out his arm and said, "Come on. I'll walk you out and we can discuss your vision for my character's wardrobe."

"What does 'the merry wanderer of the night' wear?" Lindsey asked. She didn't take his arm, so Robbie simply took her hand in his and put it through his elbow himself.

"The possibilities are endless," he said as he led her from the room. "What do you think of deep-purple velvet?"

Lindsey glanced over her shoulder and waved to the group. She could feel Sully's eyes burning on her face but she didn't have the courage to meet his gaze.

"Velvet?" she asked. "Wouldn't that be hot under the lights?"

"True," he agreed. "I suppose I could be naked."

He was pushing through the main doors to the theater's patio when he said this, and he turned to give her a lascivious grin. Lindsey couldn't help but laugh. For certain, Robbie Vine was the perfect Puck.

"You're joking," she said.

"Sadly, yes. So, tell me, fair librarian," he said. "Why didn't you audition?"

Lindsey dropped her hand from his arm and fished through her purse for the key to her bike lock. She took the lock off and put it and her bag into the basket on the back.

"I'm a watcher," she said.

"But with that glorious head of blonde hair and that striking profile, you'd be amazing on the stage," he said.

"Not if I can't act," she said. "Which I can't."

"Have you ever tried?" he asked.

"No," she said.

"Give me a sad face," he said. "A face that speaks of love lost and a heart yearning."

"I can't," Lindsey said, and as if to prove it, she giggled.

Robbie grinned. "Yes, you can. Think of having your heart broken and let your face reflect your inner pain."

Lindsey knew he wouldn't stop badgering her until she tried, so she thought about having her heart broken not once but twice over the past few years and then she turned her face to Robbie.

He studied her with one eyebrow raised.

"I said to look sad, love, not like you're going to bury an axe in some poor bugger's back."

Lindsey grinned and then tried one more time for sad. Robbie looked alarmed.

"Are you quite all right?" he asked. "You look as if you have severe indigestion or possibly appendicitis."

"Oh, you, I told you I couldn't do it." Lindsey laughed and swatted his shoulder. He caught her hand in his and tugged her close.

"Well, if you are a watcher, I'm delighted that you'll be watching me," he said.

Robbie was standing just inches away from her, and she felt his green eyes on her, absorbing every detail as if she was the most fascinating person he'd ever met.

The doors to the theater opened and out stepped Ian, Mary and Sully. The three of them paused to take in the sight of Lindsey and Robbie. Lindsey felt a ridiculous flash of guilt, and she quickly stepped away from Robbie and pulled her bike out of the rack.

"Good night, Robbie."

"Good night, fair Lindsey." Then he raised his voice, and she knew his words were for the benefit of the others when he said, "Remember, 'The course of true love never did run smooth.' "

Lindsey shook her head at him. As she climbed on her bike and pushed off the sidewalk, she said, "I think you'd better go rehearse your part, because that is Lysander's line."

Robbie looked surprised and then busted out a delighted laugh as she pedaled away. She glanced back quickly to see him grinning and Sully frowning. She heaved a sigh as she turned onto the main road, which led to her house. One thing that could not be argued—the bard sure knew what he was talking about when it came to the rough-and-tumble path of true love.

The next day, Lindsey noted that the town was abuzz with audition anxiety. Since Lindsey had moved to town two years before, she had attended many of the Briar Creek Community Theater productions. There was a high standard, no question, mostly because Violet La Rue was involved, usually in the starring role.

This season, however, it appeared that everyone from the clerk at the local bakery to the mailman to the pages who shelved books in the library had auditioned. Lindsey had no doubt that the motivating factor was the chance to be on stage with Robbie Vine.

"I bombed," Heather moaned. She was lying on the old beat-up sofa in the staff lounge, consoling herself with a Snickers and a can of Mountain Dew.

"No, you were good," Perry assured her. "I mean Dylan was the best, but he always is."

"Argh." Heather bit into her candy bar like it was Dylan's head.

"Where is Dylan?" Lindsey asked. Perry, Heather and Dylan were her library pages, and they spent their afternoons shelving books and helping out in the library as needed.

"He was going to stop by the theater," Perry said.

"The suck-up," Heather grumbled.

Perry rolled his eyes at Lindsey, and she had to press her lips together to keep from smiling.

"He said he wouldn't be more than a few minutes late," Perry said.

Lindsey glanced at the clock. The pages didn't start their shift until four, so they had ten more minutes to decompress from school.

"When you start, I believe Ms. Cole has several trucks for you to shelve," Lindsey said. "And then I was hoping you'd help me put together a display of materials by and about Shakespeare. Perry, could you work up a flyer for me, since you're so good at graphic design?"

"Don't we have a mini bust of good old Shakespeare back in storage?" Heather asked. "I think I saw it when we were storing the summer reading materials."

"If you can find it, that would be excellent," Lindsey said. "Thank you, Heather."

"Sure." The girl sighed.

"And, Heather, for what it's worth, I saw your audition last night and I thought you were terrific," Lindsey said.

"Really?"

"Really."

"Thanks, Ms. Norris," Heather said and she bounced up from the couch, looking infinitely cheered.

"How come she didn't believe me when I said that?" Perry asked Lindsey.

"Because she's a librarian," Heather answered for Lindsey as she headed out the break room door. "She knows what she's talking about."

"Oh, and I don't?" he asked, following behind her.

Lindsey watched them go in bemusement. Had she ever been that young or that mercurial in temperament? No. She was an old soul and had pretty much sailed on an even keel her whole life. Her brother Jack was the roller coaster of the family. He lived life on the edge and liked it that way, whereas Lindsey was happier to hear about his exploits but had no desire to live them.

She figured as soon as Violet posted the cast list on the theater doors, the town would calm down and things would return to normal. She found she was looking forward to it.

Lindsey left the break room and was headed into her office when she saw Ms. Cole talking with Milton Duffy. They were standing off in the DVD area, talking in low voices. Not that Lindsey was trying to hear what they were saying, but she took a detour through the new books area just to see if the displays were full.

Drat. They were, which meant that there really was no need for her to linger.

Ann Marie, one of their part-time employees, was behind the circulation desk, and Lindsey went over to say hello. Ann Marie was checking in a stack of books but she, too, kept glancing at Ms.

Cole and Milton, as if trying to make sense of what she was seeing.

When she saw Lindsey, she smiled. "In all of the years I've been working here, which is three, Ms. Cole has never—and I do mean never—left the circulation desk to go be social."

"I know," Lindsey said. "It's alarming."

"Phew, I thought it was just me," Ann Marie said. "But it's kind of freaking me out."

Lindsey laughed. "Agreed. I had no idea how accustomed I'd become to the reliability of Ms. Cole. Then again, maybe she's trying to badger a fine out of Milton."

"He doesn't have any fines," Ann Marie said. When Lindsey looked at her, she shrugged and said, "I checked."

"Weird," Lindsey said.

"What's weird?" a voice asked from behind her, and Lindsey turned around to see Beth dressed in glittery wings with a garland of flowers on her head.

"Don't tell me, let me guess," Lindsey said. "You're supposed to be Mustardseed."

"Peaseblossom, actually," Beth said.

"Ah, my mistake," Lindsey said.

"Did Violet post the parts yet?" Ann Marie asked.

"Not yet," Beth said with a frown. "I am dying of anxiety."

"Good thing faeries are immortal then," Lindsey said.

"Miss Library, why are you dressed that way?" a young girl named Casey, who was a regular attendee of Beth's family story time, asked Beth.

"I am trying out costumes in case I get picked to be in a play," Beth said.

"Are you a princess?" Casey asked.

"No, I'm a faerie," Beth said.

"A faerie princess?" Casey persisted.

"No, a faerie servant to the faerie queen," Beth answered.

Casey frowned. "I'd rather be the queen. Do you have any books about queens?"

"Real queens or make-believe?" Beth asked.

"Real," Casey said. "Because when I grow up I'm going to be a real queen."

"Follow me," Beth said. "We can start with Cleopatra and work our way through history to Queen Elizabeth, who has the same name as me."

"Elizabeth is a good name for a queen," Casey said. "You should be a queen and not a faerie."

Lindsey and Ann Marie watched them walk toward the children's area where Casey's mother stood, holding a baby.

"Why is a queen better than a faerie?" Beth asked.

"Please." Casey gave her an exasperated look. "More power."

Both Lindsey and Ann Marie ducked their heads so that Casey didn't see them laughing.

"Out of the mouths of babes," Ann Marie said.

“No doubt,” Lindsey agreed.

“So, is it true what I heard about Robbie Vine?” Ann Marie asked.

“That depends. What did you hear?”

“Well, aside from the fact that he’s a perfect male specimen, is it true that both his wife, Kitty, and his girlfriend, Lola, are here to perform in the show and that they are all renting a beach house together?”

“Violet did say something to that effect, yes. She’s hoping that the three of them can anchor the show and coach our amateur actors and actresses to a bit higher caliber, given that it’s the bard and all. I met Kitty; she’s fairly terrifying. I saw Lola in the theater yesterday but only from a distance.”

“How does a man juggle a wife and a girlfriend?” Ann Marie asked.

“From what I heard him say, his marriage is over,” Lindsey said. “And when Nancy pointed out Lola to me, she said that she’d heard that they had broken up. Whatever that means.

“Actors are different, aren’t they?”

“Yes. Yes, they are,” Lindsey agreed. “I’m going to be in my office if anyone is looking for me.”

“Would anyone include tall, fair-haired and dreamy?” Ann Marie asked.

Lindsey glanced up to see Ann Marie looking past her at the door. Lindsey turned just in time to see Robbie Vine stroll into the building.

CHAPTER 5

Deep dimples bracketed his perfect smile as soon as Robbie spotted her, and Lindsey couldn't help but smile in return. She heard Ann Marie gulp, and turned to see that the pretty brunette was staring openmouthed at Robbie.

"Oh, why did I wear this frumpy old outfit?" Ann Marie wailed. "I look like I should be scrubbing the toilets."

Lindsey glanced at her. In her khaki capris and powder-blue, collared blouse with the sleeves rolled up to her elbows, Ann Marie looked perfectly poised and professional. She'd been growing out her short hair, and it was now a nice, medium length.

"You do not," Lindsey said. "You look fantastic, really."

"You're just saying that," Ann Marie protested.

"Just saying what?" Robbie asked as he joined them. "How much you missed me?"

Lindsey rolled her eyes. "How long does it take for you to catch up to your ego when it enters a room?"

Robbie laughed. "I'll let you know when I've arrived."

Lindsey shook her head but couldn't help grinning. Even if he was completely self-involved, at least he could joke about it.

"And who is this lovely lady?" he asked as he smiled at Ann Marie.

"This is Ann Marie," Lindsey said. "She works here part-time. Ann Marie, this is Robbie Vine."

"H . . . H . . . Hi," Ann Marie panted. Then she turned and ran into the workroom.

Robbie looked at Lindsey. "Something I said?"

"She's got a condition," Lindsey said. "Something you would never be afflicted with."

"What's that?" Robbie asked. He rested his elbow on the counter and leaned against it, making himself comfortable.

"She's shy."

"Ah," he nodded his head, looking grave. "I've heard stories of that affliction. Quite terrifying."

"Hmm," Lindsey murmured. "So, what brings you to our humble little library?"

"I'm trying to acquaint myself with the local hangouts," he said. "Violet told me that the library was a popular one. Of course, when I realized that's where I'd find you, I needed no further urging to come and visit."

"Are you flattering me for a reason?" Lindsey asked.

"Yes, I find you interesting," he said.

"Interesting?"

"I didn't want to offend your smart sensibilities by telling you I found you attractive," he said. "Although, I do—very much."

Lindsey felt her face heat up. Good grief! If Sully was emotionally standoffish, than Robbie was his complete and polar opposite. Was there no middle ground? She wasn't sure she was capable of dealing with either of them.

"Is that the only reason you're here?" she asked. She was hoping he needed a book, some reader's advisory or had a reference question she could manage that would put her back into her comfort zone.

"No, I did have one other errand," he said. He raised his voice, not in a shout, but in a stage voice that resonated into every corner of the library. "I wanted to let you know that Violet has posted the cast list."

There was a squeal from the children's area as Beth and Heather clutched each other's hands and jumped up and down.

"This is it!" Beth cried. "Let's go find out if we're in."

"But we can't leave," Heather protested.

"Lindsey, we're taking our break!" Beth shouted across the room. She and Heather bolted for the door before Lindsey even had a chance to nod her approval.

"Wait for me," Perry said. Then he glanced at

Lindsey and added, "I'd better go for moral support—you know, if Heather doesn't get in, she might need consoling."

He, too, dashed out the automatic sliding doors before Lindsey could say a word. She glanced over to where Milton and Ms. Cole had been standing. He was whispering to her, but she was shaking her head.

Lindsey had no doubt that he was encouraging her to go and check the list, but Lindsey knew that, short of a fire, Ms. Cole would never leave the library during her shift, and even then it would be under duress.

"Go, Ms. Cole," she said.

The lemon looked at her and then opened her mouth to speak. Lindsey had no doubt that it would be to tell her that Lindsey's predecessor, Mr. Tupper, never let staff run out of the building in mid-shift. Lindsey decided to cut her off.

"I said, go. This is not negotiable," Lindsey ordered, and nodded her head in the direction of the door.

Ms. Cole gave her a brisk nod and hurried out of the building with Milton beside her.

Lindsey glanced around at her small library. It was practically empty, as many of the patrons had bolted out the door in the wake of Robbie's announcement.

"Well, you certainly know how to clear a room," she said. "I'll give you that."

Robbie gave her an alarmed look and asked, "Do you think this bodes ill for my career?"

He looked so genuinely concerned that Lindsey put her hand on his arm and said, "No, I was just joking."

He glanced down at her hand on his arm and back up. Then he grinned.

"Oh, you are a trickster," she said and took her hand away.

"Of course, I am," he agreed. "I'm Puck."

He assumed a dramatic pose and then bowed.

"And I'm your understudy," a voice said from behind Lindsey. She turned to see her other library page, Dylan Peet, standing behind her looking at Robbie with awestruck wonder.

"Dylan, you're in the show?" Lindsey asked. "That's wonderful."

"I'm playing First Faerie," he said. "Ms. La Rue said that I'm to study the part of Puck, too, in case Mr. Vine is unable to perform."

Robbie looked his understudy up and down with one eyebrow raised. They were nearly the same height; Robbie had an inch or two on the youth. They had the same fair coloring and green eyes, but where Robbie's hair was a reddish-blond, Dylan's was more of a deep auburn.

Robbie walked slowly around the young man as if examining him from every angle. Lindsey suspected he was doing it to test the boy's nerves. Finally, Robbie stopped in front of Dylan.

"I think you'll do nicely," Robbie said. He held out his hand and they shook. "We can run lines together, if you like."

"It would be an honor, sir," Dylan said, looking like he might faint.

"Dylan, why don't you get a drink of water?" Lindsey suggested. "Then I'm going to need you to start the shelving, as we're running behind."

"On it," Dylan said with a grin that rivaled Robbie's in charm.

As he went into the back room, Lindsey turned back to Robbie. "Don't corrupt him."

"Me?" Robbie clapped a hand to his chest as if he were mortally wounded.

"Yes, you," Lindsey said. "I know your type."

"Oh, really?" he asked. "And what type is that?"

He resumed his position against the counter and looked as if he was planning to stay awhile. Much as Lindsey enjoyed bantering with him, she really needed to get back to work. She had a weekly report to write, and there was a presentation she had to pull together for the library board.

"We did it!" Beth yelled as she danced back into the library.

"Shh!" Lindsey and Robbie said together. Then they ruined it by looking at one another and laughing.

"Peasebottom at your service," Beth said.

"Mustardseed reporting for duty," Heather announced.

“Congratulations,” Lindsey said.

“Come on, I’ve got outfit ideas,” Beth said, and she grabbed Heather by the hand and dragged her into the children’s section.

Perry came in after them, looking dejected.

“So, no comforting hugs to give?” Robbie asked him.

Perry shook his head. “Sad girls are clingy; happy girls just grab you, squeeze the breath out of you and then run off. Oh, and I’m in the play, too. I’m Moth, one of the faerie servants. What sort of name is that?”

“Chin up,” Robbie said. “You and your lady friend are two of the faeries; you can run lines together.”

“Really?” he asked.

Robbie nodded and Perry looked infinitely cheered. Then his face darkened. “Wait. Am I going to have to wear tights?”

Both Lindsey and Robbie laughed at his horrified expression.

“You’ll manage it,” Robbie said. “Some girls find them very attractive.”

Perry didn’t look like he believed him.

“Dylan could use your help in back,” Lindsey said.

“Fine,” Perry said, and he marched glumly past them.

The doors opened again and Ms. Cole entered. She looked utterly composed; Lindsey couldn’t tell if they were about to have a lemon breakdown or not.

Ms. Cole walked passed Lindsey and Robbie and assumed her usual post at the circulation desk. She slipped her reading glasses onto her nose and began checking in the stack of books that had been abandoned by Ann Marie. Lindsey glanced at Robbie, and he shrugged.

"Do you have anything you want to share, Ms. Cole?" Lindsey asked.

"No."

"Do you need some time to compose yourself?" Lindsey persisted.

Given the severity of Ms. Cole's demeanor, Lindsey was afraid the woman hadn't gotten the part and would be even more difficult to work with than usual. The thought made her shudder.

"Why on earth would I need that?" Ms. Cole snapped.

Lindsey blinked and then turned to Robbie, hoping he could offer some comforting words of encouragement. But no, the big wuss was backing up toward the door.

"Where are you going?" she asked.

"I have a . . . thing," he said.

"For an actor, you are a terrible liar."

Robbie shrugged and continued to slide toward the door. Lindsey glared at him and he made his right hand into the shape of a phone with middle fingers folded and his thumb and pinky out.

"I'll call you," he whispered.

"Chicken!" she hissed after him.

"Bock, bock," he clucked as he walked away with his knees bent, flapping his arms as he left the building.

Lindsey squashed her laugh. She needed to think about her staff. Poor Ms. Cole. Not getting the part had to be a crushing blow for the woman, who as far as Lindsey could tell, had virtually no life outside of her job at the library.

"Listen, Ms. Cole," Lindsey said as she came around the counter to stand beside her. "You are an exemplary employee when it comes to never taking a moment for yourself, which is why if you're feeling a little emotional, I completely understand if you want to take some time to regroup."

Ms. Cole turned from the stack of books she was checking in to face Lindsey. She carefully removed her glasses and let them hang on the chain from her neck while she met her boss's concerned gaze.

"I'm going to need some time off," she said.

"Of course, anything you need," Lindsey said.

"I'll need the week that the play is running," Ms. Cole said. "I will simply be too exhausted playing Titania to come into work that week."

"Ah!" Lindsey gasped. "You got it? You got the part?"

Ms. Cole bowed her head in acknowledgment.

“That’s wonderful,” Lindsey cried. Anyone else she would have hugged, but Ms. Cole was not a hugger, so Lindsey held up her hand, and said, “High five.”

Ms. Cole frowned at her.

“That’s when you slap your hand with mine,” Lindsey said.

“Why?” Ms. Cole asked.

“It’s a theater thing,” Lindsey lied. “It means, ‘Yay you.’ ”

“Oh.” Ms. Cole patted her hand against Lindsey’s.

It was quite possibly the single most awkward exchange of high fives in the history of the high five. Lindsey wasn’t sure what to do with her hand afterward, so she crossed her arms over her chest in what she hoped looked like a casual pose.

“I’ll just go make a note of your vacation days.”

“Do.” Ms. Cole turned back to her stack of books, and Lindsey made a mental note never to attempt a high five with the lemon again.

CHAPTER 6

Lindsey had to admit there was a certain tangible energy in the theater. She didn't know if it was Robbie or Violet or the cast and crew combined that made the auditorium crackle with electricity, but there was no denying the fact that there was a buzz in the air.

She had Beth, Dylan, Perry and Heather lined up in front of her while she and Nancy took their measurements. Lindsey wasn't much use with a needle, but she could accessorize the heck out of any outfit.

"Nothing too girly," Perry was saying.

"You're wearing tights," Nancy said as she measured him around the waist. "And if you give me a hard time, I'll make them hot pink."

Perry blanched, and the others laughed.

"It could be worse," Lindsey said. "If you'd been cast as Nick Bottom, you'd have to wear a donkey's head."

"That'd be okay with me," Dylan said. "He has a really cool part."

Nancy frowned at him and put her hand on his forehead. Then she made a *tsk*ing noise.

"What?" Dylan asked.

“You’ve got it bad,” she said.

“Is he getting sick?” Heather asked as she stepped away from him.

“No, he’s just got the bug,” Nancy said. “The acting bug.”

Dylan grinned at her. “I do, don’t I?”

She nodded.

“I can’t help it,” he said. “When I step on that stage, I just feel alive.”

Lindsey studied the handsome teen’s face. He looked as if someone had plugged him in.

“Faeries!” Violet called from the stage. “Front and center!”

The four of them hurried down the aisle, and Nancy looked at Lindsey and said, “About that donkey head . . .”

“Yeah?” Lindsey asked.

“You have any idea on how we’re going to pull that one off?”

“Papier-mâché?” Lindsey suggested.

Nancy slapped her on the back, which pitched Lindsey forward a few feet.

“Thanks so much for volunteering to be in charge of it,” Nancy said. “You might ask Ian if he has any of the supplies you’ll need to make it.”

Before Lindsey could rally a protest, Nancy was striding off in the direction of Milton and Ms. Cole.

“Oberon and Titania, I need your measurements!”

Lindsey glanced at Mary, who was sitting in the back row with a sketch pad, doodling ideas for character costumes.

Mary looked at her and raised both of her hands as if she was a scale.

“Measure Ms. Cole,” she said, and lowered her right hand. “Or make a papier-mâché donkey head.” Then she lowered her left hand.

Lindsey frowned and turned and went in search of Ian. Surely making a donkey head could not be that difficult. The back of the theater opened up into a large loading dock.

It was here that she found Ian and his set crew sawing wood and banging together a wooden shell that she assumed was going to be the two-level set with stairs and a cave from Nancy’s sketch.

Lindsey saw Sully hammering the steps into place and quickly looked away. She hadn’t spoken to him since the awkward evening outside the theater when he had found her talking to Robbie. She had avoided him ever since. Not because she felt guilty, she assured herself, but because she didn’t want to see any concern in his eyes—which was unwarranted, but would make her feel guilty nonetheless.

She wanted to tell him that he didn’t need to worry about her and Robbie, but given that Sully had offered her nothing but friendship, it seemed presumptive on her part to say anything. Amiable breakups were not nearly as easy to navigate as hostile ones. Sometimes it was just easier to hate your ex, but she didn't hate Sully. Far from it.

"Lindsey! Hello, earth to Lindsey."

She turned her head to find Ian standing beside her. Oh, no, how long had he been there? Had she really been staring at Sully like a lovesick twelve-year-old?

"The set is really coming along," she said, hoping he'd think she'd been scrutinizing their progress.

"Yeah, I have a solid crew," Ian said. "Especially that fine young man working on the steps there."

He had a twinkle in his eye when he pointed to Sully, which Lindsey chose to ignore.

"So, what do you know about papier-mâché?"

"For the set?"

"No, for a donkey's head."

"Hey, now, I know you're sore at Sully and all—" he began but Lindsey interrupted with a laugh.

"No, it's for the character Nick Bottom. You know, the one that Puck sees in the forest and gives the head of a donkey," she said. Then she grinned. "If it was for Sully, I wouldn't be making the front end, if you get my drift."

Ian busted up with a laugh of his own and Lindsey joined in. At least she could joke about it. When Sully appeared on her other side, Ian took one look at his friend and laughed harder. Lindsey, on the other hand, felt bad and abruptly grew serious.

"You okay, Ian?" Sully asked.

Ian nodded, and visibly tried to pull himself together. "Could you show Lindsey the supply closet?" A snort escaped as he added, "She has to work on an ass."

Sully frowned and looked at Lindsey.

"I need to make a papier-mâché donkey head," she said.

"Ah." Sully nodded. He sent his friend one more concerned look and said, "Follow me."

The supply closet was tucked into a corner backstage. Sully opened the door and yanked on a string hanging from the ceiling. A single lightbulb lit the enormous walk-in closet and Lindsey's eyes went wide at all of the stuff crammed onto the shelves.

Half-empty paint cans, drop cloths, miscellaneous props, ladders, rolls of chicken wire and bags of plaster filled the space, with no rhyme or reason. The closet was just begging to be sorted, and Lindsey's inner librarian clamored to be let loose.

"Whatever you need, should be in here—somewhere," Sully's voice trailed off doubtfully.

"Thank you." They were standing side by side in the tiny room, which seemed to shrink the more aware Lindsey became of Sully. She would have taken a step away from him, but there was no place to go.

"So, uh, holler if you need anything," he said.

He ran a hand through his hair, leaving finger trails in the thick, mahogany curls. He looked as if he wanted to say something but thought better of it.

He left the room and headed back toward the loading dock. Lindsey stood in the doorway and watched him go, feeling forlorn.

"So, it's the boat captain," a voice said from behind her.

She turned to see Robbie standing behind her, watching Sully walk away. He took a long drink out of the water bottle in his hand.

"I don't know what you mean," she said. She turned back to the closet, feeling the heat of embarrassment warm her face.

"You have a thing for the boat captain," Robbie said. He followed her into the closet. "That's why you're so resistant to my charm."

Lindsey said nothing, but began to dig through the shelves for supplies. This did not deter Robbie, who kept talking as if their conversation was still going.

"I can't say that I blame you," he said. "He really is a handsome lunk, but he doesn't say very much, does he?"

"He doesn't have to," Lindsey said. She could have kicked herself. Now it sounded like she was agreeing with him.

"Oy, so I'm right!" Robbie said. "Still, he doesn't have my accent or my celebrity aura . . ."

"Or your wife," Lindsey added. She found a small roll of chicken wire and put it aside.

"Kitty?" he asked. "We haven't been husband and wife, except on paper, for years."

"Which would explain why your girlfriend is here, too," Lindsey said.

"You've been researching me," Robbie said. He grinned at her as if pleased. "That means you're interested."

"No, it doesn't," Lindsey said. "It means you have a lot of fans in town who want to know about you, and as the librarian, I get to do their research for them."

"Well, your research is out of date," Robbie said. "My girlfriend and I broke up ages ago."

"And yet she's playing Hermia, while your wife plays Helena. Given Shakespeare's love triangle between Hermia and Lysander and Demetrius, which is then complicated by Helena, wouldn't it make more sense for you to play Lysander or Demetrius?" she asked.

"But I'm such a Robin Goodfellow," he said.

"And you all get along while doing the show?" Lindsey asked.

"Of course; we're professionals," he said. He took another long sip off of his water bottle, and Lindsey noticed it was a special brand of coconut water. So Hollywood.

"Robbie!" Violet's voice called from the stage. "We need you!"

"Sorry, love," he said. "Duty calls, but we can finish this discussion later."

Lindsey shook her head. She loved how he didn't phrase it in the form of a question. Before she could call him on it, he was gone.

She continued searching the shelves and had put aside a good amount of materials for the donkey's head mask when she heard raised voices outside of the closet.

It did not sound as if it were a part of the play. In fact, it had all the intensity of an argument, and she hesitated to leave the storage room and walk into the middle of an awkward situation.

She cleared her throat, hoping that whoever was out there would hear her. No such luck. Their voices were even louder now, drowning out any attempt she made to be heard.

"You just couldn't keep your hands off of her, could you?" a voice hissed. It was a man's voice and Lindsey tried to place it—not that she was eavesdropping, she told herself. She was trapped in a closet. It wasn't her fault if they chose to argue beside it.

"I never touched your wife, you nutter."

Lindsey recognized this voice as belonging to Robbie. The accent sort of gave him away.

"Oh, really?" the voice asked. "Then why has she been coming home late from the Blue Anchor every night, reeking of a man's cologne?"

"I really couldn't say, Brian," Robbie said,

sounding sympathetic. "Perhaps you should ask her."

Brian. Lindsey realized the man accusing Robbie of cheating with his wife was Brian Loeb, the man, ironically, cast as Nick Bottom, whom she was making the donkey's head for.

"I don't need to ask her," Brian said. "Ever since you arrived in town, all she ever talks about is Robbie Vine this and Robbie Vine that. She's obsessed with you."

Robbie chuckled, which Lindsey did not think was his best move at this juncture. And she was right.

"Don't you dare laugh at me!" Brian snapped. "I know you're having an affair with Brandy and when I can prove it, I am going to crush you like a little bug right under my shoe."

"Oh, are you now?" Robbie asked. Now he sounded mad.

If he was innocent of cheating, Lindsey couldn't really blame him. She tried to picture what Brian's wife looked like but could not place her. The Loebs weren't library users as a rule, so she'd only just met Brian when play rehearsals began. If his wife was hanging out at the Blue Anchor, however, Lindsey was sure Mary or Ian could describe her.

"Now, let me be clear," Robbie said. "When you realize it is not me who is frolicking in the daisies with your wife, I'm going to demand an apology."

"Pah!" Brian scoffed. "I'm not some stupid female who is going to fall for your charm. When I catch you with my wife, I'm going to—"

"What?" Robbie taunted him. "You're going to what?"

"Kill you," Brian hissed.

If he had shouted the words, it would have been less scary, but his quiet assuredness made the hair on Lindsey's neck stand up. She had no doubt he meant what he said.

CHAPTER 7

A crash sounded from backstage, and Lindsey jumped out of the closet to make sure Brian hadn't done anything so stupid as to harm Robbie.

She saw a door slam at the end of the stage and a curtain swirled nearby. The men appeared to have stormed off, for which she was grateful, given that she didn't want to face either of them.

Sully was standing near the closet, looking at a piece of set that appeared to have toppled over.

"Oops," he said.

"Breaking up some tension?" she asked.

He shrugged.

"So," he said.

"So," she replied.

They were both quiet. Sully looked like he wanted to say something, but naturally he didn't. Lindsey refused to be the one who breached the chasm between them. As far as she was concerned, he had done the breaking up, so it was his responsibility to do the making up.

"Did you find what you need?"

"I did." Awkward would be an understatement for the tension between them. Lindsey gestured to the piece of scenery, "Need a hand?"

"That would be great. Thanks," he said.

They moved so they were on opposite sides of the canvas framed on the wood. Together they hefted it up and propped it against the wall. Lindsey wiped her hands on her jeans.

"Lindsey, listen," Sully said.

She glanced at him and felt her chest tighten. Was he finally going to admit that breaking up was a bad idea? What should she do if he did? She wanted to throw herself at him, but figured it would be better to try to keep cool at least a little. It was really hard, though, with his brilliant-blue eyes looking at her as if . . . as if . . . hmm. As if he was about to say something she wasn't going to like.

"What is it?" she asked.

"You should probably steer clear of Robbie Vine," he said.

"And why's that?" she asked. Even to her own ears, her voice sounded so frosty she was surprised snowflakes didn't fly out of her mouth when she spoke.

"He's married, for starters," Sully said.

"I know."

"And he has a girlfriend," Sully continued.

"I know that, too."

"And you're okay with that?" He looked as outraged as if she'd just taken up spitting in public.

"I don't think it's any of my business," she said. "Or yours either, for that matter."

Sully clapped both of his hands to his head as if he was trying to keep his hair on. In all the time Lindsey had known him, she'd never seen him lose his cool. She realized it was sort of nice to see the Captain feeling an excess of emotion.

"Was that all?" she asked.

He goggled at her as if he couldn't believe his ears.

"Yes," he said.

"I'll see you around then." She turned and headed back into the closet to retrieve her materials.

"No, wait!" His voice was reluctant as if the words were being forced out of him at gunpoint.

"Yes?"

"I really think you shouldn't get involved with him, Lindsey," he said.

She wasn't sure what made her do it. Maybe it was just a frustrated need to get through his thick emotional skin. But she turned and stepped toward him until they were just inches apart.

She raised one eyebrow in what she hoped was a challenging expression and asked, “Why not?”

Sully seemed rendered speechless by her nearness, and she took a certain amount of comfort in knowing that he felt the attraction snapping between them just as strongly as she did.

Lindsey stared at the handsome face so close to hers. She loved that face. Not because it was handsome, although it was, but because it was such an honest face, so full of humor, intelligence and kindness. She had missed that face terribly over the past few months. And now, if his full lips could just form the words telling her how he felt then maybe, maybe, they would stand a chance.

He reached out and tucked a long strand of hair back behind her ear. The gesture was tender, and Lindsey felt her insides melt.

“Because he isn’t good enough for you and you’ll just get hurt,” Sully said.

Lindsey blew out a breath and stepped back. She felt as if she’d been doused with a bucket of cold water. Was it really that hard for him to tell her how he felt? Maybe he didn’t really feel the same way she felt. Maybe he was over their brief relationship and he was really just looking out for her as a friend. The thought was depressing.

"Don't worry about me," she said as she turned away. "I've been hurt before and I always bounce back."

Sully didn't come after her.

The donkey head was proving to be more difficult than Lindsey had anticipated. It did not help that she was not the craftiest person in the world. She had decided to make the donkey's head like a visor that Brian could wear on top of his head and then she would paint it gray and attach a matching cloth that could hang from the back of the mask as if it was the donkey's neck.

She was working at a table in the back of the theater while the actors rehearsed onstage. Mary and Nancy had brought two sewing machines, and they were zipping away at the costumes while Lindsey's fingers were covered in clumps of cold paste and soggy strips of newspaper. Bits of newspaper and paste coated the table and her clothes and, she suspected that there were clumps of it in her hair.

"Ah!" She tried to shake a particularly tenacious bit of newspaper off of her hand. It clung like a burr. She tried to use her other hand to pull it off, but all she managed to get were little bits of newsprint. It was maddening.

She muttered a few colorful curses under her breath and tried to wipe the paper off, but it just adhered to her other hand.

"Blech; I hate this stuff!" she said. She scraped her hands on the edge of the table, feeling at her wits' end.

"Are you all right, Ms. Norris?" Dylan asked as he stopped on his way past the table.

Lindsey noted he was standing a safe four feet away. Smart kid.

"Papier-mâché does not like me," she said. "Which is fine, because I don't like it, either."

Dylan smiled and gestured to the woman beside him. "My mom is a whiz with that stuff; maybe she can help you."

Lindsey glanced at the woman beside him. "Hi, Joanie, how are you?"

"Fine," Joanie Peet said, barely sparing Lindsey a glance.

Lindsey thought Robbie Vine might have been onto something when he said if a woman says she's fine, she is anything but. Dylan gave his mother a concerned glance, and sent Lindsey an apologetic look.

"Can we go now, Dylan?" Joanie asked. She sounded irritated. "I am very disappointed that I had to go backstage to find you. You know you are only here to rehearse and then leave. There is to be no lingering or loitering."

Lindsey frowned. She'd gotten to know Joanie Peet when she hired Dylan as a page. Joanie was usually quick with a smile, a kind word or a helping hand. She was always first on the list for the newest Debbie Macomber books, and she doted on Dylan, who was her only child.

Maybe she was a little too involved in Dylan's life, but Lindsey knew it was because Dylan was frequently ill and she needed to monitor his health very carefully. Lindsey could only imagine how stressful that was for Joanie and her husband, Tim.

"I'm sorry, Mom," Dylan said. "But don't you want to stay and watch awhile?"

"No. I told you how I felt about your participation in this play," Joanie said. "The late hours, the stress, it just can't be good for you. I don't know why you had to go against my wishes. If you get sick, you have no one to blame but yourself."

"Mom, it's my senior year of high school, and I'm graduating at the top of my class. I just wanted to do something fun for a change," he said.

"But that woman, Violet La Rue, have you heard what they say about her?" Joanie asked. She didn't even bother to keep her voice down. "She had all sorts of tawdry affairs, and even has a child out of wedlock."

Dylan rolled his eyes. "Yeah, I know. Charlene La Rue is her daughter, and she happens to be a very successful television newscaster in her own right."

Lindsey could feel her teeth clenching hard as Joanie criticized her friends.

"That's not the point," Joanie said. "She wasn't married when she had a child. There's no excuse for that sort of irresponsibility. And don't even get me started on that Robbie Vine. You are not allowed to go anywhere near him. He's completely amoral, with a wife and a girlfriend at the same time, and he probably does drugs."

"He's not that bad," Dylan said. "He's actually very nice."

Joanie's eyes looked like they were going to pop out of her head. "You've spoken to him?" she asked.

"Just to say hello," Dylan said. "You did raise me to be polite."

"Fine, but nothing more than hello," she said. "I mean it. I won't have you mixing with these sordid people."

Lindsey had never suspected that Joanie Peet could be such a judgmental shrew. She was boggled that the woman who had raised Dylan, one of the nicest kids she'd ever had work at the library, could be so awful.

Dylan looked miserable, but he nodded his head. Lindsey watched the two of them leave. She wondered if she should have leapt to her friends' defense. But then, she sort of suspected Joanie was right about Robbie. The comments about Violet, however, really chapped her.

"Lindsey, how goes the mask?"

"Huh, what?" she asked. Lindsey turned and

found Beth standing beside her. Beth was looking at her with concern.

"I think your hands are going to harden into claws," Beth said.

Lindsey looked down at the mixture on her hands. Then she glanced at the chicken wire she had been trying to wrap with the soggy newspaper strips.

"I think we can safely conclude that papier-mâché is not my forte."

Beth lifted up the chicken wire, which Lindsey had molded into the shape of a donkey head.

"I don't know," she said. "I think you've almost got it."

Lindsey watched while Beth deftly dampened a few dry strips in the bowl of paste and smoothed them over the frame. She carefully folded a few more strips around the ears and managed to fill in the sad gaps that Lindsey had missed.

"There," she said. "When this dries and you paint it, it will be fabulous."

"I'd hug you, but we'd probably get stuck together forever," Lindsey said.

Beth grinned. "Come on, let's go wash up."

The bathrooms for the cast and crew were at the back of the theater near the dressing rooms. They could hear Violet's voice directing the cast on stage mingling with the set builders, who were pounding nails on the loading dock out back.

Lindsey wondered if Sully was here tonight.

She hadn't seen him earlier—not that she was looking for him she reminded herself, refusing to acknowledge any disappointment.

Trying not to touch anything, they walked through the theater with their hands up in the air like surgeons. Beth pushed through the swinging door that led to the ladies' room with her hip, holding it open for Lindsey. The bathroom was empty, and they each took a sink.

Lindsey had just gotten the last of the goop off of her hands and was reaching for a paper towel when a crash sounded from the stage followed by several shouts. She and Beth exchanged surprised glances and hurried toward the sound of the commotion.

When they managed to push through the curtains at the side of the stage, Lindsey's heart caught in her throat when she saw Robbie sprawled on the ground with a large tree, saved from a previous play to be used in this show, lying across him.

His left leg was trapped and he was grimacing in pain. Lindsey and Beth hurried forward and knelt beside him while Sully and Ian tried to lift the round tree trunk off of him. As soon as they lifted it, she and Beth tugged Robbie out from underneath it.

Robbie grunted as they pulled. Violet hurried across the stage to join them as Beth and Lindsey gently helped him stand on the wooden stage.

"Robbie, are you all right? What happened?" Violet asked.

"Bloody hell! I was leaning against the tree just like we blocked it, and the next thing I knew it was falling on top of me."

Sully was kneeling by the base of the tree, checking the bottom of it. When he glanced at Robbie, he frowned.

"The base of this has been damaged," he said. "Any pressure on it and it was going to fall."

"Well, how did that happen?" Violet asked. "We used it last night and it was fine."

"It could have been damaged when it was moved earlier," Ian said. He was frowning like Sully, and Lindsey got the feeling he wasn't happy with the idea that the pieces of the set could be damaged so easily.

"Robbie!" a voice shrieked from the side of the stage. A buxom brunette came running across the stage and flung herself against Robbie who had just lowered himself into a seated position.

"Easy, Lola," he said. "You hit harder than the tree."

"Sorry," she said and sat back on her heels. "It's just—when I saw—are you all right?"

Robbie carefully moved his leg. He cringed as he bent his knee and put his foot flat on the floor.

"I think I'll live," he said.

"Ah!" The woman called Lola clapped a hand over her mouth and turned to scan the crowd. With a shaking hand, she pointed into the crowd that had gathered and said, "You did this!"

Lindsey glanced over to see Kitty, the same woman who had warned her away from Robbie, standing at the edge of the crowd with her arms crossed over her chest and a sour look on her face.

"Please," she said. "If I wanted to hurt Robbie, I'd get him in his wallet. After all, I'm still his wife while you're just his ex-girlfriend."

Lola narrowed her eyes and growled, "Only because you won't sign the divorce papers."

"Are you that desperate to have my sloppy seconds, Lola?" Kitty asked. "How pathetic."

Lola snarled and launched herself at the other woman. Before she reached her, Sully jumped forward and snatched her up around the waist while Ian blocked Kitty from engaging.

"Enough! Take them outside to cool off," Violet ordered.

"I don't need to—" Kitty began, but Violet gave her a menacing look that made her close her mouth in midsentence.

"Go," Violet said.

Everyone watched as Sully took Lola out toward the back door and Ian led Kitty out the front.

"Come on, let's see if you can stand." Violet gestured for Lindsey and Beth to help Robbie up.

Lindsey took his right while Beth took his left.

"Upsy daisy," Beth said.

Robbie put an arm around each of their shoulders, and together they got him up on his feet. He gingerly put weight on his left leg. Lindsey saw his mouth tighten, but his arm on her shoulder was light.

He took a few steps forward and Lindsey and Beth walked with him. He gave them both a quick squeeze and released them.

"Thank you, my lovely angels of mercy," he said. "I think it's just going to be bruised."

Violet was watching him and said, "I want you to have it checked by a doctor."

"Will do," he said.

"You might want to keep it elevated, and ice it to keep the swelling down," Beth said. "I think we have some ice in the machine in the concession stand."

"Excellent," Violet said. "Could you get him an ice pack, Beth?"

"And, Robbie, for the rest of tonight's rehearsal, you are chair-bound. Milton, could you grab a chair from backstage?"

Lindsey watched Robbie wince as he took a step in the direction of the side of the stage. She hurried over and took his arm and draped it over her shoulders.

"You really shouldn't push it, you know."

He looked at her and his face cleared and his dimples deepened when he grinned at her.

"How do you know I wasn't just using my prodigious acting skills to see if you cared?" he asked.

"You wouldn't!" she said.

"Wouldn't I?" he asked.

He looked at her and for a second Lindsey was sure he could see all the way into her soul. She blinked and looked away. Then she shook her head and laughed.

"You are the only man I've ever met who would use an injury as an opportunity to flirt."

He winked at her and Lindsey felt her face heat up. She was not going to succumb to his charm, she told herself, even as she realized that she genuinely liked Robbie as a person.

"Probably, you should sort out your wife-girlfriend situation before you try to add any more women to your life," she said.

He sighed. "I'm not very good with the closure portion of relationships."

"Clearly."

He looked at her and grinned. "But I'm unrivaled at beginnings."

Milton arrived at the side of the stage with two chairs, one for sitting and one for leg propping. As Lindsey helped Robbie into a chair, Beth arrived with the ice pack.

As Lindsey stepped away, she saw Sully had returned without Lola and was watching her with a frown. She felt a flash of guilt and then shrugged it off. Helping an injured man was nothing to feel guilty about.

As she went to leave the stage and go back to her worktable, Robbie grabbed her hand and raised the back of it to his lips.

"Thanks, love," he said.

Lindsey felt her face heat up again, but only because she knew that Sully was watching them. She glanced back to where Sully had been standing, but he was gone.

When she turned toward Robbie, she saw a twinkle in his eye and said, "You like trouble, don't you?"

CHAPTER 8

Me?" he asked. He blinked his green eyes innocently at her.

"Yes, you," she said. She was not buying what he was selling.

Violet had rolled up his pant leg and was about to put the ice pack on his leg. When Lindsey glanced down at the knot forming on Robbie's shin, she didn't have the heart to be too mad at him. He could have been seriously injured.

Lindsey left Robbie to Violet's ministrations and went back to her donkey to see how the drying process was going. When she got back to the table, she found the mask crushed as if someone had hit it repeatedly with a fist.

Beth and Mary joined her at the table as she picked up what was left of the mask and turned it over in her hands.

"What happened?" Beth gasped.

"At a guess, I'd say someone beat the hell out of it," Lindsey said. "Probably, I should be grateful that it isn't my face."

"But who—?" Mary began and then she broke off. "Oh."

"Oh?" Beth asked.

Mary looked at Lindsey and asked, "Wife or girlfriend?"

"Could be either, but I think Ian took Kitty out this way, so my guess would be that Ian left her and Kitty came back in and exorcised some misguided rage on Nick Bottom's donkey head," Lindsey said.

She glanced at the stage, where Violet was directing Robbie, who was still sitting, Ms. Cole and Milton through their parts in Act IV. She didn't have a good feeling about what had happened with Robbie. And she really didn't have a good feeling about what someone had done to her mask. Was it a warning? Were both incidents warnings? Or was she just being paranoid?

A movement in the shadows of the entrance of the theater caught her attention. Whoever was back there was carefully making their way to the door. If this was Kitty and she thought she was going to slip out after destroying Lindsey's work, she had another think coming.

"Hey!" Lindsey shouted and she ran across the theater. "Stop!"

The person in the shadows jumped and broke into a run. He was running flat out toward the emergency exit when he ran in front of a light that illuminated his particular body type: short and droopy. It was theater critic Harvey Wargus.

He slammed through the emergency exit before Lindsey could reach him. When she shoved through the door out into the cold night air, the alley was empty and she had no idea which direction he had run.

"Damn it!" she said.

"Who was that?" Beth asked as she pushed through the door after Lindsey.

"Harvey Wargus, the critic," Lindsey said.

"But what's he doing here during rehearsals?" Mary asked.

"I don't know, but I doubt that it bodes well for Violet," she said.

There was a reason that Harvey had been skulking around the theater. She knew he hated Violet and Robbie. Could he hate them enough to try to shut down the production by hurting Robbie?

"We need to tell Violet," Mary said. "She needs to be warned that he's been spying."

"But why would he?" Beth asked. "What could he possibly get out of watching us rehearse?"

"Oh, I'm sure he'll get something out of it," Lindsey said. "And it won't be pleasant."

Violet took the news that Harvey had been in the theater better than Lindsey thought, but then again, it could be Violet's skill as an actress that kept her from showing any emotion in front of the cast and crew.

"Run your lines," she directed the cast. "I need to make a call."

Lindsey could feel Robbie watching her but she pretended not to notice and retreated to her worktable, where she decided to clean up her supplies for the evening. She did not have the patience to mold chicken wire again. It would have to wait until tomorrow.

After all of the hullabaloo, she just wanted to go home to her dog, Heathcliff. A nice walk and a hot cup of tea would put her right and hopefully make her forget about the angry wife, her smashed work, the skulking critic and the frown on Sully's face.

Lindsey was up early the next morning. Heathcliff, a snuggler by nature, let out a grunt when she pushed the covers off and stepped out of the bed.

"Come on, lazy bones," she said. He stretched his furry black body across the bedspread and let out a tongue-curling yawn.

When she had gotten home the night before, she'd been too tired to go for a walk and so had played fetch with him in the yard instead. This morning she wanted to make up for it by taking him on a nice long walk before she left for work.

She had a hankering for a pumpkin-raisin muffin at the bakery, and it was giving her sufficient motivation to get moving.

Lindsey tied her long, blonde hair in a sloppy knot on top of her head, slipped on her workout clothes and sneakers and clipped Heathcliff's leash to his collar. Together, they jogged to the center of town. The small grocery store had its own bakery, which had patio seating outside. Lindsey found an empty table in the corner and tied Heathcliff's leash to one of the chairs.

Mr. and Mrs. Kendall, a retired couple, were seated at the next table. Mrs. Kendall held out her hand to Heathcliff, who immediately rolled over onto her shoes and offered his belly for pets.

"Go get your coffee, dear," she said to Lindsey. "I'll keep an eye on your baby for you."

"Thanks, Mrs. Kendall," Lindsey said. She turned to Mr. Kendall and asked, "Did you read the new Clive Cussler yet?"

"Is it in?" he asked. The eyes behind his bifocals sparkled with new-book joy.

"Just came in last week," Lindsey said. "Shall I put your name down for it?"

"Yes, please," he said.

Lindsey strode into the bakery knowing that Heathcliff was in good hands. She bought a coffee, her pumpkin muffin, and a water and doggie bagel for Heathcliff. She also picked up the local weekly paper, which had just come out today. It stuck mainly to the local events, but she always liked to check and see that the library was well represented.

Lindsey took her seat and chatted with the Kendalls for a few minutes about their dogs before they took their leave.

Lindsey sat with her feet up on the opposite chair, sipping her coffee and nibbling her muffin while Heathcliff gnawed on his bagel under the table. The sun was warm and the breeze was cool, making it a glorious autumn day.

She flipped through the paper, pausing when a picture of the front of the theater appeared in the upper-right-hand corner of page three. The headline yelled in bold letters: **Briar Creek Community Theater Doomed!** Lindsey frowned and then gasped when she saw that the byline was credited to none other than Harvey Wargus.

> Diva Violet La Rue has no business directing a puppet show, never mind a community theater production of Shakespeare's *A Midsummer Night's Dream* . . .

Lindsey continued reading, but the article just got worse. Wargus called both Violet and Robbie has-beens whose best days were long past, which was fairly ridiculous given that Robbie was barely pushing forty. He then went on to criticize the town, the theater, and the rest of the cast and crew for their shoddy showmanship and severe lack of skill and talent. The only good thing Wargus could say about the production at all was that it would, as all plays do, end.

The back door of the bakery opened and shut, but Lindsey was too busy rereading Wargus's vitriol to look up. She sat, engrossed, when the sound of a raised voice grabbed her attention.

"I'd like to beat him with a rolled-up newspaper," a voice said.

Heathcliff growled from below the table, and Lindsey immediately reached down to scratch his ears and soothe him.

Lindsey glanced over her shoulder to see Milton Duffy and Ms. Cole taking a table across the patio from hers. He was carrying a tray loaded with coffees and muffins, and she had a rolled-up copy of the *Briar Creek Gazette* in her hands.

Lindsey felt her jaw drop. Milton and Ms. Cole? At least that explained Heathcliff's reaction. He and the lemon were not fans of one another.

"Now, Eugenia," Milton said. "You can't let him get to you. He's a critic. You know what Kurt Vonnegut said about critics?"

"Yes." Ms. Cole sighed. "I believe it was something to the effect that 'Any reviewer who expresses . . . loathing for a novel is preposterous. He . . . is like a person who has put on full armor and attacked a hot fudge sundae.' But Vonnegut was talking about novels, not plays."

"Yes, but can't you just see that little butterball Wargus dressed in armor going after a sundae with his pen?" Milton asked and grinned at her.

To Lindsey's shock and amazement, Ms. Cole actually chortled. "I can!" she cried. "You're so right. We should just ignore him, but if he comes into the library again . . ."

Her voice trailed off, and Milton patted her hand and said, "You'll be the consummate professional that you always are and not let him get to you. Besides, the best revenge will be to put on the show of a lifetime."

Ms. Cole heaved a put-upon sigh and nodded her head. "You're right. Shall we run our lines?"

"I'd love to," Milton said.

Lindsey wondered if she should go over to their table and say hello. Normally, she wouldn't have given it much thought, but the relationship between her and Ms. Cole was a delicate one, and she didn't want to do anything to make it more awkward than it already was.

Still, she didn't want to be rude to Milton, either. Then again, if they hadn't seen her, and it was pretty clear that they hadn't, was it being rude to leave them to their rehearsal? She thought not. As a few more people came out onto the patio, Lindsey took the opportunity to slip away unnoticed.

As she strolled back to her house to change and get ready for work, she thought about last night's rehearsal. Who had smashed her donkey head? Probably Kitty. Was Robbie all right? And what was the deal with Lola? She seemed to think she and Robbie were still together while he was pretty clear that he had cut her loose. And why did Lindsey care, since she had no interest in dating anyone right now? Right?

She thought about Sully and sighed. Why was it so complicated with him? She knew that she cared for him, and she suspected that he cared for her, but he never said so, which made the whole situation impossible. She didn't want to spend her life trying to guess how someone was feeling.

When they had first gotten together, it had been she who announced her feelings for him. At the time she had felt quite bold and daring and had been relieved when he had said that he liked her, too. But when her ex had shown up trying to win her affections back, an impossibility rivaled only by turning iron into gold, Sully had done a full retreat and dumped her. Fine.

She thought she'd handled the dumping pretty well. She didn't cry—in public—and she had gone about her life exactly as it had been before she'd started dating him. The unfortunate thing was that she missed him—really bad.

She loved that he was well read and they could talk about anything. They both loved old movies and hanging out at the Blue Anchor with their friends. He'd even begun to teach her how to sail a boat.

She glanced down at the dog trotting happily beside her. She knew that even though Heathcliff couldn't say it, he missed Sully as well. Okay, maybe she was projecting there, but she didn't think so.

When she arrived back at her house, she found Nancy and Charlie standing on the front porch. They each had steaming mugs of coffee, and Nancy was reading to Charlie from the *Briar Creek Gazette*. Lindsey had no doubt about which article Nancy was reading.

When Heathcliff caught sight of them, he barked and strained at his leash. Lindsey unclipped him so he could go and greet two of his favorite people. As soon as he was free, he broke into a run. He jumped up on Charlie first and then Nancy. They both paused to pet him, and he wiggled and wagged and then raced back to Lindsey.

"Good morning," she said as she stepped onto the porch. She held up her own copy of the paper. "How did you like the Wargus article?"

"I didn't," Nancy grumped. "I thought he was

writing for a fancy-schmancy paper owned by that Buchanan fellow. What's he doing writing for the *Gazette*?"

"The editors probably figured he's a big name and it would draw advertisers," Charlie said. "It's all about the mighty dollar, man."

Charlie was a struggling musician who worked seasonally for Sully. By mutual agreement, he and Lindsey never talked about his day job. Charlie was a good, hardworking guy in his early twenties with long, stringy black hair and a varied collection of tattoos and piercings all over his body. Lindsey liked him, even when the band practices he held in his apartment made her furniture rumba across the floor.

"I'm afraid you're right," she said. "If the *Gazette* can turn the community theater production into a scandal sheet for the next few issues, they'll be sure to lock in new advertising."

"I can't say that I blame them, with newspapers closing everywhere, but still, I hate seeing Violet's name in here," Nancy said.

"Unless it drums up enough interest in the play to get more people to attend," Lindsey said. "They can prove Wargus wrong with sold-out shows and an amazing performance."

"You're right," Nancy said. "That'll shut up that horse's ass."

"Whew, go Naners," Charlie said. He held up his fist and they exchanged knuckle bumps.

"Will you be there tonight to work on costumes?" Nancy asked Lindsey.

"Yeah, I have to re-create my donkey head," she said.

"I'll help you," Nancy offered.

"No, I've got it," Lindsey said. "It's sort of become a personal challenge now."

Nancy nodded. "I understand."

"Of course, if Robbie's wife comes near my stuff again, I might need you for an alibi," Lindsey said.

Nancy rubbed her hands together. "Oh, Charlie and I could come up with a good one, don't you think, Charlie?"

"We could always say you were off getting a tattoo," he offered.

"Wouldn't I then need a tattoo to show for it?" Lindsey asked.

"You're right." He smacked his forehead. "Hey, maybe you should go get one so you have it in advance."

Lindsey shook her head. Charlie had been pestering her to get a tattoo since she moved in.

"I'm not getting a tattoo," she said.

"Why not? Naners has one," he said.

CHAPTER 9

Lindsey turned wide eyes to her landlady.

Nancy's blue eyes twinkled at her. "It's true. It's a tramp stamp right on my . . ."

"It is not!" Charlie protested with a laugh.

Nancy grinned. "Well, that would be something, wouldn't it? And I think your uncle Jake would have approved."

"Your tattoo is much more romantic than that," Charlie said with a soft smile.

Nancy's husband, Jake Peyton, was a ferry boat captain who had gone down with his ship. Nancy had never really gotten over it and during really bad storms she frequently had nightmares. Charlie lived in the middle apartment in her three-family captain house, to keep watch over his beloved aunt.

"My tattoo is a small lighthouse, just an inch tall," Nancy said. "It's on my right hip, where Jake always kept his hand when he slept. I had it put there to lead him home."

Lindsey felt her eyes get wet and her throat tighten up. She looked at Charlie and saw he had a suspicious sheen to his eyes as well.

"Aw, Naners," he said on a sigh. He opened

his arms and pulled her into a solid hug.

Nancy patted his back. “Don’t fret, Charlie, I’m okay.”

“I’m not.” Charlie let out a sniff, which made both of them laugh, breaking the sadness that had begun to envelope them. Then he looked at Lindsey and said, “See? Tattoos can give you an insight into the most significant moments or relationships of a person’s life.”

“Tell that to all the guys who got Celtic armband tattoos in the eighties,” Lindsey said.

“Tattoo art was just developing then,” Charlie protested.

“Fine, but I still don’t see me getting one,” Lindsey said. “I can’t even commit to a shade of eyeliner, never mind a permanent-ink pictorial. And don’t even get me started on where I’d have it put. Too many decisions.”

“We’ll see,” Charlie said.

“And on that note, I have to get ready for work,” Lindsey said.

“Come on, buddy,” Nancy said. “We’re baking coconut bars today.”

Heathcliff hopped up and wagged. He did love spending his days with Nancy. Since Heathcliff’s arrival the previous winter, he had chosen Lindsey as his primary caretaker, but Nancy and Charlie had quickly become a part of his pack as well. It made Lindsey feel much less guilty when she had to be at work all day.

• • •

When Lindsey arrived at the library to start her shift, she found Ms. Cole already at the circulation desk checking in the materials from the book drop. She tried to reconcile the forbidding-looking woman at the desk with the one who had been sharing coffee with Milton. It was almost as if they were two different people.

"Good morning, Ms. Cole," Lindsey said.

Ms. Cole nodded at her, which Lindsey knew was the best she could hope for. She shook her head and headed into her office. She had several book orders to submit and had been thinking about offering an e-reader class at the library, since they had been spending more and more time trying to help patrons use their e-readers to download books.

She owned an e-reader herself, but the book-loving part of her felt the same surge of panic she always felt at the thought that all books in the future would be in electronic form and there would be no more cloth bindings and paper pages to be held, but then she shook it off.

The electronic book was not going to eradicate hard-copy books. There was an art to the book that would never disappear, and the mere fact that it didn't require batteries would keep the book alive. She was sure of it . . . mostly.

The morning passed in a blur of e-mail, book orders and program planning. Lindsey wasn't sure how they could teach a class when there were so many different types of e-readers out there. Frustrated, she decided to take a break and went out to the library to see what was happening.

The library was eerily quiet. In fact, as she scanned the room, there wasn't a soul to be seen. Not even Ms. Cole.

"Hello?" Lindsey called out.

The sound of applause was her only answer. Frowning, Lindsey followed the noise to the story time room in the back of the children's area.

Lindsey glanced through the window in the door and saw that the room was packed with kids, parents and staff. At the front of the room, Robbie Vine was giving a performance for the kids. The overhead light shown on his reddish-blond hair and his dimples flashed as he grinned at the kids, who squealed with excitement.

Lindsey eased the door open and crept into the room to watch. Robbie was magnetic. Even on this small stage in this cramped room with an audience of wiggly toddlers, he commanded his audience's attention, giving off an energy that made it impossible to look away.

She leaned against the back wall and watched, enraptured. When Robbie finished his piece, which had been a recitation of classic nursery rhymes, the room broke into enthusiastic applause and Robbie took several deep bows. When he rose, he glanced across the crowd and his gaze met Lindsey's.

It was like getting hit with a bolt of lightning. Lindsey felt it all the way down to her shoes. Oh, this was bad. She could not be here, looking at him, feeling this feeling.

She glanced down the wall and saw Ms. Cole at the back of the room, as well as their part-time library assistant Jessica Gallo, who should have been minding the reference desk. She tried to make her voice sound stern and said, “I think we all need to get back to the main library.”

“Yes, you’re right. Sorry,” Jessica said.

Ms. Cole said nothing but merely led the way out of the room. Lindsey followed, and did not look back.

“Isn’t he brilliant?” Jessica gushed. “He had the kids entranced while he performed. It was amazing.”

“Yes, he’s a wonderful actor,” Lindsey said, although she wasn’t sure who she was reminding, Jessica or herself.

Once the others were back at their desks, she returned to her office. She tried to tell herself she wasn’t hiding, but she knew it was a lie.

She had no business being attracted to a man like Robbie Vine. He was married. He had a girlfriend. He was married. He was an actor. He was married. She put her head down on her desk and tried to figure out where her common sense had gone.

A knock on the door made her snap upright.

"Come in," she said. She began to straighten her already meticulous desk.

The door opened; it was Charlene. Lindsey was disappointed that it wasn't Robbie, and was annoyed with herself for her reaction. She smiled even brighter at her friend, determined to get her head on straight.

"Charlene," she said. "What a surprise."

Being a television news reporter kept Charlene so busy they rarely saw her unless it was for their Thursday crafternoon meetings, and even those she occasionally had to miss.

"Hi, Lindsey." Charlene came in and shut the door behind her. "Do you have a minute?"

"For you? Always," Lindsey said. "Sit down."

Charlene took a seat across from her desk, and Lindsey noticed that her friend's usually flawless face had small worry lines pinching the corner of her eyes.

"What's wrong?" Lindsey asked.

"I'm worried about my mom," Charlene said. "This production, the bad press, my father sending that vile reporter here, I think it is too much for her to have to handle."

"So, you think your father did have a hand in sending Harvey Wargus here?" Lindsey asked.

"I don't know," Charlene said. "I've been trying to investigate without my father finding out, but so far, no luck."

"Why would your father want to pester your

mother now?" Lindsey asked. "She's retired from Broadway; she lives a quiet life here in Briar Creek. I just don't see what he has to gain by antagonizing her."

"He doesn't like to lose," Charlene said.

"But didn't he lose when he chose not to be a part of your life?" Lindsey asked.

Charlene gave her a warm smile. "Spoken like a true friend."

"No, I don't have to be your friend to see what he lost," Lindsey said. "Look at you. You're a beautiful, charming, intelligent woman. You're an excellent reporter, an amazing wife and mother and a fabulous friend. I pity your father."

"Well, I thank you," Charlene said. "But I don't think this is about me, and if it is, it is only in a peripheral way."

Lindsey gave her a questioning glance.

"Mom's birthday was back in July," she said.

"Yes, we had the luau." Lindsey grinned. Then she frowned. Sully had been there, too, and they hadn't spoken once all night. Very annoying.

"Well, do you remember the flower delivery that she got?"

"Oh yeah, the purple roses," Lindsey said. "Kind of hard to forget a bouquet as big as a Buick."

"I think it was from my dad."

"No."

"Yes."

"Why?"

Charlene just looked at her and Lindsey said, "Oh. Oh. Oh!"

"I think he wants to get back together," Charlene said. "There have been other things, too."

"Do you think she's interested?"

Charlene gave her a fretful look. "I don't know. She hasn't said anything."

"Have you asked her about this?" Lindsey pressed. She leaned forward, resting her arms on her desk. "You and your mother are so close. You know you can talk to her about anything."

"Except what if she wants to see him again?" Charlene asked. "I don't think she'd tell me because she knows how I feel about him."

"She'd tell you," Lindsey said. "Violet is the most honest person I know, and you are the most important person in the world to her. She'd tell you if she wanted to see your father."

Charlene was quiet for a minute. Then she nodded. "You're right. I know you're right. I did have one other theory. It's in the exact opposite direction."

"What's that?"

"Well, if my mother rejected my father completely, do you think he might be out for revenge? And that he might sabotage the show to get even?"

CHAPTER 10

"Whoa," Lindsey said. "You did say your father doesn't like to lose. Is he vindictive like that?"

Charlene shrugged. "I don't know that I have the most objective opinion of him."

They were both quiet for a bit. Lindsey told herself she was just asking questions to be thorough, but she knew there was a silly part of her that was fishing. She chose to ignore it.

"Have you talked to Robbie about all of this?" she asked. She was pleased that her voice sounded perfectly casual.

"Actually, I stopped by because I heard he was here, but I must have missed him."

"Oh, is he already gone?" Lindsey asked. She refused to acknowledge even a flicker of disappointment that he hadn't stopped by her office.

"Beth said he was meeting his understudy on the pier to run over some lines," Charlene said.

Lindsey thought about how unhappy Dylan's mother would be to hear this. She had made it very clear that she didn't like Dylan spending time with the theater people. Then she realized that this was probably why Dylan and Robbie were meeting at the pier. It would be very hard to be seen out there, especially if they practiced on one of the lower docks.

"Well, maybe you can catch him out there," Lindsey said. "He and your mother seem close enough that she would tell him if she was worried about your father messing with the production."

"True," Charlene said. "Mom and Robbie are very close."

"And if not Robbie, then maybe Nancy knows," Lindsey said.

"I thought of that, but since Nancy is Mom's best friend, I didn't want to put her in an awkward spot," Charlene said.

"Oh, well, than definitely ask Robbie," Lindsey said. "He seems to thrive on awkward spots."

Charlene tipped her head and studied Lindsey. "He likes you, doesn't he?"

Lindsey glanced down at the top of her desk. "I have no idea what you mean."

Charlene laughed. "Yes, you do. Robbie likes you and he's got you all flustered, doesn't he?"

"Ugh." Lindsey thumped her head down on her desk. "I feel like such an idiot. He probably does this to every woman he meets, and let's not forget that he's married."

Charlene reached across the desk and brushed back the long, curly strands of Lindsey's blonde hair in a comforting mother-to-a-child sort of way. "Robbie's marriage has been over forever," she said. "Just not legally."

Lindsey turned her head to the side and gave Charlene a baleful look. "And he has a girlfriend."

"Oh, no, they broke up months ago," Charlene said. "Lola is just sort of a barnacle. She'll keep clinging to Robbie until she finds someone else to attach herself to."

Lindsey sighed and pushed herself back into a seated position. "Still, it's too complicated for me."

"Maybe," Charlene said. She stood and crossed to the door. "But maybe you don't need to get involved with Robbie. Maybe having him interested in you will motivate a certain boat captain we know to get his act together."

Lindsey clapped her hands over her face. "Oh, horror. That scenario requires entirely too much drama."

"Well, it is theater season," Charlene said with a laugh. "Thanks for listening, Lindsey."

"Anytime," she said. "Let me know what happens."

"I will," Charlene promised.

She closed the door softly behind her, and Lindsey forced herself to get back to work. It was a relief to have her brain taken up with concrete matters like dispensing the budget and cataloging old issues of newspapers and magazines. Lindsey found it very comforting to be able to instill order in at least one part of her life.

• • •

"You will bend to my will," Lindsey muttered. "Or I will use the snips on you."

"Do you find that threatening chicken wire makes it more pliable?"

Lindsey whirled around to find Robbie standing behind her. He was grinning, and she tried to ignore the way it made her heart skip. She was determined to maintain a healthy boundary with the actor.

"Well." She cleared her throat. "I tried bribing it with the immortality of being a donkey's head, but that didn't seem to work."

"Perhaps it finds the prospect of life on Brian's buggery head more than it can bear," Robbie said. He was holding his usual bottle of coconut water, and unscrewed the cap and took a long drink.

"I inadvertently overheard your tiff the other day. Brian seemed unhappy with you," Lindsey said.

"He thinks I slept with his wife," Robbie said. "Ridiculous!"

"So you didn't?" Lindsey asked before she could think better of it.

He gave her an exasperated look. He crossed his arms over his chest, and she noted that his long-sleeved T-shirt sat well on his broad shoulders.

"Is that what you think of me?" he asked. He wasn't smiling now; Lindsey wondered if she had hurt his feelings.

"You do have a reputation," she said.

"Most of which I haven't earned," he said. His green eyes studied her face and he leaned close and whispered, "Now, if I could earn the reputation of being the plunderer of pretty, blonde librarians, well, that's a reputation I could live with."

A small squeak came out of Lindsey's mouth, which she tried to cover with a cough. His grin was decidedly wicked now, and she had the sinking feeling that she was in way over her head.

"Lindsey!" a voice called from behind her.

She turned to find Sully striding toward them. Robbie straightened up, and Lindsey felt a hot heat fill her face. Again, she had a twinge of guilt, which was ludicrous, since she and Sully were no more.

"Yes?" she asked. She hoped she sounded casual but judging by the flat stare Sully was giving her, she didn't.

"Nancy sent me to find you," he said. "She's holding a meeting for costumes in the back room."

"Oh, that's right." Lindsey turned back to Robbie. "Sorry, I have to go."

"That's okay," he said. "We'll talk more later."

How did he make such a simple sentence sound so laden with innuendo?

"All right," she said. She turned back around and went to pass Sully, who fell into step beside her.

The theater had several back rooms used for storage and rehearsals that ran along one side of the building. She pushed through the door on the far side of the theater, which led to a dark, narrow hallway. She had assumed Sully would return to the backstage area where the set crew worked, but he didn't. Instead he stayed right beside her.

She glanced at him out of the corner of her eye and felt her heart pinch. His jeans and T-shirt were covered in sawdust, and his thick, mahogany curls were pushed back by a blue bandanna he had tied around his forehead, probably to keep the sweat from dripping into his eyes. His jaw was set tight and his mouth was in a narrow, straight line. He did not look happy.

"Thanks for coming to get me," she said. The room where the meeting was to be held was on her left, and the hallway would take Sully back to the loading dock.

"No problem," he said. His voice made it sound as if it was anything but.

"Are you mad at me?" she asked.

"Nope," he said. "Why would I be mad?"

"I can't imagine," Lindsey said. "But you sure seem cranky."

"Well, maybe it's because every time I see you, you've got Robbie Vine twisted around you."

His voice rose in volume and Lindsey blinked. Sully never raised his voice. He was the calmest person she had ever known. Frankly, it was nice to see a display of emotion even though his ire made her defensive and she found herself snapping back.

"I don't see why you care, since you dumped me!"

"I didn't dump you," he argued. He turned so he was facing her. "I wanted to give you time."

"Time I didn't ask for," she said. "Which, for your information, makes it a dumping."

"You were supposed to be figuring out how you felt about your ex," he said.

"I didn't need to figure anything out about him," she said. She threw her hands up in the air, mostly to keep from wrapping them around his neck. "I knew how I felt. I was perfectly clear about how I felt."

Sully leaned in close so that his face was just inches from hers. "Yeah, I saw how you felt when you thought he was dead."

He opened his mouth as if to say more but then he stepped back and shook his head. "You're right. It's none of my business. Do whatever makes you happy. Have a great time with your little actor buddy."

He turned and strode down the hallway, anger thumping in his every step.

"Argh!" Lindsey growled and turned and smacked the concrete wall with her hand. Ouch! Okay, that was dumb.

She was shaking out her hand when the door

opened and Nancy's and Mary's heads popped out.

"Was that . . . um . . . Sully we heard?" Nancy asked.

"Yes," Lindsey said. She glanced at Mary to see how she was handling the thought of Lindsey and her brother mixing it up in the hallway.

"Good," Mary said. She did not seem fazed in the least. "About time he got off his duff."

She stepped back into the room and motioned for Lindsey to enter. The three of them sat down at a small table in the center of the room. Nancy had brought a pitcher of lemonade and there was a plate loaded with oatmeal raisin cookies. Lindsey sat down and Nancy poured her a glass while Lindsey helped herself to three cookies.

"So, did you two clear the air?" Nancy asked.

"No, I think we just fogged it up even more." Lindsey shrugged. "That man is hard to read."

"That's because he keeps it all bottled up," Mary said. "He always has, ever since we were kids."

"That can't be good for the digestion," Nancy observed. "No wonder he's feeling ornery. I should make him some pumpkin cookies."

Mary and Lindsey both smiled at Nancy's home remedy, and the tension was broken.

"I don't know about his digestion, but he certainly seems to have a strong opinion about Robbie Vine," Lindsey said.

"That's because he's jealous," Mary said.

“Of what?” Lindsey scoffed. “The man is married.”

“Sort of,” Nancy qualified.

“That’s like being sort of pregnant,” Lindsey said. “Married is married, whether they live together or not, and I am not dating a married man.”

“Good for you,” Nancy said. “It’s much less complicated that way.”

“I don’t know,” Mary said. “The way that Robbie has been looking at you, you might be the motivation he needs to cut loose the old ball and chain.”

“Oh, I don’t think so,” Lindsey said. “Robbie is . . . mesmerizing. Of that, there is no question, but if I interest him at all it’s just as a curiosity. I don’t imagine a life in the theater gives an actor much exposure to librarians, and as everyone knows, we are a fascinating bunch.”

“No doubt,” Nancy agreed, ignoring Lindsey’s teasing tone. “But don’t sell yourself short.”

“Yeah,” Mary agreed. “Not only do you have Robbie interested, you’re the only woman I’ve ever known to make Sully pine.”

Lindsey raised an eyebrow and studied her ex-boyfriend’s sister. “Pine?”

“He has been as mopey as a lovesick puppy all summer long,” Mary confirmed. “Ask Ian if you don’t believe me.”

“Then why—?” Lindsey was about to ask Mary

why Sully had dumped her, but she stopped herself. Sully was the one who needed to tell her whatever was going on in that male brain of his. "So, are we really having a meeting or was this just an excuse to gorge ourselves on cookies and lemonade?"

"Excuse to gorge," Nancy admitted. "But since we're here, I suppose we should review where we are with each of the costumes."

She retrieved a three-inch red binder from a tote bag by her feet. The binder had tabs separating each character and their costume requirements.

She started with the main characters, and they reviewed what needed to be done for each one, working their way through the book. There were only a few characters left when the lights went out.

The darkness was so complete that Lindsey couldn't even see Nancy and Mary, although they were seated just a few feet away. A small emergency exit light was the only thing visible in the room, but while it illuminated the door it did nothing to cut through the gloom.

"Do you think it's the whole building?" Mary asked.

"I don't see any light coming from the hallway, so I think so," Nancy said.

"I'm going to see if anyone knows what happened," Lindsey said.

She stood up and felt for the wall. She bumped

her leg into another table and stumbled, but her fingers found the concrete wall and she followed it toward the door.

She traced the outside of the door frame until she felt the doorknob. She pulled the door open and noted that the hallway was just as dark as the room behind her.

"Do you see any light?" Nancy asked from the table.

"Nothing yet," Lindsey said. "Wait here, maybe I can rustle up a flashlight."

She stepped out into the hallway. She could hear the excited murmur of voices coming from the stage area. She felt her way along the wall, trying to remember where the door into the auditorium was.

Her fingers closed on a door handle and she pulled it open.

She stepped into the room just as a scuffle and a shout sounded from the stage.

"Get off!" a voice that was unmistakably Robbie's shouted. "Hey! Ah!"

There was the sound of a thud as if a body had just collapsed against the stage.

"Robbie? Was that you?"

"Who's there?"

"Ouch!"

"Hey, what's going on?"

"Could somebody please hit the breaker?"

There were too many voices to pick out any one

voice. Lindsey hurried forward, but it was still pitch-black and she slammed into a row of seats, almost knocking herself down. She began to feel her way along the seat backs, trying to get to the stage.

"Quiet!" Violet's voice commanded. "Everyone be still. If you move in the dark, you could hurt yourself."

The loud voices and shouts quieted to a low murmur. Lindsey took the opportunity to step into the aisle, which had small yellow floor lights that would lead her down to the stage. She was getting close when a beam of light snapped on near the stage.

It swept the stage, catching everyone in the position they had been in presumably when the lights went out. Then it swung back and lowered. Lying on the stage was Robbie; a dark stain marred his white shirt, and it took Lindsey just a moment to realize that it was blood pooling from a gash in his arm.

As Robbie was illuminated by the light, a scream sounded and the entire room erupted into chaos. Lindsey rushed forward and clambered up onto the stage, reaching Robbie first. Violet knelt beside her.

"Robbie, are you all right?" Lindsey asked. Her hands were shaking and she blinked. "Ugh, sorry. Clearly, you're not."

He glanced up at her from where he lay. "No,

no, it's just a flesh wound in my arm, but I was afraid to move lest I meet my adversary's knife point again."

"What are you saying?" Violet asked.

"Someone stabbed me, love," he said. His voice was low so that only the two of them and the person next to Violet with the flashlight could hear him. "Shortly after the lights went out the knife went in."

CHAPTER 11

Shine the light here, please," Lindsey said.

The person holding the flashlight knelt down, and she saw that it was Sully. He shined the light onto the gash on Robbie's arm. It looked like a messy stabbing. Robbie's shirtsleeve was ripped and soaked in blood. When Lindsey pulled back the edge of the fabric, she could see that the cut was a deep slice made by a very sharp knife.

She glanced up and met Sully's gaze in the glow of the light. Her own concern was mirrored in his eyes.

"It's still bleeding," she said. "I need something to tie it off."

"There's a first aid kit out on the loading dock," Sully said. "I'll go get it."

He handed the flashlight to Violet and disappeared.

"Moves like a shadow, he does," Robbie said as they watched Sully leave. "Impressive for such a big man."

Lindsey frowned at him. Surely he was not implying that Sully had been the one with the knife?

"I think your shirt is beyond repair," she said. "Do you mind if I use it to stop the blood flow?"

"Be my guest," he said.

Lindsey tore the sleeve off where the fabric had been slashed by the knife. She folded it into a pad and pressed it onto the cut. She hoped the pressure would slow the bleeding.

"I don't understand," Violet said. "How could this happen?"

"Really, Violet?" Robbie asked. "I know you don't cook, but surely the purpose of a knife hasn't escaped you."

"You know what I mean—" Violet began but she was cut off as a body came tripping toward them out of the dark.

"Robbie!" Lola crouched down on his other side and hugged him close. "Are you all right? What happened? Did you fall?"

"I'm fine," he said. He spoke through gritted teeth, and Lindsey realized the jostling Lola was giving him was causing him severe pain.

"How about the lights?" Violet turned and

yelled up toward the balcony. "Ian, any luck?"

Another beam of light shone down from the balcony for a second before it vanished again.

"I'm working on it," Ian yelled. There was the sound of banging and some cursing.

"Here, let me help you up," Lola said. Her long, brown hair was tied back and she wore a low-cut blouse, which gave Lindsey an eyeful of cleavage when she bent over to lift Robbie up by the underarms.

Robbie let out a hiss when Lola tried to drag him to his feet. Lindsey moved with them to keep the pressure on his arm. She looked at the wadded-up shirtsleeve and noted it was saturated in blood.

"Lola, get off of him," Violet snapped. "In fact, back up and move away. Everyone else sit ti—"

In a flash, light filled the theater again. Lindsey blinked and glanced around the stage. She caught a glimpse of Milton and Ms. Cole holding hands just before Ms. Cole snatched her hand away. Beth was huddled in a corner with Dylan, Perry and Heather, while several crew members were stranded on the piece of set they'd been painting at the back.

"Robbie, your arm. Oh, my god, you've been cut!" Lola said. She looked closely at the blood-soaked rag and then slumped on top of him in a dead faint.

"Oh, good grief," Violet said. "Someone check her, please."

Sully wound his way back to Lindsey and handed her the first aid kit. Without a word, he rolled Lola off of Robbie's chest. Her face was pale, but she was breathing.

"Fainted," Sully said. "Luckily, Vine broke her fall."

"Can you take her to get some air?" Violet asked. "In fact, everyone go out front for a few minutes and get some fresh air. We'll call you when we're ready to rehearse again."

The voices of the cast and crew rose and fell as they scattered from the stage. Lindsey watched as Sully lifted Lola up into his arms as if she weighed no more than a child and carried her out front with the others. She felt a twinge of what she suspected was jealousy but she refused to acknowledge it. Sully was just helping the woman; besides, whatever Sully did was no business of hers.

She turned back to Robbie. "Can you sit up?"

"Sure," he said. She and Violet spotted him while he pushed himself up into a sitting position. Gently, they shifted him so that he was leaning against a piece of the set designed to look like a cave.

"I'm going to get some rags for that blood," Violet said. "Be right back."

"Hold this," Lindsey said to Robbie. He put his hand over the shirtsleeve still pressed to his cut.

Lindsey popped open the metal first aid kit. It

had disinfectant wipes, rolls of gauze and assorted bandages. It would do until Robbie got the wound dressed by a professional.

She glanced at his arm. What remained of his sleeve needed to be rolled up, so she tentatively began to fold back the shirt.

The bottom of a tattoo appeared, and curious, Lindsey pushed the fabric up a bit more so she could see it. It was a stylized sun done in reds and yellows with a blue outline. In the center of the sun was a date: 10-23-95.

"Nice tattoo," she said.

"It marks the most significant day of my life," he said, "although I didn't know it at the time."

Lindsey remembered Nancy's lighthouse tattoo and she felt her throat get tight. What was it Charlie had said? A person's tattoos could give insight into the most important events of his life?

"Sometimes dates are like that," she said. "You don't know it's important until later."

"Indeed," Robbie agreed. "Sort of like September fourteenth of this year."

Lindsey looked at him. "What happened on that day?"

"I met you."

His gaze met and held hers, and Lindsey felt her pulse pound in her ears. She wasn't ready. She couldn't feel that way about someone yet. And he was so far out of her league. Her thoughts chased each other around in her head until she couldn't think.

She glanced down at his cut, breaking the moment.

"Let me know if I hurt you," she said.

He didn't answer, and she glanced up to make certain he heard her. Their faces were just inches apart.

"You won't," he said.

Lindsey blew out a breath and took the wadded-up fabric off of his cut. She then reached into the kit and took out the alcohol wipes.

"This is probably going to sting," she said.

The cut was a clean slice and probably it was going to require stitches, but the worst of the bleeding seemed to be over.

Lindsey shook out one of the wipes and gently dabbed at the cut. Robbie sucked in a breath through his teeth and she cringed, knowing it was going to get worse before it got better.

She held his arm still with one hand and ran the cloth over the cut with the other. She felt his muscles bunch beneath her fingers, and he let loose a string of mild curses while he kicked at the floor with one of his feet.

"I'm sorry, I'm so sorry," Lindsey said. "I know it hurts. Just one more pass and it'll be good, I think."

She swabbed the cut one last time and Robbie let out a shout.

"Are you all right?" she asked. "Is there anything I can do?"

"One thing," he said through gritted teeth. And before Lindsey realized his intent, Robbie cupped the back of her head and kissed her.

Lindsey was too surprised to move and the kiss was over before she could even register what had happened. In fact, the only thing that convinced her of what had actually just happened was the fact that her lips were still tingling. Well, that and the fact that Sully had returned to the stage and was glaring at them.

"Okay, then, let's get that bandaged up, shall we?" she asked.

Robbie grinned at her. It was a wicked grin, the sort that bespoke all sorts of trouble for the person on the receiving end of it. Lindsey found herself grinning back, although she knew if she'd had any sense of self-preservation she wouldn't have.

While she wrapped Robbie's arm, she was increasingly aware of Sully, who had been joined by Ian and Violet. The three of them were having a low, murmured conversation, but she couldn't make out what was being said.

"You seem to be having a lot of bad luck on the stage lately," she said to Robbie.

"Agreed." He sighed. "I'm getting the feeling that someone is not interested in seeing me play Puck."

"Well, you are—" Lindsey stopped before she finished her sentence.

"I am what?" he asked.

Lindsey paused while wrapping the gauze around his arm and met his gaze.

"You are a bit of a polarizing personality," she said.

"Me?" he asked. He looked so surprised at this that Lindsey had to laugh.

"Surely you've noticed," she said. "You seem to bring out either the absolute best in people or the worst."

Robbie watched her while she fastened a strip of adhesive tape around his arm to keep the gauze in place.

"I hadn't thought of it like that," he said. "I guess my only question now is—"

"Who do you bring out the worst in and why would they want to harm you?" she asked.

"No, actually," he said. Lindsey glanced at him in surprise and again she was overly aware of their close proximity. Up close, the green in his eyes was as vibrant as a new leaf, and she noted that his eyelashes were blond on the tips.

His voice was lower when he continued, "My question is what do I bring out in you, Lindsey? The best or the worst?"

Lindsey felt her throat go dry. She swallowed hard, trying to think of a way to answer that didn't encourage him, but then she wondered if that was really what she wanted.

"Time to go see a doctor, Vine," a voice said from behind them.

Lindsey snapped her head up and saw Sully standing behind Robbie with his arms crossed over his chest and an annoyed look on his face.

"Oh, I think Lindsey has patched me up just fine," Robbie said. His eyes were still on Lindsey and he made no move to rise.

"Sorry, Violet's orders. Here let me help you," Sully said. He didn't wait for Robbie to stand but hooked him under the arms and hauled him to his feet.

"Thanks, mate," Robbie said, although Lindsey noted that he sounded more annoyed than grateful.

"You should have a doctor look at it, just to be on the safe side," she said. She stood beside them, clutching the first aid kit to her chest.

"After you," Sully said. He nudged Robbie in the direction of the stairs—and he was none too gentle about it.

"Well, I see what you mean about the worst," Robbie muttered to Lindsey as he passed her. He made a mock horrified look at Sully, and Lindsey smiled.

"Thanks for taking care of me," he said. Then he blew her a kiss and Lindsey felt her face get hot.

She watched as he walked up the aisle and pushed through the door to the lobby. She barely caught a glimpse of Lola as she pounced on Robbie once he stepped outside. She knew it shouldn't bother her, but still she turned away from the sight.

Sully was standing there watching her, and Lindsey felt inexplicably irritated with him. "Go ahead and say it."

"Say what?" he asked. His voice was mild as if he had no idea what she was talking about. This made her even more annoyed.

"Go ahead and tell me that Robbie is bad news and I should stay away—you know, the whole spiel. Get it off of your chest," she said.

"I wasn't going to say that," he said. He looked genuinely hurt and Lindsey felt her annoyance slip away.

"No?" she asked.

"No," he said. He shoved his hands into his pants pockets and blew out a breath. "You should do whatever makes you happy. You deserve to be happy."

Lindsey stared at him. All she could think when she studied his handsome face was, *you make me happy*. But of course she didn't say it. Instead, she said, "Thanks for taking him to the doctor. That's very good of you."

Sully stepped close to her, and she could smell that particular scent that was his: a citrusy, sea air–soaked smell that filled her senses and made her dizzy.

“Just be careful, Lindsey,” he said. “Like I said, you deserve to be happy, but I’d hate to see you get hurt.”

She watched as he left through the doors to the lobby.

“Do you think it’s safe enough to have everyone come back in?” Violet asked Ian.

They were walking across the stage toward Lindsey, and she turned to see Ian run a hand over his bald head.

“I think so,” he said. “But Violet, whoever tampered with the circuit breaker meant business. We need to call Chief Plewicki and tell her what happened.”

“Do you think whoever damaged the circuit breaker did it to get to Robbie?” Lindsey asked. The coincidence was just too much.

Violet and Ian both looked worried and Lindsey knew that was her answer.

“But why would someone want to stab him?” Lindsey said. “I mean I understand that he puts some people off, but to cut him, I mean, that’s . . . well . . . scary.”

“It’s worse than that, I’m afraid,” Violet said.

“What do you mean?” Lindsey asked.

“We don’t think they meant to just stab him,” Ian said. “We think they planned to murder him.”

CHAPTER 12

Murder?" Lindsey gasped. "Surely it was just a warning of some sort, maybe, from someone who wants to stop the show?"

"Lindsey, you dressed the wound," Ian said. "If it had been over just a few more inches, it would have been his heart."

"And the attack wasn't made using a prop sword, either," Violet added.

"No," Lindsey agreed. "That cut was most definitely made by a very sharp blade."

Violet let out a deep sigh. She crossed one arm over her middle and rested her head on the fingertips of her other hand.

"This is a nightmare," she said. "I suppose I should call Chief Plewicki."

"She'll definitely want to know what's happening," Lindsey said. "And Robbie should file a report."

"Speaking of our favorite thespian, someone should keep an eye on him," Ian said. He glanced at Lindsey. "Shall I volunteer Sully for the task?"

"Oh, I don't see that going well," she said.

"Hey, where did everyone go?" Nancy asked as she and Mary arrived from the hallway with costumes draped over their shoulders. "We were hoping to do some fittings."

"There was an incident," Ian said as he moved to stand beside his wife. He put his hand on her shoulder as if to reassure himself that she was okay. "Robbie was cut with a knife."

"On purpose?" Nancy asked. Her blue eyes were wide as she looked at Violet in horror.

"We suspect so," Violet said with a nod of her head. "Between the stabbing tonight and the set falling on him the other day, I'd say someone is not too happy with him. Still, I can't imagine who would—"

"Oh, can't you?" Ian asked. "How about his wife, Kitty?"

"Or his girlfriend, Lola," Mary added.

"Harvey Wargus certainly is not a fan," Nancy said.

"Or Brian Loeb, who seems to think that Robbie slept with his wife," Lindsey added.

"Yes, Robbie does have a few jealous males with him in their sights, doesn't he?" Ian asked. He was looking at Lindsey, but she refused to acknowledge his thinly veiled reference to Sully. If there was one thing she was certain of, it was that Sully had nothing to do with Robbie's injury. Sully was much too honest and direct for that.

"Well, I guess I'll send everyone home for the night and call the police in to investigate," Violet said. "I know Robbie can be . . . well, a handful, but he's one of my closest friends and I will not let any harm come to him when he's been good enough to help me stage this production."

The others nodded, but then Lindsey paused.

"Violet, I hate to suggest this, but do you think it could be your ex-husband, Sterling Buchanan?" Lindsey asked. "Do you think he'd go after Robbie to hurt you?"

Violet paled. "I don't . . . that's a very good question. It seems I have several calls to make. If you will excuse me?"

"I'll come with you," Nancy said. "I can make a pot of tea and sit with you while you make your calls."

Violet looked at her friend and squeezed her arm. "Thank you."

"Do you want me to close up the theater for the night?" Ian asked.

"Leave the stage lights on," Violet said. "I'll be in the office and I want to show the police where everything happened. But please send everyone home and go ahead and lock up the rest of the rooms."

"Will do," Ian said.

"Do you want a lift home?" Mary asked Lindsey.

"Oh, thanks, but Beth and I rode our bikes," Lindsey said. "I'm going to go outside and see if I can find her."

"Lindsey, be careful," Ian said. "If someone

does have it in for Robbie Vine, they might not like that he seems to have taken a shine to you."

Lindsey nodded and Mary gave her a quick hug. She could only hope that Ian was wrong. She went back to the wardrobe room to retrieve her things. She wondered what Emma Plewicki would make of the situation and if she would recommend closing the show.

A few of the cast and crew were still loitering about outside. She saw Beth standing with Dylan and Heather and made her way over to them. She assumed Perry must have already left.

Dylan was the first to spot her. "Ms. Norris, will Mr. Vine be all right?"

He looked pale and shaky, and she realized it was probably the first time these teens had seen anything like this.

"I think so," she said. "The wound wasn't deep and the bleeding had pretty much stopped."

"Is it true that he was stabbed on purpose?" Heather asked. "Did someone try to kill Mr. Vine?"

Lindsey blew out a breath. She didn't want to scare them but she didn't want to give them false platitudes, either.

"I honestly don't know," she said. "The police have been called and I'm sure they're going to check into it."

Just then an SUV pulled up. Lindsey saw that it was Joanie, Dylan's mother. Under the streetlight that shined through the window, she looked decidedly unhappy, and Lindsey wondered if word of what had happened in the theater had already spread through the small community.

"My mom is here," Dylan said. "I'll see you all tomorrow."

He opened the door and climbed into the passenger seat. Lindsey and Beth both waved to Joanie, but she immediately began speaking to Dylan and didn't see them. Judging from the expression on her face, she was not happy.

"I think it's safe to say that Dylan does not get his charm from his mother," Beth said.

"He's adopted," Heather said. Lindsey and Beth both looked at her. "He told me the other night after his mom yelled at him for being backstage when he was supposed to be out front."

"I wonder if she'll make him quit the show," Beth said.

"She can't!" Heather cried. "He loves it and he's a really, really good actor."

"He is very naturally talented," Beth agreed. "But I didn't get the sense from his mother that she approves of his desire to be on stage."

Another car pulled up; Heather's mom. Unlike Dylan's mother, she rolled down her window and chatted with Lindsey and Beth before they left.

"So, now that they're gone," Beth said as they walked toward the bike rack, "tell me what you really think. Did someone try to harm Robbie on purpose?"

Lindsey bent over to unlock her bike. She put the lock in the back basket and lifted the bike out of the rack. She waited while Beth did the same. As they walked their bikes to the curb, she pondered Beth's question.

"It looks like it, but I honestly don't know," she said. "There are a lot of people who have reason to dislike Robbie, but murder? That's pretty harsh for the merry wanderer of the night."

Lindsey was in her office at the library the next morning when the Chief Plewicki stopped by. Emma was a dark-haired beauty with a heart-shaped face and a wide, warm smile.

When Chief Daniels had retired over the summer, Emma had applied for his position and been hired as the new Briar Creek chief of police. She also had the distinction of being the town's first female chief of police. Lindsey had noted that during Emma's first few months, she had been quick to enforce the rules that had gone a bit lax under the former chief's watch. Lindsey wondered if the pressure of being the first female made Emma more strict or if it was just because she was new.

As a native Creeker, Emma knew most everyone in town and knew how to work the small-town politics to her advantage. Lindsey liked having one more woman in the town department head meetings, as it evened out the boardroom.

"Hi, Lindsey, do you have minute?"

"For the chief of police?" Lindsey asked. "Always."

"That never gets old," Emma said. She grinned at Lindsey as she came in and sat down.

"Chief Plewicki does have a nice ring to it," Lindsey said. "What can I do for you?"

"I went to see Robbie Vine today," Emma said. "He's quite a charmer."

"Agreed," Lindsey said. She felt her face get warm at the memory of his kiss but she pushed the thought aside. He had been teasing her, she was sure of it. Okay, mostly sure of it.

"What's your take on what happened last night?" Emma asked.

Lindsey blew out a breath. "It was scary. The lights went out. Everyone was stranded in their spot, and then Robbie was stabbed."

"So you don't think it was an accident?" Emma asked. "Maybe he jabbed himself on a piece of set in the dark? Maybe one of the set builders jabbed him with a tool by mistake?"

Lindsey looked at Emma and considered what she said. Could the whole thing have been a freak accident? Then she remembered the gash on Robbie's arm.

"No," Lindsey said. "Admittedly, I know nothing about wounds, but it looked too clean to me."

"The doctor who stitched up his arm agrees with your assessment," Emma said. "Definitely a knife."

"Then why are you asking if it was a piece of set?"

"Because I wanted your impression, and I'd really have liked for it to have been an accident," Emma said.

"So someone is trying to harm Robbie?" she asked.

"Quite possibly," Emma said. "It could also be that they are trying to ruin the show, given that Robbie's the star, and hurting him would be an effective way to shut it down."

"Oh dear, poor Violet," Lindsey said. "Will she cancel the show?"

"She thought about it," Emma said. "But Robbie insisted that the show must go on."

Lindsey could see him doing that. He was so very passionate about the stage.

"I don't think that's the wisest choice," Lindsey said.

"Agreed." Emma nodded. "Listen, Lindsey, I don't want to put you in an awkward position, but Robbie seems particularly fond of you, so I was hoping you would be willing to keep an eye on him."

"How do you mean?"

"Well, he managed to work you into the conversation when I talked to him last night and again this morning."

Lindsey felt the heat of embarrassment creep into her face but decided to ignore it and hoped that Emma would do the same. "No, I meant how do you want me to keep an eye on him?"

"Don't do anything that would put you in harm's way. Just if you see anyone in the theater who seems angry with him, talks bad about him or threatens him, or seems to want to cause him harm, could you let me know?"

"I can start you out with a few names right now." Lindsey recounted her conversation with Violet, Nancy, Mary, and Ian from the evening before. After naming Kitty, Lola, Brian the jealous actor, and droopy Harvey Wargus, Lindsey felt better.

"Violet gave me the same names," Emma said. "I've got some officers out talking to them already, and I'll follow up by questioning them myself. It sounds like it could be any one of the four of them. But I don't want to fixate on them and miss someone else. If you see anyone approach Robbie in a threatening manner, will you report it to me immediately?"

"Absolutely," Lindsey said. "Is there anything else I can do?"

"Not yet, but I'll let you know," Emma said as she rose from her seat. "I'm really hoping this was just a person acting out and that it doesn't get any more serious. My officers and I will be taking shifts at the theater, so that might prove to be enough of a deterrent."

"Let's hope," Lindsey agreed.

Emma rose from her seat and walked to the door. She turned and looked at Lindsey.

"There was one thing I wanted to know," Emma said.

"Yes?"

"Do you know where Sully was at the time that Robbie was stabbed?"

"What?"

"You heard me," Emma said.

Her face wore a mild expression, but Lindsey knew the other woman well enough to know that she was cataloging Lindsey's every reaction.

"Emma, if you think Sully would ever harm anyone—" Lindsey began, feeling indignant on Sully's behalf.

"No, I don't," Emma interrupted. "But I had to be sure, and as his former girlfriend, I figured you'd know if he might be having turf issues because of Robbie."

"No," Lindsey said. "As far as I know, there are no turf issues. In fact, when we spoke the other night, Sully was very clear that I should do whatever made me happy."

The words were harder to get out than Lindsey would have thought. Emma pressed her lips together in understanding.

"I'm sorry," she said.

"No need," Lindsey said. "I know you're just doing your job."

Emma nodded and left the office, leaving Lindsey feeling sad. She hadn't thought much about her conversation with Sully because it depressed her, but now, at least it made him look free and clear of the incidents with Robbie.

Now that Emma and her officers were going to be at the theater, Lindsey couldn't help but wonder what tonight's rehearsal would bring. She hoped a whole lot of nothing.

Three nights later, the tension level in the theater had diminished and once again everyone was beginning to feel at ease. There had been no further incidents involving falling scenery, the lights going out or actors suffering knife wounds.

Lindsey had finally gotten her papier-mâché donkey head to look like a donkey and was happily painting it gray while she watched the cast rehearse on stage under Violet's watchful eye.

She had seen Sully earlier, and while he had greeted her as if everything was fine, she couldn't help but feel like there was a growing chasm of distance between them. She missed him. She missed what they'd been together and she missed him as her friend. She didn't see how she could change things; maybe it was only something time could manage.

Robbie, on the other hand, had been constantly underfoot when he wasn't on stage. He was funny and charming and Lindsey couldn't help but like him. He never mentioned their kiss from the other evening, and he didn't try to kiss her again, either.

Instead, he asked her what books she liked to read and what movies she liked to watch. He asked her about her childhood and what her favorite flowers were. Being on the receiving end of his attention was very flattering, but Lindsey couldn't help but think that she was just a passing distraction for him.

They talked about the actors he had worked with and the experiences he'd had. Lindsey was particularly enthralled when he told about being presented to the queen of England. Robbie, of course, made a joke about it, but she could tell he was proud.

As she capped her paint, she looked up from her donkey's head to watch Robbie on stage as he delivered his lines. He didn't just say the lines; he made them come to life.

As if he sensed her eyes on him, he turned and delivered the last of his lines right to her. When he was finished, Violet and the others clapped and he gave a short bow.

"Why don't we all take a short break," Violet said. "Be back in five."

"You're not kidding when you said short," Robbie said. He picked up his bottle of coconut water and shook it. It was empty.

Lindsey glanced back down at her donkey head

and wondered if she could scrounge up a blow dryer to make the coat of paint dry more quickly.

She decided to go ask Nancy when there was a terrible gurgling sound from the stage. She glanced up and saw Robbie stumble. He caught himself on a piece of the set and pushed himself upright.

"Mr. Vine, are you all right?" Dylan asked from across the stage.

"Huh?" Robbie squinted at the boy. "Yeah, I'm fine."

Lindsey frowned. Robbie looked anything but fine. As if to prove her right, he let out a groan and sat down—or, more accurately, fell down on the stage.

"Robbie, get up!" Kitty snapped from the front of the theater.

"Don't tell me what to do, you harpy," Robbie snapped. But he wobbled even while sitting and his voice sounded slurred.

"Robbie, are you drunk?" Violet asked. She sounded annoyed.

"No!" Robbie said. Then he clutched his forehead and said, "Gah, my head is splitting!"

Lindsey wondered if she had any pain medicine in her purse. She was about to go check when Robbie pitched over backward onto the stage.

"Robbie!" Violet shouted.

She ran forward and knelt beside him, and Lindsey hurried from her position at the back of the theater. Emma Plewicki had been sitting in the back row, but she ran up onto the stage and knelt on Robbie's other side.

"Robbie!" Violet cried his name and patted his face. Everyone else in the theater stood frozen. Emma checked the pulse in his wrist and his neck. Then she rested her right ear on his rib cage as if listening for a heartbeat or to feel the rise and fall of his chest.

In moments she was sitting up and she snatched the radio out of its holder on her shoulder. Lindsey heard her call for an ambulance. In the meantime, she started to give Robbie CPR. She was doing chest compressions, and Lindsey could see the sweat bead up on her forehead.

Violet was whispering low in Robbie's ear words of encouragement and cajoling. Time seemed to stand still as everyone looked on in horror. Emma kept up the chest compressions, but there was no sign from Robbie that they were making any difference.

Five minutes later, the EMTs burst through the door at the back of the theater, pushing a stretcher down the aisle.

As soon as they hopped up onto the stage, Emma moved over to give them room.

She glanced at Lindsey and snapped, "Get everyone out of here!"

Feeling as if she were in a trance, Lindsey turned and glanced at the cast and crew, who stood in a trancelike state watching the real-life drama playing out in front of them.

"Everyone, move," Lindsey said. Her voice was stronger than she would have thought. She held her arms out wide and walked toward the group. They all looked around her at the EMTs.

"You heard the chief," Lindsey said. "Let's clear the area."

She saw Milton and Ms. Cole standing by the side of the stage. Her gaze met Milton's and he gave her a small nod of understanding. He turned and whispered something to Ms. Cole. She nodded and together they began to encourage the cast and crew to leave the stage.

Lindsey heard the EMTs talking about Adrenalin and a defibrillator, and she could hear them give one another commands, but she didn't turn around. Not until after the last of the cast and crew had gone through the door, did she turn back to the stage.

She saw one EMT, listening through a stethoscope to Robbie's chest. The seconds stretched into minutes, which felt like hours. Finally, he sat back on his heels.

He looked grim as he glanced at his watch. He turned to Emma and said, "I'm sorry, he's dead."

CHAPTER 13

"What?" Violet cried. "No, there's been a mistake. He's just unconscious. Check him again."

"Ma'am, I'm sorry," the paramedic said. He looked at Emma and said, "We're going to need to move him now."

"Of course," she said.

"No! Robbie, no!" Violet cried. She looked as if she'd launch herself at his body, but Emma caught her by the arms and held her.

"Violet, it's no use," Emma said. Violet let loose a desperate, keening cry and collapsed into Emma's arms.

Lindsey couldn't catch her breath. She could feel her heartbeat rushing in her ears and closing out all sound, as if it could drum out the paramedic's words. It couldn't be true. He couldn't be dead. But there was no denying the still, lifeless form of Robbie Vine.

She tried to speak, but her throat was raw, as if her vocal chords had been severed and couldn't push out the words.

She cleared her throat and tried again, "Violet, I'm so sorry."

Emma glanced up and waved her over. When

Lindsey knelt beside them, Emma handed Violet over to Lindsey and said, "I'm going to have to interview everyone. No one leaves."

"I understand," Lindsey said.

The paramedics loaded Robbie onto a stretcher. Violet reached out and gripped his lifeless hand in hers for just a moment. Lindsey found herself staring at Robbie's handsome face. She saw flashes of him smiling, laughing and teasing her. When they draped a sheet over his head, she wanted to yell for them to stop. Like Violet, she simply couldn't believe that a spirit as bright and vibrant as Robbie's could have been extinguished.

Instead, she leaned close to his covered head and whispered in a voice that was rough with unshed tears, "Good-bye, merry wanderer of the night."

The paramedics wheeled him away, and Violet continued to sob. Lindsey held her close and rocked her. There were no words of comfort that she could give. All she could do was give her friend a comforting circle of arms in which to weep.

Emma left with the paramedics. While she was gone, Nancy came running onto the stage from the back room with Mary right behind her.

"We snuck out of the green room and were eavesdropping," she cried. "Oh, Violet, oh, I'm so sorry."

Violet raised her head, and Lindsey moved so

that Nancy could sit and take her post as chief comforter.

Mary looked closely at Lindsey and asked, “Are you all right?”

“Yeah,” Lindsey lied. She bit the inside of her cheek to keep from crying, but her eyes stung and her throat burned from the effort.

“Lindsey!” Sully came tearing onto the stage from the loading dock at the back with Ian right behind him. “Are you all right? What happened?”

He grabbed her by the arms and held her so that he could get a good look at her face. His blue eyes missed nothing, and he said, “Oh, damn.”

He pulled her close and held her tight. It was the kindness in his eyes and the secure feeling in his arms that were her undoing.

Lindsey began to cry. She didn’t mean to, but once the floodgates burst, there was no holding back and she was hiccupping into Sully’s shoulder while he ran a hand up and down her back, soothing her while she cried it out.

“Sorry,” she said. She pulled away and sniffed. “I just . . . it was . . . I can’t believe it.”

Sully cupped her face, his thumb stroking her cheek. His voice was tender when he said, “I know.”

Emma Plewicki came back into the theater. Her face was set in hard lines as she strode toward the stage.

“Violet, are you all right?” she asked.

Violet was sitting on the edge of the stage with Nancy beside her. One look at her tear-ravaged face and Emma rephrased her question.

"What I mean by that is are you up to talking about what happened or do you need more time?"

"No, I can talk about it," she said. She looked shaky, and she fretted a tissue between her fingers.

"If you'll excuse us," Emma said. "I'd like to talk to everyone one at a time." Her voice was gentle but firm.

Nancy looked at Violet. "Do you want me to stay with you?"

"No, I'll be all right," Violet said. She patted her friend's hand.

Nancy looked reluctant but she left the stage and joined the others. As they started to walk up the aisle, Emma turned and called after them, "Don't go too far, Lindsey. I want to talk to you next."

Lindsey stumbled but Sully steadied her. "I gotcha."

"Thanks," she said.

"Come on, let's get some air," Sully said. He looked at Ian and said, "I'm taking Lindsey outside for air if Emma wants her."

Ian glanced at Lindsey and gave her a sympathetic smile.

"We'll come get you."

The side door to the theater let out into a narrow alley. A cold breeze blew in from the water; it was damp and heavy, and she sucked in big gulps of it, grateful for its bracing effects. It lifted the hair off of her hot neck, and she pressed the heels of her hands against her eyes, trying to keep from crying.

Sully stood quietly beside her. He didn't say anything but his presence was strong and sure and she knew she could lean on him if she needed it. Knowing this steadied her.

"I can't believe he's dead," she said. "I can't believe I watched him die."

"Come here," Sully said.

He opened his arms and just like that, she fell into them. He rested his head against her hair and Lindsey soaked up his strength, not caring that they'd been at odds for months. She was just grateful that he was here now.

"Emma's a good cop," he said. "She'll figure it out."

Lindsey leaned back and looked at him. "You don't think it was a random heart attack, do you?"

Sully blew out a breath. "No."

"Poor Violet," she said. She stepped away from him, wrapped her arms around herself and began to pace. "He was like family to her. I can't even imagine how Charlene is going to take it."

"Badly, I would guess," Sully said.

The side door opened and Mary peered out. "Emma wants to talk to you, Lindsey."

"Oh, all right," she said. She turned back to Sully and rested her hand on his arm. "Thanks."

"Anytime," he said.

Lindsey would have liked to have said more, but things had changed between them. They weren't dating and they'd been too distant with one another over the past few months to be friends, so she was left not knowing what to say.

With an unsatisfactory nod, she took a deep breath and went back into the theater. She tried not to look at the place where Robbie had fallen but of course that's exactly where her gaze went.

There was no sign of Violet. In fact, the only people in the theater were Emma and what appeared to be some crime scene techs, who were investigating the stage where Robbie had fallen. Emma was sitting in the front row, and she gestured for Lindsey to join her.

Lindsey took a seat and turned slightly to face Emma. "How's Violet holding up?"

"She'll be all right," Emma said. "Right now I'm worried about you. How are you doing?"

"I've been better," Lindsey said. "I can't believe one minute he was swigging his coconut water and the next he's dead on the stage."

"His what?" Emma asked, suddenly sitting up.

"Coconut water," Lindsey said. "He always had a bottle on hand."

Emma glanced over at the techs. One of them was looking at Lindsey, and he turned and nodded at Emma.

"We found two empty bottles up here," he said. "We'll have them tested."

“Tested for what?” Lindsey asked.

“We don’t know yet,” Emma said. “But my first guess would be poison.”

“You think Robbie was poisoned?” Lindsey asked.

Emma was silent for moment and then she let out a sigh. “I would like you to keep that to yourself, but yes, I do believe he was poisoned.”

“Which means his death was murder,” Lindsey said.

“Yes,” Emma confirmed.

It was like a punch to the gut, but Lindsey couldn’t deny that there were a lot of people who had issues with Robbie. He did not manage his personal life very well, and it seemed that for every person who adored him another loathed him.

Lindsey spent the next few minutes describing everything she had seen that night as Emma took notes. It seemed to Lindsey she was building a chronology of the evening’s events. It was going to take her a long time to get through the cast and crew but maybe at the end of it, she’d have her suspect.

“If you think of anything else, call me,” Emma said as she rose to leave.

Lindsey made her way out of the theater, wondering if the others were outside. They weren’t. It was just Sully, sitting on the bike rack, waiting.

“Want a lift home?” he asked.

"Are you allowed to leave?"

"Emma's only questioning the people who were in the theater when it happened," he said. "The rest of us were questioned by one of her officers, presumably to establish our whereabouts."

"Did Violet go home?"

"Nancy took her to go break the news to Charlene."

"In that case, I'd really appreciate a ride home," she said.

Sully stood up, and Lindsey unfastened her bike. She wheeled it around the building to the parking lot, where Sully had his truck. He hefted it up into the back for her, and Lindsey climbed into the passenger seat.

It had been a long time since she'd gotten a lift from Sully, and it felt nice to be with him again. They were quiet on the ride. In fact, the whole town seemed quiet as if maintaining a respectful hush after such a horrible tragedy.

It was a short drive and Lindsey was grateful. All she wanted to do was go and hug her dog. When Sully pulled into the driveway, Heathcliff came barreling around the house from the backyard.

Lindsey and Sully both got out of the truck. Heathcliff wrapped his front paws around Lindsey's leg and hugged her tight. Then he barked and ran around the truck to do the same thing to Sully.

Charlie came around the house at a jog. "Heathcliff, hey!"

"Hi, Charlie," Lindsey said.

"Oh, it's you. I might have known. I swear, that dog can sense when you're a quarter of a mile away."

Charlie glanced past Lindsey to where Sully was hauling her bike out of the back. He raised his eyebrows at Lindsey. Lindsey gave a quick shake of her head.

Charlie raised his hands in the universal sign of *What gives?* Lindsey shook her head again and jerked her head toward the house to let him know they would discuss it later.

Lindsey knew Charlie was torn because while they were neighbors and friends, Sully was his boss and a friend, plus the two of them had known each other a lot longer. Charlie had never come out and directly accused Lindsey of breaking Sully's heart, but she sometimes thought he believed that, even though he knew full well that Sully had been the one to end their relationship.

Charlie shook his head back at her and pointed to the ground as if to say *Explain now*.

Lindsey bugged her eyes at him and tried to look threatening.

"Are you two done with your sign language now?" Sully asked as he plopped the bike down next to Lindsey.

She jumped and turned to look at him in surprise.

"We weren't—" Charlie began but Lindsey interrupted him.

"Yes, we're done," she said.

Sully gave her a slow smile and she found herself returning it, even though she knew hers was probably hampered by the overwhelming shock and sadness that seemed to weigh her down with all the grace of a cinderblock.

Sully looked at Charlie and said, "We've got some bad news. Robbie Vine is dead and it looks like someone killed him."

"Oh, boss, you didn't!" Charlie cried.

CHAPTER 14

"What?" Sully asked. "No, I didn't! What would make you even think a thing like that?"

"Well, he was moving in on your girl," Charlie said.

"Oh, my god, do you not have a filter for that mouth?" Lindsey asked him.

She snatched her bike from Sully and wheeled it through the side door of the garage. When she came back out, Sully was glaring at Charlie, who was looking sheepish.

“It’s just—” Charlie began but Lindsey held up her hand to stop him before he said something even more incredibly stupid.

“Come on, Heathcliff,” Charlie said. “Looks like I’m sharing your doghouse.”

Heathcliff jumped on Sully one more time before following Charlie into the house.

“Sorry about that,” Lindsey said.

“No need for you to be,” Sully said. “Charlie leads with his mouth. That’s what makes him such a good rock singer.”

Lindsey smiled. “Well, thanks again for the ride.”

“Anytime,” he said.

She gave him a small wave and turned and headed to the house. Maybe if nothing else, she and Sully were reestablishing their friendship. The thought made the heaviness in her chest ease just the tiniest bit. But then she thought of Robbie and she felt taken out at the knees once again. How could someone as vibrant as Robbie Vine be dead?

“Lindsey, wake up!” a voice called, accompanied by a fist pounding on her apartment door.

Heathcliff bounded off of the bed and out of the bedroom, and skidded across the wooden floor of the living room to the front door, barking all the way.

Lindsey squinted at the clock. It was seven

o'clock in the morning but it felt like the middle of the night. Sleep had been impossible last night and she hadn't drifted off until the wee hours of the morning.

"Lindsey!" the voice called again.

She was wearing her favorite blue-and-green-plaid pajama bottoms with a matching solid green top. She glanced down and decided she was decent enough to let in whoever was outside and so followed Heathcliff to the door.

"Who is it?" she called.

"Charlie."

Definitely decent enough; Charlie had seen her in her jammies a million times.

She unlatched the chain and turned the deadbolt. She pulled the door open and Heathcliff shot out to greet Charlie with a hug around the knees and some furious wagging of his tail.

"Hey there, boy," Charlie said as he scratched Heathcliff's ears.

"What is it, Charlie? Is Nancy okay?"

"No, Nancy is fine," he said. "She's already over at Violet's, going full mother hen on her."

Lindsey nodded.

"But you have to turn on the news," he said. "Emma Plewicki is about to give a press conference about Robbie Vine's death."

"Oh! Oh!" Lindsey turned and hurried back into her apartment. She grabbed her remote and flipped on the local news channel.

Sure enough, there was live footage of Emma Plewicki at the police station. Lindsey turned up the volume.

"At seven forty-seven last night," Emma said, "Mr. Robert Vine took ill while performing on the Briar Creek Community Theater stage."

The sound of cameras snapping pictures of Emma buzzed like a swarm of angry bees. Lindsey was pleased to see that Emma kept her composure. Charlie came to stand beside her.

"She's representin'," he said as he nodded with approval.

Lindsey gave him a sideways look and turned back to the television.

"Mr. Vine was rushed to the hospital for further treatment," Emma said. "I want to assure his adoring fans that everything has been done to give Mr. Vine the best possible care. Because we have been unable to locate Mr. Vine's immediate family, we ask that you respect their privacy until we can fully inform them of the situation."

"Chief Plewicki, was it a drug overdose?" one reporter shouted.

"I am not at liberty to discuss the case any further," she said. She was very firm, and Lindsey was proud to see her shut down the reporters without losing her cool.

"Was it a self-inflicted condition or do you suspect foul play?" another reporter asked.

"Again, I can give no further details until I have

been in communication with his family," she said.

The reporters continued to shout questions at her even as Emma walked away from the front desk at the station and back into her office.

A reporter, Kili Peters, stepped in front of the camera. She was a blonde bubblehead whom Lindsey had had the misfortune to have stalking the library several months back when Beth's ex-boyfriend had been slain. Lindsey was not a fan.

"Well, there you have it," Kili said. "Robbie Vine was rushed to the hospital last night. Reports from people on the scene say that he took his last breath on the stage, but this has yet to be confirmed by the police. It sounds as if it won't be until they can locate his family."

"Thank you, Kili," the male news anchor said. "Please keep us up to date as the story unfolds."

"Will do, Jim," Kili said. "This is Kili Peters, reporting live from Briar Creek."

Lindsey switched off the television and turned to face Charlie. "What do they mean they can't locate his family? Wouldn't that be Kitty?"

"According to Nancy, it's actually his mother they're trying to get into contact with," Charlie said. "She's on vacation in Italy and they're hoping to reach her before the news media does."

"Oh, poor thing," Lindsey said. "What a horrible way to find out that your son is dead by having a reporter scream it at you while they try to take your photograph."

“Agreed,” Charlie said. “So, how are you doing?”

“Fine; no, that’s a lie,” she said. She pulled out the fixings for coffee and held them up. Charlie nodded, and Lindsey began to brew a double pot of coffee. “I feel like road kill actually.”

“You liked Robbie,” he said. He sat at the counter and watched her while she scooped coffee into the filter.

“He was very likable,” she said.

“I’m sorry,” Charlie said.

“Me, too. I’m more worried about Violet and Charlene, however. I got the distinct impression that Robbie was like family for them. They have to be devastated.”

“What do you think will happen to the theater if they cancel the show?” Charlie asked. “I mean, don’t they need the advertising and ticket sale revenue to keep the mortgage paid on the theater?”

“They do,” Lindsey said. “But maybe the bank will be forgiving in light of the tragedy.”

Charlie gave her a flat stare as she poured his coffee. “Yeah, because banks are really known for that.”

Lindsey sighed as she poured her own cup. The boy had a point. So now, on top of losing her friend, poor Violet was probably going to lose her theater as well.

A meeting was called for all of the cast and crew for seven o’clock that evening. Lindsey was one of the last to arrive, as she'd gotten caught up with helping Mrs. Fisk research the legal forms she needed to give her daughter power of attorney when she died.

Mrs. Fisk was nowhere near death. She was only fifty-five, but she was a nervous sort who liked to have everything in order just in case.

As Lindsey walked her bike from the library to the theater, she couldn't really fault Mrs. Fisk. Given that Robbie, who had only been in his late thirties, was now dead, it was pretty clear that you never knew when your number was up and it was good to be prepared. Lindsey wondered who would inherit Robbie's fortune. If Kitty was his beneficiary, it certainly gave her a heck of a motive to kill him.

She locked up her bike and then slipped through the door to take a seat with the rest of the crew. Mary and Nancy were sitting with Ian and Sully. The cast was sitting closer to the stage, and she could just make out Beth's spiky black hair in the second row.

Violet was in front of the stage. She looked pale and tired, and Lindsey imagined that she hadn't gotten much, if any, sleep.

"How's she holding up?" Lindsey asked.

"As well as can be expected," Nancy said.

"Good evening, everyone," Violet said. "Thank you all for coming."

There were murmured greetings in return.

Lindsey scanned the room to see who had shown up. She saw Lola sitting down in front with the cast, but there was no sign of Kitty. She wondered if Robbie's wife was too grief struck to attend or if she had been detained by the police.

"Now, I know that most of you have heard the rumor that Robbie is dead. I'm sad to say it is true." Violet paused. There were a few mutters, but mostly the room absorbed the news without surprise.

"I imagine many of you think that without Robbie, we will cancel the show," Violet said. "But I refuse to do that. I'm sure you have all heard the stories that Robbie's death was no accident. Well, I'm here to tell you that those rumors are also true."

A gasp rippled through the crowd. Surprised, Lindsey returned her attention to Violet. She didn't think that Emma had announced the cause of Robbie's death and she was surprised that Violet was saying anything that hadn't been confirmed by the police as yet. Then again, Robbie had been a close personal friend to Violet, so her grief was probably getting the better of her.

Like the others, Lindsey had assumed the show would be canceled. She noted, however, that Violet's posture had changed in the past few minutes. She wasn't hunched over with sadness anymore. Instead, she was standing tall with her chin tilted up.

"Robbie was taken from us, and the loss of my friend to me and to the theater world is almost too much to bear." Violet's voice broke and she paused to collect herself. "But I refuse to cower and crumble from this sick and twisted act of treachery. Robbie and I performed together on some of the greatest stages in the world, and I know that he would not want me to cancel this show. In fact, he will probably haunt me if I do."

A ripple of muted whispers raced through the room.

"And so, I propose that we put on *A Midsummer Night's Dream* for Robbie, in his memory and in his name. We will honor him with the greatest performance of our lives."

The room erupted into applause and Violet struck a triumphant pose at the front and center of the stage.

Lindsey turned surprised eyes on Nancy and Mary. They did not look as surprised, and Lindsey figured that Violet had already told Nancy her plans. Ian and Sully didn't look surprised, either, and Lindsey wondered if she was the only one out of the loop.

"Dylan," Violet addressed the teen sitting next to Beth. "Are you willing to step out of your role as understudy and take on the role of Puck?"

Lindsey saw him turn to Beth with wide eyes as if asking her if he could do it. Beth nodded and he turned back to Violet and said, "Yes, for Mr. Vine, I'll do my best."

"Excellent," Violet said. She beamed at the group and said, "Well, let's get started. We have a lot of work to do."

As one, the crowd rose from their seats. There was a dull roar of chatter and it was a moment before one lone voice rang out over the crowd.

"Ms. La Rue," a man's voice called repeatedly. "Ms. La Rue!"

Violet turned away from Dylan, who had climbed up onto the stage to stand beside her, and faced the person in the theater.

"Yes?" she asked.

"Is it true, Ms. La Rue, that Robbie Vine was poisoned to death and died right here on this stage?"

CHAPTER 15

Who is that?" Violet asked. She was squinting against the light that was shining onto the stage from the balcony.

"It's me, your old pal Harvey," he said. "So, is it true?"

"Harvey Wargus?" she asked. "How did you get in here? This rehearsal is closed to the public, and

I thought I made it clear that you are not welcome in my theater."

"You said Robbie was taken from you," Harvey continued. "Do you believe the preliminary reports that he was poisoned?"

"You'll have to confirm that with the authorities," Violet said. Her face was flushed, and Lindsey could tell she was angry. "Please leave, Harvey."

"But I'm sure Robbie's fans will be so moved to hear about you dedicating this show to his memory," Harvey said. "Would you care to give me an exclusive about your feelings on your friend's death—you know, for old time's sake?"

"Get out," Violet snapped.

"Aw, what's the matter, Violet? Are you afraid your little theater won't survive the scandal?" Harvey actually cackled with a manic delight. "Tell me, who do you think did the egotistical no-talent in, anyway? Surely you have some ideas."

His words were cut off as Sully caught him by the back of the collar and hoisted him out of the seating area. With one hand on the back of his shirt and one on the back of his pants, he carted Harvey to the side door, which Ian helpfully opened. With one great heave, Sully tossed him out and Ian let the door slam back into position.

"All right, Violet?" Sully asked.

"Never better," she said and she gave him a tight smile.

Ian and Sully headed down the hall that led to the back of the stage and the loading dock to resume work on the set.

"Come on," Nancy said as she looped her arm through Lindsey's. "We have a new Puck to outfit."

Mary, Nancy and Lindsey were in the back room working on the costumes when Lindsey paused and frowned at the other two.

"Is it just me or do you think it's weird that Harvey asked Violet about the theater being able to survive the scandal?"

"Harvey Wargus is a liver-spotted wart on a toad's bottom," Nancy said.

Mary laughed. "Nice bardesque put-down."

"Thank you," Nancy said. "But honestly, the man is vile. He hated Robbie and he hates Violet, and he'd like nothing more than to see them suffer."

"Well, one down then," Mary said.

"Do you think he might have killed Robbie?" Lindsey asked. "And if so, will he go after Violet next?"

"No," Nancy said, and then her eyes widened. "Maybe."

"I think we need to keep an eye on her," Lindsey said.

"Agreed," Mary said. "In fact, I'll go out there right now. I can hem this doublet in the theater while they rehearse."

She gathered her supplies and draped the costume over her shoulder.

"I'll make sure Ian and Sully are in the loop," she said. The door shut behind her, and Lindsey turned to face Nancy.

"I hope I'm just being paranoid," she said.

"No, I don't think so," Nancy said. "And even if you are, it's better to be safe than sorry."

"I suppose," she said. "I'll go tell Beth what's going on. The more people keeping an eye on Violet, the better."

Lindsey made her way backstage. She found Beth with Heather and Perry and the new cast member who had taken Dylan's place as one of the lesser fairies. They were going over their blocking for Act II.

"Sorry to interrupt," Lindsey said. "Beth, can I talk to you?"

"Sure," she said. "Walk Molly through it, guys, and I'll be right back."

She and Lindsey moved out of the way of the actors playing Theseus and Hippolyta. Beth watched them go by with a wistful look, and Lindsey wondered if it was because she wanted the part of Hippolyta or because Hippolyta had a fine-looking partner in Theseus.

"So, how goes the costuming?" Beth asked. "Do you need help?"

"No, thankfully Mary and Nancy really have it under control."

"Oh, I don't know. I saw your donkey mask, and I was impressed."

"Please. It looks like a gray waffle with ears," Lindsey said. Beth laughed and Lindsey smiled. "But I'm confident I can bend it to my will before the dress rehearsal."

"That's my girl," Beth said. "So, how can I help?"

"Actually, I was hoping you could help keep an eye on Violet," Lindsey said.

Beth raised her eyebrows and Lindsey explained what she had discussed with Nancy and Mary.

"Do you really think this is about more than Robbie?" Beth asked.

"I don't know," Lindsey said. "I know there were a lot of people who had issues with him, but murder seems awfully harsh. I wonder if it isn't bigger than that, like maybe someone wants the theater gone or they want revenge."

"But if what you're saying is true, then you think Violet could be next," Beth said.

"I'm afraid she might be," Lindsey said. "That Wargus guy sure seems to have it in for her, and Sterling Buchanan did hire him to cover the show. Maybe there is more going on here than even Violet is aware of."

"Whoa," Beth said. "Well, count me in. I won't let her out of my sight."

"And make sure she doesn't eat or drink anything unless she knows its point of origin."

Beth nodded. Then she looked at Lindsey. "How are you holding up?"

"I'm okay," Lindsey said. "Feels weird without him here though, doesn't it?"

"Yes, he brought a certain energy to the theater that is sadly lacking now."

"How is Dylan doing?"

"Like a duck to water," Beth said. "It was great that Robbie spent so much time working with him before. It'll make the transition into the bigger part much easier for him."

"How about his mother?" Lindsey asked. "She seemed unhappy that he was spending so much time here."

"She was in earlier and seemed quite proud that he had such an important role. Maybe now that he's one of the stars, she approves."

"Ah." Lindsey nodded. "Maybe she has a bit of the stage mother in her."

"Oh, I hope not," Beth said. "We already have Heather's mother trying to push her into a bigger part. She even tried to have Heather take the role of Puck."

"How does Heather feel about it?"

"Mortified," Beth said. "She's happy with her bit part."

"Poor kid."

"It's okay. Violet can manage the stagestruck mom," Beth said. "So far, she's sent her for coffee, had her painting sets and last I saw she sent her on an errand to go look for a scepter for Oberon."

"I thought Nancy already had one."

Beth shrugged.

"Fairies, front and center," Violet called out from the stage.

"Gotta go," Beth said and she squeezed Lindsey's arm. "Don't worry, I can keep a good eye on Violet from the stage."

"Thanks," Lindsey said.

She left the backstage area and made her way to the hallway. As she turned the corner, she bumped into Lola, who was leaning against the wall, looking lost.

"Oh, I'm sorry." Lindsey steadied herself on the wall. "I didn't see you."

"No one ever sees me," Lola mumbled. Then she burst into tears.

Lindsey glanced around the dimly lit hallway, hoping someone, anyone, would show up. The place was as abandoned as a graveyard.

"It'll be okay, really," she said. "It just takes time."

"You don't understand. No one cared about me like Robbie did," Lola sniffed. "He looked after me. Now I have no one."

Lindsey looked at the woman next to her. She was a dark-haired beauty who had the helpless and vulnerable thing down pat. Is that what Robbie had seen in her?

"Oh, please," a voice said from the end of the hall. "Robbie's dead. There's no one to come to your rescue. Surely you can cease the waterworks now."

Lola wailed louder, and Kitty strode toward them in knee-high black leather boots, a miniskirt and a sweater that dipped low in the front and hugged her figure tight.

"You wouldn't understand," Lola sobbed. "What Robbie and I had was real; you were just his business partner."

"That's right," Kitty said. "I managed his career. I made all of our lives better because of my fabulous business sense, but without Robbie, my business no longer exists. So, if anyone should be crying, it would be me—which is exactly what I told the police and why they let me go."

Lindsey gave her a surprised look, and Kitty glared at her.

"What?" she asked. "Did you think I busted out of jail?"

"No, but being the spouse . . ." Lindsey's voice trailed off.

"Yeah, yeah, I'm the chief suspect," Kitty said. "I got that. Fortunately, even the pea-brained police in this podunk town can see that as Robbie's manager, it really made no sense for me to kill him. Sort of like cutting off my right arm. Stupid."

"That doesn't mean you didn't do it," Lola said.

"It could have been a crime of passion. You just couldn't bear that he loves me now."

"Ha!" Kitty let out a mirthless laugh. "In case you didn't notice, dearie, Robbie was already looking to replace you. Or did the fact that he dumped your lame ass escape you?"

"He didn't dump me!" Lola wailed. "He just wanted to take a break. Lots of couples do that."

"You're pathetic," Kitty sneered. "If Robbie wanted a break, it means he was done with you. In fact, I do believe it was our lovely librarian here who caught his eye."

"No, I—" Lindsey protested but Lola's crying drowned out her words.

"He would have gotten sick of her," Lola said. She sniffed and wiped her nose on her sleeve. "She's not a theater person. Robbie never liked anyone outside of the theater. He said they didn't understand our world. She was just a plaything to him."

"Plaything?" Lindsey asked. Now she was getting irritated.

"Now you've done it," Kitty said. "You've made the book nerd mad."

"I'm not mad," Lindsey said.

"Then why is your face red?" Kitty asked.

"It's hot in here," Lindsey said.

"And getting hotter," Kitty taunted her. "So, were you interested in Robbie? Did you fancy yourself as his next girlfriend?"

"No!" Lindsey protested. "He was charming, but I had no intention of dating him."

"I don't believe you," Lola said. She had stopped crying and was eyeing Lindsey like she'd like to do her some harm. "Everyone loved Robbie. Women were always throwing themselves at him, even when he was with me."

"Same here," Kitty said. "Even when our marriage was happy, which, all told, was about six months long, women would chase him down the street, show up naked at our front door, send him expensive presents."

"Remember that one woman who tried to kidnap him?" Lola asked.

"That was on your watch," Kitty said.

"I know, but who expected a team of men to shimmy down from a hovering helicopter and scoop him up from the breakfast table?" Lola asked. "I really wasn't prepared for that."

"What happened?" Lindsey asked in awe.

"Some rich woman decided that Robbie was going to be her shiny new toy," she said. "He had to make a run for it."

"But he got away?" Lindsey asked.

"Oh yeah," Kitty said. "He just had to go hide out for a while. You wouldn't believe some of the crazy things women do to get noticed." She paused and looked at Lindsey. "Maybe that's why he took a shine to you. You're not like that."

"Thanks, I think," Lindsey said. The three of

them were silent for a moment. Lindsey was trying to wrap her head around the stories Lola and Kitty told her and the strange relationship they seemed to share.

"What are you two going to do now?" Lindsey asked.

"Well, the police have told us we can't leave town until they're done with the investigation," Kitty said. "So, we will perform in the play just like we would have, and I will handle the business end of things just like I did before Robbie—"

For the first time, Kitty showed a flash of vulnerability, but she scrunched up her face and took a deep, fortifying breath.

"Come on, sad sack, we need to rehearse," she said. She took Lola by the arm and hauled her up the stairs toward the stage.

Lindsey watched them go. Could Kitty have killed Robbie in a jealous fit? It seemed unlikely, but maybe she had a financial motive. What about Lola? She was obviously still in love with Robbie; if he had tried to break it off with her, she might have killed him out of spite.

Then again, all of the incidents with Robbie had happened at the theater. If it had been Kitty or Lola, wouldn't she have killed him where she had easy access to him, like in the house they were all renting? Unless, of course, killing him at the theater gave them an alibi of sorts.

And what about the crazy female fans they

talked about? If a woman was crazy enough to try to kidnap a man, certainly she might turn into a killer if she didn't get what she wanted.

Lindsey made her way back to the costume room, more confused than ever. If she looked at who had the most to gain by Robbie being dead, then, if what Kitty said was true, it wasn't her. Lola didn't seem to have enough oomph in her to commit a murder, but then again, how much oomph did you need to poison someone?

Lindsey felt as if the more she learned, the less she was certain of and there was only one thing she could do about it: research. It was time for the skeletons to come out of Robbie's closet once and for all.

CHAPTER 16

I love this database, Lindsey thought as she sat at her desk looking at the unending list of articles that had been brought up using the magazine and newspaper search option in the library's online catalog. Now she just needed to narrow her parameters to weed out the fluff pieces.

More than twenty thousand articles had been written about Robbie Vine. This sure beat using a lame Internet search engine and getting random web pages, or even worse, some unverifiable bits of information cobbled together by a collection of self-proclaimed "experts."

If she sorted out all of the articles that were reviews of his shows and movies, that should trim it down. She revised her search. Wow. Still a lot of articles, but if she was looking to know about Robbie's past, she was betting she wanted the interviews from when he was a breakout star and had been less cautious with his words.

A knock sounded on her door, and she called, "Come in."

Emma Plewicki walked in, and Lindsey suddenly felt like the kid caught reading a comic book in history class. She leaned forward, covering her monitor.

"Hi, Emma, how's it going?" she asked.

"Why do you look weird?"

"Weird? What do you mean?"

Emma narrowed her eyes. "Chief Daniels warned me about you. Are you being a buttinsky?"

Lindsey sat back in outrage. "Did he call me that? Because that's just rude."

"Is that an article search on Robbie Vine?" Emma asked. She leaned around Lindsey to see her computer. "He was right; you are a buttinsky."

"I'm not—okay, I am," Lindsey said. She dropped her head into her hands and then peeked at Emma through her fingers. "I can't help myself.

Seeking information is an occupational hazard."

"Or interfering with police work," Emma said. "Depending upon your point of view."

Lindsey raised her right hand. "I swear I've done no interfering of any kind."

Emma took the seat across from her desk and said, "Are you quite certain?"

"Yes, it's just . . . well, I can't help wondering who could have had such a grudge against Robbie that they would kill him," Lindsey said. "Yes, he was arrogant and a narcissist, but from what I could tell from Kitty and Lola, they both still cared for him."

"I thought you said you weren't interfering." Emma sat up straight and glared at Lindsey. "What were you doing talking to Lola and Kitty?"

"I just ran into them in the theater," Lindsey said. "And by that, I do mean literally ran into them. I came around a corner and Lola was standing there crying, then Kitty came up and they both started talking about Robbie."

Emma raised one eyebrow and stared at Lindsey. "And now you're looking up articles about him?"

"Well, it doesn't seem like either of them had a reason to kill him if you take the whole crime of passion equation out, and a poisoning does seem a bit too plotted to be a crime of passion. But then there are the two incidents with him getting hit by a piece of set and then stabbed in the dark."

"Either of those two could have been a crime of passion, but I agree, it seems unlikely," Emma said. "Statistically speaking, in a crime of passion the weapon is usually something that was at hand, which is why you get the blunt-object trauma so often in those scenarios."

"Really? I had no idea," Lindsey said. "I would have guessed a gun or a knife."

"No, that would indicate premeditation," Emma said. "Which would not be a crime of passion."

"Huh," Lindsey said. "Is it wrong that I find this fascinating and horrifying at the same time?"

"I wouldn't say wrong, necessarily," Emma said. "Human beings and what they are capable of doing to one another is intriguing and repellant."

"So, you're pretty clear that it wasn't a jilted lover who did Robbie in?" Lindsey asked.

"Yes; in fact, it's why I came to see you," Emma said.

"Me?"

"Everyone says Robbie was showing an interest in you," Emma said. "Did he say anything about anyone to you, anyone who was giving him grief or causing him concern or anything like that?"

"No, he didn't mention anyone specifically," Lindsey said. "I did overhear him in an argument with Brian Loeb."

Emma raised her eyebrows but was silent, letting Lindsey continue.

"Brian accused Robbie of having an affair with

his wife, Brandy," Lindsey said. "Robbie denied it, but Brian didn't seem to believe him."

"Did Brian threaten him?" Emma asked.

Lindsey thought back to the argument. It had been a nasty one. "Yes," she said. "He did threaten him. First he said he was going to squash him like a bug. Robbie laughed him off and then—"

"Then?" Emma prompted her.

"Brian said that he was going to kill Robbie when he caught him with Brandy," she said.

Emma pursed her lips. "As far as you know, did Brian ever catch Robbie with Brandy?"

"No, not that I know of," she said.

"Can you think of anyone else who might have wanted to harm Robbie?"

"Other than Harvey Wargus, the critic, no," Lindsey said.

"I've already had him in for questioning," Emma said. "He's a squirmy little fellow."

"Right," Lindsey agreed. "And I don't like him. Did Violet talk to you at all about her ex?"

Lindsey felt as if she were betraying her friend by mentioning him, but how could she not when he could very well be the reason that Robbie was dead?

"Yes, both she and Charlene mentioned that Sterling Buchanan could be vindictive when he doesn't get what he wants."

"Robbie was like family to them," Lindsey said. "Do you think Buchanan would have been angry enough to have him harmed in order to hurt them?"

"I don't know," Charlene said. "But I have made inquiries in that direction. The man has so much money that he's made himself quite untouchable. Good thing I'm not easily deterred."

Lindsey smiled. No, she didn't imagine that Emma would be easily put off.

"If you think of anything else, let me know," Emma said as she rose to leave. "Oh, and if you find anything of interest in those articles about Robbie—"

"I'll be sure to let you know," Lindsey promised.

"Thanks," Emma said, and Lindsey was pretty sure that it was non-ironic.

She spent her lunch hour eating a tuna fish sandwich at her desk while reading the articles. The later ones all read pretty much the same about a boy born in Manchester being raised by a single mom who got a scholarship to the Italia Conti Academy of Theater Arts in London. The articles glossed over his rebellious youth, his troubles with the law and a stint in jail. The earlier articles had more meat and more bite, since Robbie was not yet a huge star with PR handlers who could cushion and bend his interviews to their will.

It was an article in the *Times* that caught Lindsey's attention. Robbie had just starred in Noël Coward's *Design for Living* at the Gielgud

Theatre on Shaftesbury Avenue to rave reviews. The reporter joined Robbie for breakfast and found him quite distraught. He had just been informed that he was to be a father. He was not happy about the news. He told the reporter that he and the mother, an American soap opera actress, had just had a fling, one that hadn't been good enough that he'd want a reminder of it for the rest of his life.

Lindsey cringed. He was young in the article, true, but he came off as harsh, selfish and frankly nasty. He did not sound like the charming man she had come to know. She wondered if the PR firms took over his press shortly after this mess.

She scanned the next two years' worth of articles. There was no mention of a wife until he'd married Kitty ten years ago. Kitty was American, but Lindsey doubted she was the mother of Robbie's unnamed child; as far as she knew, they had had no children.

Lindsey wondered what had happened to the mother and child. She checked the date of the article and she figured the baby would be somewhere in its late teens now. She scanned the next few years of articles. The pieces were much less invasive. It was easy to see that Robbie had control of his interviews now, and he gave away nothing that he didn't want known.

The actress was out of the business. She had married a tycoon and moved to Austria. There was nothing current about her, but Lindsey looked up the story line to the soap opera and her character had been pregnant at the same time she would have been. Had they written it into the show just for her? It seemed likely.

Violet had known Robbie since before his debut on Shaftesbury Avenue in London when she had been a guest teacher at his acting school. Lindsey wondered if they'd been close back then and if so, did Violet know he'd fathered a child?

She hated to disturb her when she was under so much stress, but there was only one way to find out if Robbie's child or its mother had ever resurfaced in Robbie's life and that was to ask Violet. She had a feeling Charlene would know, too.

She knew from Beth that Charlene had taken a few days off from the television station to deal with what had happened. She and her three kids were at their cabin on Wishbone Island, one of the smaller Thumb Islands out in the bay. Lindsey suspected that Charlene was trying to protect her kids from the media scrutiny surrounding Robbie's death.

In fact, before Lindsey had come into work, she had baked a batch of pumpkin squares that she had hoped to bring to Charlene and her family. She had been wondering how Charlene had been handling Robbie's death. This would give her a good reason to pop in and see her friend. Lindsey was off the clock at six, and left the library in the very capable hands of her library assistant, Jessica Gallo. Beth and Ms. Cole both headed straight to the theater while Lindsey stopped by the house and retrieved Heathcliff for a walk. Charlie was home and Lindsey rapped on his door on her way out.

"Door's open," Charlie called.

"Charlie, I need to run an errand," Lindsey said as she entered the apartment into his living room.

He was sprawled on his neon orange velvet couch reading *Mad* magazine. Heathcliff did not hesitate but launched himself on top of Charlie and began to lick his face.

"Okay, okay." Charlie laughed. "I'm petting you. See? Lots of pets. Ugh, why does he always lick me on the mouth?"

Lindsey laughed.

"Sorry about that," she said. "He has boundary issues."

"As in, he doesn't have any?" Charlie asked with a grin. He rubbed Heathcliff's head and said, "Love me less, little dude."

"About my errand . . ."

"Did you want to use my van?"

"Uh . . . no," Lindsey said with a shudder.

She had borrowed his van once and it had taken her three washings to get the man stink out of her clothes. Charlie's decrepit van was used primarily to schlep his band to all of its gigs, and the smell of stage sweat and stale beer permeated its shag interior.

"But thanks for the offer," she said. "This errand is actually a run to Charlene's cabin on Wishbone Island."

Charlie glanced up at her from the magazine still in his free hand and said, "Oh, so you need a boat?"

CHAPTER 17

"Yep." Lindsey nodded. She clutched the Tupperware tub full of pumpkin squares to her chest and tried to look the part of the concerned friend.

"You're in luck. I'm on call for the water taxi tonight, since both Sully and Ian are working on the set for the play," he said. "I'm getting double overtime. Let's go."

"Can I bring Heathcliff?" Lindsey asked.

"Sure, he loves the taxi," Charlie said.

"When did he go out on the taxi?" Lindsey asked.

"Oh, um . . ." Charlie grabbed his jacket off of a nearby chair. Lindsey already had hers on.

"Charlie," she said in a warning voice.

"Well, sometimes when I'm watching him for

you, I take him down to visit Sully and we go for a ride on the taxi," Charlie said. He made a face like he was expecting her to slug him. "He missed Sully and I know Sully missed him, too, since you two—"

"Since Sully dumped me," she said. "It's fine. I'm not mad. Much."

Heathcliff's ears perked up at the name *Sully,* and he did a happy dance.

"No, we're not going to see him," she said. Heathcliff sat back down and gave her a sulky look from under his bushy eyebrows. "I'm not going to cave in, so forget it."

"Come on, boy. They'll get back together, you'll see," Charlie said.

"Charlie!" Lindsey protested.

"What?" he asked. "You, Sully and Heathcliff are like PB &J. You just go together."

"Whatever," Lindsey said. She knew it was pointless to argue with him.

"Cheer up, buddy," Charlie said to Heathcliff as he led the way out the door. "At least you still get to ride in the boat."

The air was cold out on the water, and Lindsey's nose began to run. She had forgotten to wear gloves and kept her hands jammed into her pockets when she wasn't blowing her nose.

Wishbone Island was halfway out into the islands, so it only took a little over twenty minutes to reach. Heathcliff loved it. He had his own spot on the boat where he stood and rested his paws on the side; he barked at the wind and tried to bite the waves that splashed up against the boat, and he never stopped wagging.

Lindsey sat in the seat next to him, keeping a hand on his leash just in case a stray wave knocked him overboard. She realized it was unnecessary, as he seemed to have better sea legs than she did, but still, he was her baby.

"Charlie, exactly how many times has he been out on this boat?" she called.

Charlie looked at her and then cupped a hand to his ear and yelled, "Huh?"

Lindsey knew he could hear her. The engine and wind weren't that loud. She shook her head at him, not buying his dodging of the question.

"Oh, look," Charlie cried. "Here we are."

He cut the engine back and turned the wheel to follow the perimeter of the island toward Charlene's cabin. Wishbone Island was named for its shape, and Charlene and Martin's cabin was at the pointy end of the wishbone.

Although the line of the island was rocky, the island itself was lush with trees. There were several cabins on it, as it was one of the few of the Thumb Islands that had electricity. Given the modern conveniences and boat-only access, it was a perfect getaway spot, especially for a local celebrity like Charlene. Lindsey knew that

Charlene loved the peace and quiet that her family could get on the island, away from her life as a busy news anchor.

Charlie brought the boat right into the long dock that belonged to Charlene's cabin. Heathcliff jumped out as soon as he could, and Lindsey scrambled out to tie the boat while Charlie shut down the engine.

Heathcliff was dancing on his feet and Lindsey finally said, "Okay, go ahead."

Heathcliff took off at a run, down the dock and up the stairs that led to a large deck. From there he crossed the deck to scratch against the door, which led into the cozy red cabin with the white trim nestled against a thick thatch of fir trees.

Lindsey waited for Charlie, and together they made their way up the steps. Lindsey had just reached the landing when she saw Charlene come out the door, shutting it behind her.

Charlene was a tall, lithe black woman, who while strikingly good looking, also possessed a keen intelligence that was easy to see in the spark in her eyes. She carried herself with an air of confidence, and she was a successful news anchor quite simply because people trusted her. They trusted her to report the facts and keep them informed about their world.

Right now, she was a casual version of her usual self in jeans and a black turtleneck sweater with her shoulder-length hair tied back by a plaid scarf. She glanced at Lindsey with a worried look.

"Lindsey! Charlie!" she cried when she saw them. "When Heathcliff showed up at the door, I didn't know what to think. Is everything all right?"

"It's fine," Lindsey assured her. "I didn't mean to startle you. I just wanted to check and see that you are doing all right?"

"So you came all the way out here in a boat with your dog?" Charlene asked. "Cell phones reach the islands, you know."

"I know, but I wanted to see you for myself," she said.

"Well, as you can see I'm fine," Charlene said.

Lindsey glanced at Charlie and he shrugged. Charlene was definitely not herself. Lindsey had expected her to be sad or distraught; instead, she seemed stressed and slightly irritated.

Lindsey held out the Tupperware tub she'd brought with her. "I made you pumpkin squares. I thought the kids would like them, and they're somewhat healthy."

Charlene's shoulders slumped. "I'm sorry. This was so nice of you and I'm, well, I'm just out of sorts."

"That's okay; you're grieving," Lindsey said. "It's perfectly normal to feel angry, scared, sad, all of that."

She reached out and hugged her friend around the tub of cookies. Charlene gave her a firm squeeze back, and Lindsey pressed the tub into Charlene's arms.

"How are the kids? Are they doing all right?" she asked.

A squeal of laughter sounded from the open window of the cabin, and Charlene glanced over her shoulder at the house.

"Yes, I haven't really told them anything," Charlene said in a low voice. "I've been waiting."

"Kids are tougher than people think," Charlie said. "They'll be okay."

"Maybe," Charlene said. "How are you doing, Lindsey?"

"Me?" Lindsey asked.

"Yes, I know that you and Robbie seemed to really hit it off," she said.

"Oh, I—" Lindsey glanced at Charlie and saw his outraged look. He had been very clear over the past few months that he fully expected her and Sully to get back together.

"Explain," he said.

"Well, Robbie certainly was a charmer. I'd be lying if I said I wasn't flattered to be noticed by him and I was very sad about, well—" Lindsey's throat got tight and she realized she didn't even want to utter the words that he was gone. She shook her head. She had a purpose here more than just to check on her friend.

"You cared for him a lot, didn't you?" Charlene asked.

"Yeah," Lindsey admitted, ignoring Charlie's huff of indignation.

"I understand," Charlene said. Her voice was so sympathetic that Lindsey was afraid she would burst into tears.

"Look, I don't want to keep you," she said. "I'm sure the kids must be getting ready for bed, but I feel better now that I've seen you. Will you please call me if you need anything?"

"I will absolutely," Charlene said. She took Lindsey's hand and squeezed it in hers. "You're a good friend."

"Thanks," Lindsey said. She turned to Charlie and Heathcliff, who was busily sniffing all of the corners of the deck. "Charlie, why don't you take Heathcliff down to the boat? I'll be right there."

"All right," he said. "Good night, Charlene, and I'm sorry for your loss."

Charlene gave him a small smile. "Thank you, Charlie."

Lindsey waited until they had started down the stairs before she turned back to Charlene.

"What is it, Lindsey?" Charlene asked. "What's on your mind?"

"Charlene, did you know that Robbie fathered a child?" she asked.

Charlene's eyes went wide and she blew out a breath. "Did Robbie tell you that?"

Lindsey lowered her head. "No, I was reading

some old articles about him and it was mentioned in an old *Times* interview."

Charlene put the tub of pumpkin squares on the table and crossed her arms over her chest. She did not look happy.

"Why are you digging into Robbie's past?" she asked.

"Because I'm a buttinsky?" Lindsey suggested.

The sound of laughter came from the cabin and Lindsey cringed. She sincerely hoped that was from the television and not because the kids were eavesdropping and laughing at her.

"Yes, you are," Charlene said. "But given that I'm a reporter, I can't really fault you for it. You need to stay away from this situation, however."

"I promise I'm not getting involved," Lindsey said. "It's just that someone was out to get Robbie and that someone is still out there, and I'm worried—"

"Worried about what?" Charlene asked. She was watching Lindsey closely under the yellow porch light, and Lindsey wished she had just kept her mouth shut. Charlene had enough to deal with without getting all riled that her mother might be a target, too.

"Nothing," Lindsey lied.

"Oh, no, you started to say something," Charlene said. "You need to finish it."

Lindsey blew out a breath. She was going to go for vague and hope that Charlene didn't put it together. "All right, I'm just worried that Robbie wasn't the only target."

"Meaning you think my mother might be next?"

CHAPTER 18

"Well, you weren't supposed to get it that quick," Lindsey said.

"It's nothing I hadn't thought myself," Charlene said. "Mom, of course, refuses to listen."

"Of course," Lindsey agreed. "That's why we've all agreed to keep watch over her. She won't be allowed out of our sight."

Charlene smiled. "I might have known. Meanwhile, I've been nagging Emma to assign an undercover officer to tail her twenty-four-seven."

"Excellent. Between all of us, she should be safe."

Charlene nodded. She looked as if she wanted to say more but she held back.

"I did know that Robbie fathered a child," Charlene said, "but I don't think that had anything to do with what happened."

"Does Emma know?" Lindsey asked.

"I don't know," Charlene said. "I don't feel right telling Emma about Robbie's personal business."

She looped her arm through Lindsey's and led her away from the house. "It was so many years ago, and Mom said when he refused to get married and settle down, the mother put the baby up for adoption. It was before Robbie was famous, so the mother probably didn't think he'd be a contributing factor and she couldn't do it alone. They were just kids themselves."

"Don't worry," Lindsey said. "I'm not judging. It just made me think that maybe, given his success, the mother might have come looking for him."

"No, not that I know of," Charlene said. "I mean, I would think he'd have mentioned it if she had."

"I suppose so," Lindsey said.

"What does Sully think about your interest in Robbie's background?" Charlene asked.

"Nothing as far as I know," Lindsey said. "I mean, Sully and I don't talk that much anymore, so it's not like I mentioned to him that I've been reading articles about Robbie to see if they shed any light on who might have a vendetta against him."

"So, are you and Sully really over?" Charlene asked.

Lindsey glanced down the stairs and across the small dock to the boat where Charlie and Heathcliff sat waiting. Was her relationship with Sully done for good? The thought was a tough one to process. She didn't like it but she didn't see much hope for them if Sully didn't learn to better communicate.

"I don't know, but it doesn't look good," she said.

Charlene glanced over her shoulder at the cabin as if to be sure that the kids were all right and then back at Lindsey. She studied her for moment and then asked, "Do you think you would have dated Robbie, you know, if—"

"If he hadn't been murdered?" Lindsey clarified. "Hard to say, but I did like him. Yes, I'm admitting it; I really, really liked him, despite my good sense. Why do you ask?"

"I was just wondering," Charlene said. "If Robbie hadn't, well, if things had been different and you fell for each other, then Robbie would have stayed here and we could all have lived happily ever after."

"Yeah, his wife might have had something to say about that . . . oh, and his girlfriend, too," Lindsey said.

She could feel her face get warm at the thought of having Robbie Vine for a boyfriend—which was ridiculous, since he was gone—but the thought that she never got to have him be something more in her life made her sad.

"Yeah, well, it would have been nice," Charlene said. "Don't you think?"

"Yeah," Lindsey said. She suspected Charlene

just needed to hear that Robbie's story could have had an alternate ending. "I am so sorry for your loss."

"Thanks," Charlene said, and she hugged Lindsey close. "For everything."

"That's what friends are for," she said. "Call me if you need me."

"I promise," Charlene said.

Lindsey hurried down the stairs and untied the boat. She gave the boat a shove and scrambled aboard while Charlie fired up the engine.

Twenty minutes later, they were pulling up to the dock. Lindsey was about to hustle out when she recognized the tall figure standing on the dock waiting for them. Sully.

Heathcliff went right into spasms of joy, and Lindsey felt her own heart do a skip and a jump. Why was it whenever she thought she was getting over him, he showed up and she was knocked flat all over again?

He grabbed the side of the boat and tied it up while Lindsey and Heathcliff jumped out. Charlie followed as soon as he switched off the engine. Sully didn't say anything but glanced between Charlie and Lindsey, obviously waiting for an explanation.

Lindsey just glanced at him and then at her watch. She wanted to get over to the theater and help Nancy and Mary.

"Charlie, are you heading home?" she asked.

"Yes," he said. "I have the phone here forwarded to my cell so I'll get any taxi calls wherever I am."

"Would you mind taking Heathcliff with you?" she asked. "I want to stop by the theater and see how things are going."

"Sure, me and the dog dude can hang out and watch Animal Planet. He digs the *Gator Boys*," Charlie said. Then he eyed Sully with a wary glance. "Everything all right, boss?"

"Huh?" Sully glanced between them. "Yeah, it's fine. I just stopped by the office for a minute for a paperwork thing."

"Cool," Charlie said. "So, I'll see you later, Lindsey. See ya, boss."

She nodded and waved as Charlie and Heathcliff set off toward home. Lindsey turned in the opposite direction and headed to the theater. Halfway down the pier, Sully fell into step beside her.

"So, you needed the taxi?" he asked.

"Yep."

Silence fell between them, and Lindsey sighed. She didn't like how things were between them now. It was all awkward and wrong. She couldn't help but feel that Sully didn't say what he was thinking and she was afraid that if Sully didn't learn now to say what he was thinking, then if they got back together she would always feel emotionally detached from him. And she just didn't see that as a happy-ever-after.

"I'm guessing you went to see Charlene," he said.

"I did."

"Probably brought her a banana bread."

"Pumpkin squares, actually," she said.

"Oh, man, you didn't give any to Charlie, did you?"

"No, why?"

"Because if he made out just because he was on taxi duty tonight, I would be seriously annoyed," he said. Under the streetlights, Lindsey could see the teasing twinkle in his eyes; she remembered this Sully, the one who made her laugh, and she smiled.

"He didn't get pumpkin squares, just a healthy tip," she said.

They continued down the street to the theater, and things felt more like it used to feel between them. Lindsey felt the tension in her shoulders ease. Maybe she and Sully could find a way back to where they'd once been after all. Of course, that was assuming he was interested.

"So, how are you holding up?" he asked.

"I'm okay," she said. "I've never seen anyone die before, so that's been kind of tough to process, but I imagine we all feel that way."

"Somewhat," Sully said. "But I don't think the rest of us knew him as well as you did."

Lindsey raised her eyebrows and gave him an inquiring look. "How well do you think I knew him?"

Sully gave her a rueful smile. "Not as well as he would have liked."

They paused in front of the theater. The breeze blowing in from the water pushed his dark curls forward over his forehead. Lindsey wanted to push them back, but she didn't.

"I think I was just a novelty for him," she said.

"I disagree," Sully said. "I think he saw something wonderful in you, the same way I do when I look at you."

Lindsey felt her breath catch and when she looked into his eyes, she was undone. She wasn't sure which one of them started it, but she realized they were leaning toward one another, caught up in the moment.

"Hey, you big shirker!" Ian yelled as he banged open the theater door and popped his head out. "I've been looking for you. Get in here! We have a set to finish for dress rehearsal tomorrow night."

Sully muttered something under his breath that did not flatter Ian, and Lindsey bit her lower lip to keep from smiling.

"Excuse me, duty calls," Sully said.

Together they strode in through the door that Ian held open, and Lindsey could swear she saw a mischievous sparkle glinting in Ian's eye.

Ian and Sully jostled one another as they strode down the side aisle that led backstage. Lindsey shook her head and went across the theater toward the costume room.

Once she got there, Nancy grabbed her by the arm and said, "Thank goodness you're here. Dress rehearsal is tomorrow and I swear Brian has put on ten pounds since I measured him for his costume. Could you let it out?"

Without waiting for an answer, Nancy shoved the costume into Lindsey's hands and grabbed a rolling rack of costumes, which she began to push toward the stage.

"Let me help you," Lindsey said. She draped Brian's tunic over her shoulder, grabbed the back of the rack and helped Nancy wheel it out the door toward the stage.

The costume-changing area backstage was a small one, but most of the players had few costume changes, and they were at staggered times, so the rolling rack would provide all of the cover they might need. There was also a small makeup table for touch-ups.

Nancy wheeled the rack into position, and then had the actors playing Demetrius and Helena, come and try on their costumes. Kitty was playing Helena and Lindsey was pleased to see that although she looked a bit down, she was polite to Nancy during the costuming and even managed to thank her.

One of Lindsey's favorite parts of *A Midsummer Night's Dream* was the complicated love lives of Shakespeare's young lovers. Hermia loves Lysander, but her father wants her to marry

Demetrius, and he has Theseus threaten her with a convent or death if she doesn't comply with her father's wishes. So, of course, Helena, who was thrown over by Demetrius when he fell for Hermia, rats out Lysander and Hermia when they plan to elope. It was great stuff.

Lindsey helped the actors with their costumes, and when everything was a go, Nancy sent them away and called in the actors playing Hermia and Lysander. Lola was playing Hermia, and Lindsey was pleased to see that she hadn't quit the show despite her grief.

"How are you holding up?" she asked the fragile-looking brunette as she adjusted the actress's headpiece.

Lola tipped her chin up and said, "I know Robbie would want me to give the performance of my life. So that's what I plan to do."

"That's the spirit," Lindsey said. She watched as Lola walked out onto the stage to have Violet approve her final costume.

While Nancy cinched Lysander's tunic, Lindsey heard harsh whispers coming from behind her. She turned her head, trying to see in the gloomy light. No luck. She went into the shadows and paused.

"Don't lie to me," a man said.

Lindsey peeped around a large canvas backdrop and saw Brian standing there, looking red-faced and angry, with his hands on his hips.

"I'm not lying," a woman answered.

Lindsey leaned farther forward and saw that it was Brian's wife, Brandy.

"I didn't sleep with Robbie," she said. Her voice sounded weary, as if she'd had this argument so many times she was utterly bored by it.

"You're lying," Brian snapped. "Do you think I can't tell? You don't want me to touch you anymore. You're always tired or have a headache."

"Why do you suppose that is?" Brandy asked. "You exhaust me with your crazy, jealous hysteria."

Before Brandy could react, Brian grabbed her by the throat and shoved her up against the wall. Lindsey jumped forward as Brandy clawed at Brian's hand.

"Let her go!" Lindsey snapped.

"Mind your own business!" Brian retorted, but he released Brandy, who was gasping. "Stick to papier-mâché, Lindsey, or you'll regret it."

"Like Robbie did?" she asked.

He narrowed his eyes and reached out to grab Brandy's hand.

"Don't touch me!" she snarled. "Ever again."

"What are you saying?" he asked.

"I want a divorce," Brandy said.

"You can't do that," he argued.

"Oh, yes, I can," she said. "Because now I have bruises and a witness."

Brian's face crumpled and he looked as if he

were about to cry. Brandy stepped up close to him and said, “We’re through, and just so you know, I never slept with Robbie.” She glanced at Lindsey. “His interest was elsewhere, but if he had ever offered, oh yeah, I’d have been with him in a heartbeat.”

Brian swung his arm back and Brandy clenched herself tight while Lindsey stepped forward to stop the blow. It never came.

Instead, Brian’s arm was twisted behind his back, and he dropped to his knees with a yelp of pain.

CHAPTER 19

I never could stomach a man who would hit a woman,” Emma Plewicki said. She bent over and cuffed Brian’s hands behind his back. “Come on, we’re going to take a little stroll over to the station.”

She hauled Brian up to his feet and dragged him out behind the curtain onto the stage. Lindsey and Brandy followed as if to be certain that he was being taken off of the premises.

“You can’t arrest me!” Brian protested. “I’m in the show.”

“Not anymore you’re not,” Emma said. “Violet,

you're going to need a replacement for the part of Nick Bottom. This one was roughing up his wife, so I think we need to go have a little chat about his anger management issues."

Violet took in the scene at a glance. One eyebrow was raised in silent question.

"I'll let you know," Emma said.

Lindsey knew the unspoken question was whether Brian was Robbie's killer or not.

"Fine," Violet said. "Brian, you're out. Do not return to this theater again or you'll be arrested for trespassing. Am I clear?"

"What? No!" Brian protested. "It's her fault!" He nodded his head toward Brandy. "If she wasn't such a slut, I wouldn't have had to do it."

"Brian Loeb, you have the right to remain silent . . ." Emma read him his Miranda rights while she dragged him up the main aisle to the front of the theater.

"All right," Violet said. "We need a new Nick Bottom. Who was slated to understudy that part?"

The cast on stage looked at one another. No one stepped forward. Violet frowned and looked down at her legal pad, where she kept all of her notes.

"Oh, my god," she cried. "I never assigned an understudy to that part because Brian was such an ass—literally—that I knew he'd rather die than miss his performance. Opening night is two days away. What am I going to do?"

"Don't panic." Nancy stepped from behind the

curtain and crouched down at the edge of the stage, in front of which Violet was now pacing. "We'll figure it out."

"How?" Violet cried. "Who here knows Nick Bottom's part? Anyone?"

" 'That will ask some tears in the true performing of it: if I do it, let the audience look to their eyes; I will move storms, I will condole in some measure,' " a deep voice said from the back of the stage.

"What?" Violet looked up. "Who said that? That's Bottom's part in Act I, Scene II. Continue!"

Ian Murphy strode forward and bowed. Then he continued, " 'To the rest: yet my chief humour is for a tyrant: I could play Ercles rarely, or a part to tear a cat in, to make all split.' "

"Ian Murphy, I could kiss you, you brilliant man," Violet said. "Why haven't you auditioned before?"

Ian looked down as he scuffed the toe of his shoe on the wooden floor of the stage. "I'm shy."

"Ha!" Violet laughed. "Well, now you're a star. Lindsey, take him to Mary to get fitted. Ian, I want you back here in fifteen minutes for a run-through."

"Yes ma'am," they said together. Ian gave Violet a snappy salute and jumped off the stage to stand beside Lindsey.

Lindsey led him to the back room, where Mary stood finalizing the stitching on one of the faerie costumes. She glanced up in surprise and looked questioningly at Ian.

"Mary, meet our new Nick Bottom," Lindsey said. "I think you might be familiar with his measurements."

"What?" Mary asked. "Ian, what is she talking about?"

"Brian, the original Nick Bottom has been fired," Ian said. "Apparently Violet didn't assign anyone as understudy, so she needed someone who knew the part."

"You do?" Mary asked. She looked at Lindsey. "How do I not know this about my husband?"

Lindsey shrugged.

"So, I need a costume," Ian said. "What do you think of a pair of leopard-print tights and a gold lamé tunic or is that too much?"

Mary grinned at him and shook her head. "Well, the donkey mask will certainly be appropriate."

"Hee-haw." Ian brayed and pranced around his wife while she laughed.

"Don't forget, you have fifteen minutes until Violet wants you on stage," Lindsey said.

"Oh yeah, that's right. I have to admit, I'm a little afraid of Violet," Ian said. He stopped prancing while Mary got out her measuring tape.

"We all are," Mary agreed.

Lindsey left the room and went back into the theater to see if Nancy needed any help. The players were on the stage and Dylan was practicing his final speech as Puck.

"'If we shadows have offended, think but this and all is mended, That you have but slumber'd here. While these visions did appear.'"

Not wanting to interrupt, Lindsey sat and watched him. He was a perfect Puck: less polished than Robbie, but he had the same twinkle in his eye and the same perfect pitch with his delivery.

She saw his mother sitting in the row in front of her. She was mouthing the lines with her son, and Lindsey thought it was remarkable how her tune had changed with his advancement to a larger role.

When Dylan finished, Violet called him forward. "That was excellent," she said. "You've really nailed it."

Dylan beamed at her, and Lindsey noted that his mother looked quite pleased. She found this ironic given how much she had previously expressed her dislike of Violet and her immoral lifestyle.

As Joanie Peet rose, Lindsey leaned forward and said, "He really is a wonderful actor. He must have some very strong acting DNA."

Joanie frowned at her. "Why do you say that?"

"He just seems gifted," she said. "He almost looks like Robbie Vine up there."

"I don't see any resemblance," Joanie said. "In fact, I think Mr. Vine's talents were always a bit overrated."

"Oh, well, I'm sorry," Lindsey said. "I meant it as a compliment. Dylan is very talented for a seventeen-year-old."

"He'll be eighteen in a few weeks," she said. "He's very mature for his age."

"Yes, well, he's really something special," Lindsey said. She was getting the feeling that Joanie was annoyed with her, but she couldn't for the life of her think why unless she really resented having her son compared to Robbie Vine.

"I'm fully aware of how special my son is," Joanie said. She moved around Lindsey. "I haven't spent all these years nursing my sickly boy back to health to not know what a gift he is. Please, excuse me."

Lindsey watched as she approached her son. He was crouched on the edge of the stage, listening to directions from Violet. When he turned his head, the lighting lit up his reddish-brown hair and he grinned a sort of sideways smile that looked so much like Robbie Vine's that Lindsey felt her breath catch.

Suddenly, Lindsey remembered the tattoo on Robbie's arm. It was a stylized sun with a date in the middle of it. He had told her that the date was a reminder of the most significant day of his life.

It had been 10-23-95, just a few weeks short of being eighteen years ago. Lindsey had assumed it was the date of a big show or maybe the first lead role Robbie had gotten, but looking at Dylan and remembering the article about Robbie having fathered a child, she wondered.

She must be crazy. No, it was impossible. But hadn't Heather said that Dylan told her he was adopted? Still, the odds that he was Robbie's son were slim to none. And yet, she couldn't help but wonder if perhaps it was true. There was only one way to be sure.

She made her way down to the edge of the stage, where Joanie was listening in on Violet's instructions to Dylan.

"Now remember," Violet was saying, "you are Puck, the merry wanderer of the night. When you cross the stage, it needs to have a certain ethereal magic to it."

"You aren't suggesting he prance and mince his steps, are you?" Joanie asked. "That would make him look silly."

Violet turned her head to look at her. Lindsey knew Violet well enough to know that she was not pleased to have Joanie adding her two cents to her directions.

The fire in her eyes made it quite clear that if Joanie didn't shut her yap, she was going to go the way of Brian Loeb and be banned from the theater for the duration of the show.

Lindsey stepped forward. "Dylan, you were wonderful. Robbie would be very proud."

Dylan flushed and looked down at the stage. Lindsey couldn't tell if it was pleasure or embarrassment making him shy. She hoped it was the former.

"Thank you, Ms. Norris," he said.

"Your mother tells me you're having a birthday soon," she said. "What date is it? I'll be sure to have cupcakes at the library just for you, our star."

"It's the twenty-third of October," he said.

Lindsey had to concentrate on keeping her expression completely neutral. She could feel her blood pounding through her body. She did not believe in coincidences, and this was a huge one.

"I'll be sure to note it on the calendar," she said.

"If you two don't mind," Violet said, "Dylan and I have work to do."

"Yes, of course," Lindsey said. "I'm heading back to wardrobe right now."

Violet turned to Joanie and asked, "Aren't you assisting with ticket sales and ushering?" Her point that Joanie needed to go find something else to do was lost on no one. Joanie's mouth turned down in the corners.

"Yes, I am." She turned to her son. "I'll meet you here after rehearsal."

"Thanks, Mom," he said.

Lindsey watched as Dylan's mother made her way up to the front of the theater, where the ticket office was. She knew that several of the spouses and parents of the cast and crew were helping to take turns selling tickets and working as ushers on the nights of the performance. Right now they were all meeting in the lobby of the theater for training.

"Your mother seems very excited about your part in the play," Lindsey said.

"She's done so much for me," Dylan said. "I'd do anything to repay her."

He had a fierce light in his eye, and Lindsey felt a sense of unease drape over her like a cloak. She couldn't help but wonder exactly how far he would go to repay his mother for all her years of care.

CHAPTER 20

Dylan? *Our* Dylan?" Beth asked. "You can't be serious."

"You should have seen his face," Lindsey said. "He looked as if he would do anything for his mother."

"Wanting to please your parents does not make you a murderer," Beth said.

They were seated in the staff lounge of the library, enjoying a lunch of clam chowder and clam fritters, which Beth had picked up at the Blue Anchor.

Lindsey dunked her fritter into the hot chowder

before taking a bite of the chewy, broth-soaked cake. Delicious.

"But what if he is Robbie's son?" Lindsey asked when she finished chewing. "Wouldn't you hate your father for abandoning you, especially if your father turned out to be a rich and famous star?"

"Maybe," Beth said.

She sounded reluctant. Beth loved their teen workers and always took it personally if any of them ever got into trouble, which they frequently did with Ms. Cole.

"But I thought Brian was the chief suspect now, since he was so angry about his wife and Robbie."

"As far as I know, he's still in custody," Lindsey said. "But I can't shake the feeling that Robbie's death has something to do with Dylan."

"Just because Dylan's birth date is the same date tattooed on Robbie's arm doesn't mean that there is a connection."

"Even though the tattoo is of a sun?" Lindsey asked. "You know, sun could represent son."

"Reaching," Beth said. She spooned up some chowder. "Besides, Robbie's gone. It's not like you can ask him what the tattoo signified."

"No, but I bet Kitty knows," she said.

"She hates you," Beth said.

"I don't know that I would say hate, exactly," Lindsey said.

"Oh, no, it's definitely hate, loathing, abhorrence, antipathy . . ."

"Okay, I get it," Lindsey said. "You can stop now, really."

Beth shrugged and spooned up more chowder.

Lindsey frowned into her cardboard to-go bowl. She watched the potatoes and chunks of clam swirl around as she stirred. Was Beth right? Did Kitty hate her that much? And if so, how was she going to get her to talk?

There was no help for it. She'd just have to go to the beach house that she knew Robbie, Kitty and Lola had been renting and try to charm Kitty into telling her about the tattoo on Robbie's arm. She doubted that Lola knew what it meant.

Kitty had been Robbie's wife, and even though their marriage was apparently in name only, Lindsey had gotten the feeling that Robbie confided in Kitty. Lola, on the other hand, seemed entirely too fragile.

"Uh-oh," Beth said.

"What?" Lindsey looked up from her chowder.

"You've got that look in your eye," she said.

"What look?"

"The one that says you're going to go stick your nose where it does not belong."

"I am not," she protested. "I am merely going to visit Kitty and see what she can tell me about the tattoo."

"She won't talk to you," Beth said.

"How will I know until I try?"

Lindsey paused to dunk another clam fritter into her chowder.

"Why don't you let me go and talk to her?" Beth asked.

Lindsey paused with the dripping fritter halfway to her mouth. "Really?"

"I think Kitty likes me," Beth said. "At least, I'm pretty sure she doesn't hate me."

"I don't know, I sort of got the feeling that she hated everyone," Lindsey said.

"Some more than others," Beth said, giving her a significant look. "If you could cover the children's desk this afternoon, I could pop over there and see what I can find out."

"Ms. Cole would have a field day if you took off in the middle of a workday," Lindsey said. "She'll report us both to human resources."

Beth frowned and said, "I don't know. I have to say that since the play has been under way, the lemon hasn't been quite as puckered as usual."

Lindsey thought back to the night the lights went out in the theater, the night that Robbie was stabbed. When Ian had fixed the breaker, Ms. Cole and Milton had been holding hands. At the time Lindsey had thought it was just to brace each other in the dark, but now she wondered.

"All right, I can watch the children's desk," she said. "How are you going to get her to talk to you?"

"I can be very persuasive," Beth said.

"You're going to bug her and keep bugging her until she cracks," Lindsey said.

"Yeah, and I thought I'd bring her some chocolate," Beth said.

"Belly bribery. I like it," Lindsey said.

Lindsey sat at the children's desk while Beth ducked out to go visit Kitty. In a way, Lindsey felt as if she were sending Beth into the lion pit with an aluminum sword, but then again, Beth managed thirty hyper toddlers in her story times. Surely she could handle one surly middle-aged woman.

"I want the pumpkin book," a little voice said from behind her.

Lindsey swiveled in her chair to see a little girl wearing a frilly, light-blue dress and sparkly pink shoes standing right behind her. The girl's hair looked windblown, and her red sweater was hanging off of one shoulder. She had a spray of freckles running across her nose, round cheeks and enormous blue eyes. She looked to be about five years old.

"Well, hello," Lindsey said. "What's your name?"

"Lila," the girl said. She did not smile. "And I want the pumpkin book."

"Well, Lila, I'm Ms. Norris."

The girl stared at her, unblinking. Lindsey could tell that this child really didn't give a hoot what her name was. She just wanted her book. Okay, then.

"Do you remember the name of the pumpkin book?" she asked.

"No. It had a big pumpkin on it," Lila said.

Lindsey glanced at the autumn display Beth had put up in the corner. The display unit was three shelves; she had decorated it with corn stalks and autumn leaf garlands, and it featured books about leaves changing colors, pumpkin patches and harvests.

"Did you see it on those shelves?" Lindsey asked. "We have lots of books about pumpkins."

"No, not there." Lila shook her head and made an annoyed face that left Lindsey in no doubt that Lila found her lacking in the smarts department.

"I don't suppose you know who wrote it?" Lindsey asked.

Lila just stared at her.

"Do you remember the story?" Lindsey asked. "If you tell me about it, maybe we can find it that way."

"It had a pumpkin and horses on it," Lila said.

"Oh. Was it about a farm?"

Lila glanced at the ceiling as if searching for patience.

"No," she said. Her blue eyes went back to staring at Lindsey as if trying to bend her to her will.

"Okay," Lindsey said. She had to take a deep breath and blow it out slowly so as to keep from using an impatient tone with the kid. "Let's try again. What do you remember about the story in the book?"

"The pumpkin," Lila said.

Lindsey bent forward in her chair until her face was just inches from Lila's, then she returned the girl's stare with equal intensity. They were going to have a mind meld and she was going to find this kid's book if it was the last thing she did.

"What happened to the pumpkin?" Lindsey asked.

"It turns into a carriage that's pulled by the horses," Lila said.

Lindsey sat back and blinked. "That sounds like *Cinderella*. Was there a princess in this book with a glass shoe?"

"Yes, I think so." Lila blinked and the intense stare ended.

"So, it's *Cinderella* that you're looking for?" Lindsey asked.

"No, I like the fairy godmother," Lila said. "I'm going to be one when I grow up, and I'll be able to turn pumpkins into carriages and mice into horses. It's going to be cool."

"So, that whole princess thing doesn't really work for you?" Lindsey asked. She turned to her computer and opened up the online catalog. She put in *Cinderella* and brought up the list of all of the versions of the fairy tale by the Grimm Brothers that the library owned.

"No way," Lila said. "It's much better to be magical."

"I agree." Lindsey looked at her and smiled.

With the intensity of her stare and the strength of her will, Lila certainly possessed her own brand of magic. Lindsey moved so that Lila could see the list on the monitor, each title included a thumbnail picture of the cover and she hoped Lila could pick out the one she wanted.

"Do any of these look like the book you're looking for?" she asked.

Lila pointed to one about halfway down the page. It was an older, Wonder Books version of the classic fairy tale illustrated by Ruth Ives and it was listed as checked in.

"Come with me," Lindsey said. "It should be over here."

Together they went into the fairy tale section. It was a bit lesser used than the picture books and so the books held up a bit longer. Sure enough, there sat the classic version of the story. Lindsey handed it to Lila and she hugged it to her chest.

"Oh, thank you," Lila breathed. "I'm going to show my mom."

She took off to the baby section of the room where they had a thick rubber mat on the floor and shelves of board books for the under-two set. Lindsey watched while she flopped down next to her mother and began to flip through the book. The mother glanced from Lila to Lindsey and gave her a warm smile. Lindsey headed back to the desk, fully understanding why Beth loved being a children's librarian so much. For children, books were still magical.

When she returned to her desk, she opened up her e-mail and began reading. She had several e-mails from the personnel department about the amount of hours her part-time staff could work per week. Part-time staff was not paid for vacation time, so Lindsey had hoped to bank those hours and use them to staff the library during its annual book sale.

The dragon lady who ran personnel, however, did not, as she put it, want her to "hoard" hours. It made Lindsey clench her teeth, so she forwarded the e-mail to the mayor's assistant, Herb Gunderson, hoping he could explain to the dragon that the hours still belonged to Lindsey. Herb was higher up than Lindsey, and the dragon was less likely to argue with Herb.

She had just hit send when she felt the floor shake. Earthquakes very rarely happened in Connecticut, so she glanced at the window to see if they were having a sudden turn in the weather.

The colorful leaves outside moved quietly in the gentle breeze and the sky that was visible was a crisp, cool blue that looked like it could be scooped and served on an ice cream cone. She glanced back at the library and that's when she saw *her* coming. Kitty Vine was stomping toward her, looking like she wanted to do some damage. Uh-oh.

CHAPTER 21

How dare you!" Kitty seethed. "How dare you send one of your minions to come and question me!"

Lindsey glanced over Kitty's shoulder and saw Beth hurrying toward her, waving her arms as if to indicate that Lindsey should exit through the nearest available door.

Lindsey looked back at Kitty and kept her expression bland. "Why, whatever do you mean?"

"That"—Kitty paused, turned and pointed at Beth—"showed up at my house just now, full of all sorts of questions about Robbie. Now, as far as I know, Robbie barely knew her name, so why would she be interested in him? But then I remembered that you two are besties, aren't you?"

Lindsey didn't answer but just kept staring at her. Kitty looked even more angry. Maybe Lila was onto something with the penetrating stare.

"This really isn't the place for this conversation, is it?" Lindsey asked.

"Oh, I think it's perfect!" Kitty snapped. "Since you're acting like a child and we're in the children's area. Suddenly, it all makes perfect sense."

Lindsey felt a tug on her sleeve, and she turned to find Lila there. Lila motioned her close and Lindsey leaned over so Lila could whisper in her ear.

"Do you want me to turn her into a pumpkin for you?" she asked. "I've been practicing on my baby brother."

Lindsey laughed. She put her arm around the girl and said, "I really appreciate the offer, but I wouldn't want you to get into trouble. Probably, you shouldn't try to turn your brother into a pumpkin, either."

"Stick to the dog?" Lila asked.

"Or maybe a chair," Lindsey suggested.

Lila gave her a nod of understanding and went back to her mother.

"Kitty, if you want to talk, and by that I mean talk and not yell at me, we can go to my office," Lindsey said.

"Fine." Kitty glared.

Lindsey flashed back to the first day she'd met Robbie, when he'd said that when a woman says she's fine, she is anything but. She wondered if he'd learned that from Kitty.

"Beth, do you mind taking the desk?"

"No, happy to," Beth said. She looked immensely

grateful to sit in her familiar chair in her natural habitat.

"Follow me, please," Lindsey said as she led the way to her office.

They passed the circulation desk, where Ms. Cole was checking in a cart of books from the book drop. She glanced at Kitty with a disapproving look, and Lindsey felt oddly relieved that Ms. Cole disliked someone more than her for a change.

"Can I get you anything?" Lindsey asked as they went into her office. "Water? Coffee?"

Kitty gave her a suspicious look. "No, thank you. After Robbie . . . well, I swore I'd never drink anything that I didn't know the point of origin for."

"Understandable," Lindsey said. "I do have sealed bottles of plain water."

"Well, all right," Kitty said grudgingly.

Lindsey went into the staff room and took two bottles out of her personal stash from the large refrigerator in the corner. She returned to find Kitty examining the pictures on the shelf behind her desk.

"Cute guy," Kitty said. "Is he your boyfriend?"

Lindsey glanced at the frames. There were only two, one of her parents and one of her brother.

"Brother, actually," she said. "Jack."

"So, you're single?" Kitty asked. "I figured, but it's good to have it confirmed."

Lindsey glanced down at her desk. She and Sully hadn't been going together long enough to make the framed photo shelf. The thought depressed her.

She sat down and Kitty took the seat opposite her desk.

Kitty examined her water bottle as if trying to determine whether or not it had been tampered with.

"I would not poison you," Lindsey said. "I promise."

Kitty met her gaze and seemed to make up her mind. She uncapped the bottle and took a long sip.

"So, why did you send the little cutie pie over to my house instead of coming yourself?" Kitty asked.

"Beth," Lindsey emphasized her name, "wanted to go. She made the argument that you might talk more freely with her than with me."

"Why would I talk to her *or* you?" Kitty asked. "Robbie's past is no one's business. It needs to stay in the past."

"So you knew he had a son?" Lindsey asked.

"He had a child," Kitty said. "It was the result of a crazy love affair in his youth."

"Robbie was almost twenty," Lindsey said. "The child would be eighteen in a matter of weeks."

"How do you know that?" Kitty was clutching the water bottle in her hands so tight that her knuckles were turning white.

"The sun tattoo on his arm has the child's birth date in it," Lindsey said. "Sun meaning a son."

"That's ridiculous," Kitty scoffed. It sounded forced. "The child was given up for adoption as soon as it was born. He never even laid eyes on it. He doesn't know whether it's a boy or a girl."

"But there was a child born on that day," Lindsey pressed.

"No. I don't know," Kitty said. "You'd have to contact the mother. Oh, that's right: you can't, because no one knows who she is."

"Susan Dalton," Lindsey said.

Kitty's jaw dropped open.

"Really not that hard to figure out if you do some research," Lindsey said. "She was an American soap opera star and Robbie's girlfriend for six months. The child was born about five months after their breakup."

"That doesn't mean she's the mother," Kitty protested. "It could be that she found out he'd fathered a child with someone else and dumped him."

"Yeah, but I looked up the story line of her soap opera and her character in particular. Funny how her character was written as being pregnant at the same time the mother of Robbie's child would have been, don't you think?"

"I think librarians have too much time on their hands," Kitty snapped.

"No, we just have some very formidable

research skills," Lindsey said. "Either way, it shouldn't be that hard to prove that she was pregnant in real life."

Lindsey was bluffing. She didn't think there was any way she could hunt down the former soap star and find out if she'd given birth almost eighteen years ago, but if she convinced Kitty that she could, well, it might be all the leverage she needed.

"So what?" Kitty asked. "Why do you even care? Were you that taken with Robbie that you now have to console yourself by scouring his past? I mean, what relevance does it have?"

Lindsey glanced down at the desktop. How much did she want to tell Kitty? That Robbie's child was alive and well and quite possibly here in Briar Creek? How would Kitty react to that information? Then again, did she already know?

"I think his child is here," Lindsey said. "In fact, I'm sure of it."

"What?" Kitty asked. But her voice didn't sound as shocked as it should have.

"But you already knew that, didn't you?" she asked.

"I have no idea what you're talking about," Kitty insisted.

"Dylan," Lindsey said.

Her eyes never left Kitty's face, but Kitty broke eye contact and glanced at anything but Lindsey.

"Dylan Peet is his son, isn't he?" Lindsey persisted. "Did Robbie know?"

"You're crazy!" Kitty said as she shot up from her chair. "There is no child. The actress being pregnant on her soap opera was just a story line. In fact, probably that's why people thought Robbie fathered her child, because they were dating and she was portraying a pregnancy on the show. Yeah, that's it."

"And you called me crazy?" Lindsey asked. "That's mental."

"You need to leave this alone!" Kitty said.

"Why?" Lindsey asked. "Are you afraid that your cut of Robbie's estate will be taken away from you if it's discovered that he has a child?"

Kitty glared at her.

"Oh, my god, that's it, isn't it," Lindsey said. "You're afraid you're going to lose your inheritance if it becomes known that Robbie has a child."

"Wrong." Kitty slammed her water bottle down on the desk. "Not that it's any of your business, but I know exactly what his will states, and his estate is not going to me. The bulk of his fortune was left to someone else."

Lindsey opened her mouth to ask who, but Kitty held up her hand, stopping her.

"I will not tell you," Kitty said. "You'll just have to wait to find out with everyone else when the estate is settled, but rest assured I am not the beneficiary."

"Is it his child?" Lindsey asked. Kitty's gaze slid away from hers, and Lindsey knew her guess was correct. "You have to tell."

"No, I don't," Kitty said.

"But don't you see?" Lindsey protested. "Who has the most to gain from Robbie's death? If it's not you, then—"

"But Dylan didn't know—" Kitty clapped a hand over her mouth.

"Didn't know what?" Lindsey asked. "Come on, Kitty, you've come this far."

"No!" Kitty raged. "Look, I promised Robbie I wouldn't say anything and now that he's gone . . ."

Her voice broke as if she didn't have the strength to keep going and for the first time, Lindsey saw the grief that Kitty was feeling at the death of her husband and business partner. Lindsey felt sorry for her, truly she did, but Robbie had been murdered, which meant his killer was out there and Kitty couldn't keep his secrets anymore.

"Kitty, have you considered the possibility that Robbie's child might have figured out who his father was?"

Kitty looked at her. Her light-brown eyes were watery with unshed tears.

"Think about it," Lindsey said. "How would you feel if you were a seventeen-year-old boy with a famous father who just abandoned you? Wouldn't you be angry? Wouldn't you want revenge?"

"No," Kitty said. "I made a promise to Robbie to keep his secret safe. I won't break it no matter what you say. It's the last thing I can do for him."

She strode out of the office, slamming the door behind her. It really didn't matter. Kitty had confirmed enough for Lindsey to go and talk to Emma Plewicki.

She hated to think that Dylan had anything to do with Robbie's death, but there was no way she couldn't tell Emma what she knew if it meant catching Robbie's killer. Even if the killer was his own son.

CHAPTER 22

Emma was not in the station when Lindsey stopped by. The officer on duty let her leave a note for Emma to call her, and promised to get it to the chief as soon as she came in. Lindsey couldn't deny that she was relieved. She really didn't want to tell Emma about Dylan's probable connection to Robbie, and even though she knew it was the right thing to do, she was loath to do it.

Dress rehearsal was scheduled for seven o'clock, and Lindsey knew it was an all-hands-on-deck sort of evening. She glanced at her cell phone and noted that she had an hour until she had to be at the theater.

There was a nip in the air and the temperatures were supposed to drop into the forties tonight. She glanced across the street at the Blue Anchor. She could feel the lure of Mary's stuffed flounder calling her with the little cheesy potatoes and steamed broccoli on the side paired with a nice, crisp glass of white wine. Yes, definitely. If she was going to get through tonight, she needed to fortify herself.

Lindsey hurried across the street and cut through the small town park. She was almost at the restaurant when she saw the familiar, stumpy figure of Harvey Wargus striding across the parking lot ahead of her. He stopped beside a big Lincoln Town Car with commercial plates. The window in back rolled down and Harvey leaned close to talk to the occupant. Interesting.

Lindsey knew Violet had banned Harvey from coming into the theater. There was nothing she could do, however, about stopping him from buying a ticket for opening night. Lindsey studied the car. Who in Briar Creek would have a driver? There were a few New Yorkers who owned summer houses and were driven up from the city for long weekends and short vacations, but they wouldn't be here in the off season unless it was a holiday.

No, this was someone who knew Harvey, someone who was wealthy; and with the tinted windows, Lindsey could only surmise that it was someone who didn't want to be seen. Someone like Charlene's father, Sterling Buchanan.

Without pausing to think it through, Lindsey crossed the parking lot and leaned into the open window beside Harvey. She wanted to get a good look at the man who had broken Violet's heart, abandoned his daughter and now, according to Charlene, seemed to think he had a right to have it all back.

"Well, hello, Harvey," she said. "Whatcha doing?"

Harvey jumped and banged his head on the top of the door frame.

"What? Huh?" he asked. He clapped a hand on the top of his head and rubbed the sore spot. Then he glowered at her. "What are you doing here?"

"Just being neighborly," Lindsey answered. She didn't look at him. Her gaze was fastened on the man in the backseat. If there was a stereotype of the narcissistic, egomaniacal corporate billionaire, Sterling Buchanan fit it to perfection.

He was dressed in a suit that probably cost as much as Lindsey made in a year. Large, square diamonds flashed at his cuffs and on his tie. His fingernails were buffed and polished, and his gray hair was cut with such precision that Lindsey wondered if his stylist had used a level to make sure it was perfect.

This was a man who was not only wealthy but clearly felt the need to let everyone else know precisely how wealthy he was. When she'd been working at Yale, Lindsey had come to know many alumni who were wealthy, and her favorites were always the ones who looked as comfortable in jeans and sweaters as they did in suits and gowns.

"How do you do, Mr. Buchanan?" she asked.

He raised his eyes in surprise. "This was a private conversation."

"Like I said, I'm just being neighborly," Lindsey said. "And I'm sure my dear friends will be interested to hear that you're in town. So, are you just passing through or staying awhile?"

He glared at her. "I'm sorry. Who are you?"

"Lindsey Norris, the town librarian." She extended her hand, which he ignored with disdain, making her feel as if she was something that just crawled out of the compost heap. Nice. "Harvey and I are old friends. Right, Harvey?"

He swallowed and looked panicked. "No! I just use the library, that's all. I hardly even know her."

"Aw, really, Harvey?" Lindsey asked, batting her eyelashes at him. "After all that we've meant to each other."

Harvey looked like he'd swallowed a golf ball whole.

"Well, Ms. Norris," Sterling said. "We wouldn't want to keep you."

Lindsey knew that this was his way of

dismissing her. It was fine. She was pretty sure she wasn't going to get any information out of either of them, but it was interesting that Sterling was in town. And it gave her hope—a small, flickering flame of hope—that maybe there was someone who wanted Robbie dead more than Dylan.

"So thoughtful of you," Lindsey said. "But I imagine I'll see you both at the show?"

Harvey glanced away, but Sterling just stared at her. His eyes were cold, and Lindsey wondered what the warm and vivacious Violet ever could have seen in him.

She stepped away from the car and continued on to the Blue Anchor. She pulled her phone out of her purse to see if Emma had called. She hadn't, but Lindsey figured she now had two things to tell the chief of police and she sincerely hoped that she was right about one of them.

Lindsey pulled open the door and stepped into the restaurant. Ian was working behind the bar and greeted her with a wave.

Mary was in the corner, talking to their assistant manager, Kelly Martin, who would oversee the operation of the restaurant while Ian and Mary were at the theater. Lindsey took a seat at the bar, and Ian strolled over with her glass of wine already in hand.

"Lindsey, what can I get you to eat?" he asked. "Or do you need a menu?"

“Stuffed flounder, please,” Lindsey said.

“I like a woman who knows her own mind,” Ian said. He turned around and hollered her dinner order through the small square window that overlooked the kitchen.

“Are you ready for dress rehearsal tonight?” she asked when he came back.

“Oh yeah,” he said. “I’m looking forward to it.”

“Why didn’t you audition earlier?” Lindsey asked.

“You mean, aside from my horrible case of bashfulness?” he asked. Lindsey laughed. Ian was about as bashful as a Kardashian.

“No, really,” she said.

“Honestly, I didn’t think I’d have time,” he said. “The restaurant business is never ending, you know.”

“Well, it was great of you to step up,” Lindsey said. “You’re really saving the day.”

“Don’t praise him,” a voice said from behind her. “He can barely get his swelled donkey head through the door as it is.”

“Well, it takes an ass to know an ass,” Ian quipped.

Lindsey spun on her stool to find Sully standing behind her. He grinned at Ian and then at Lindsey, and she felt her insides do the same cartwheel they always did when he looked at her just that way.

“Hi, Sully,” she said.

"Hi," he said. "Mind if I join you?"

"No, please do," she said.

"What are you having?" he asked.

"The stuffed flounder," she said.

Sully looked at Ian. "Make that two."

"On it." Ian glanced between them with an affectionate smile. He poured Sully's usual beer and put it on the bar before strolling off to check on his other customers.

"So, how are you?" Sully asked.

"I'm all right," Lindsey said. She glanced down at the bar. This was awkward, given that the last time she had seen him, she had come very close to kissing him.

"Has Emma made any progress?" he asked.

"Not that I've heard," she said. "Apparently, there were quite a lot of people who would have preferred Robbie Vine to be no more."

"You know I'm not one of them, right?" he asked.

Lindsey glanced at him and knew just like she always had that Sully could never have harmed Robbie.

"I know," she said.

"Not that I didn't want to punch him in the jaw a couple of times," Sully said. "But even if you had chosen to be with him in the end, I hope you know I only want you to be happy."

She wasn't sure why Sully was being so forthcoming with her but she liked it. She put her hand on his arm where it rested on the bar. "Thanks."

They stared at one another for a few moments and Lindsey felt as if Sully was letting her see a side of him that he usually kept to himself. He was letting her know that it had bothered him that she and Robbie had developed a friendship, but that he would never begrudge her happiness.

She smiled at him, and he leaned close and said, "I've really missed you."

Lindsey opened her mouth to tell him the same but she was interrupted.

"Dinner is served." Ian put two plates down on the bar in front of them.

Lindsey leaned back from Sully and smiled at Ian. Sully glared at him, and Ian asked, "What? That's what you ordered, isn't it?"

"Yeah, a heaping plate of lousy timing," Sully said.

Ian glanced between them and grinned. "Nothing worth having is acquired easily, and I should know. It took me three solid years of begging to get your sister to agree to marry me."

"That's because she's too good for you," Sully said. "If it were up to me, you'd still be begging Mary to make an honest man of you."

"Spoken like a true older brother," Ian said. "Tell me, Lindsey, do you have an older brother I should be calling?"

Lindsey laughed as she took her silverware out

of her napkin roll. "My brother, Jack, is much too busy gallivanting all over the world. He only comes when I sound a distress call."

"Which you are too proud to do," Sully said. He put his napkin on one knee while he tucked into his cheesy potatoes with his fork.

"Not too proud," Lindsey said. "Just waiting until I really need him."

She broke off a piece of the flaky fish and popped it into her mouth with a little bit of the crabmeat stuffing. It was warm and moist and seasoned perfectly.

"So, how is it?" Ian asked.

"Excellent," she said.

"Terrific," Sully agreed.

Ian beamed at them and then moved down the bar to refill another patron's drink.

"So, you never told your brother when you and your ex broke up?" Sully asked.

"Oh, I told him," she said. "But I didn't make a big deal out of it. Relationships end. It happens."

"Did you ever tell him about us?" Sully asked. He wasn't looking at her but instead studying his plate. Lindsey got the feeling this was important to him.

"Yeah, I told him when we started dating," she said. "He liked that you were a boat captain."

"I like him already," Sully said.

"I also told him when we broke up," she said.

"Oh."

"Yeah, and I cried," she said. "Then he wanted to sink your boat."

"You cried?" Sully's voice was soft and he looked at her with eyes that were narrowed with guilt and pain.

"Yes, but I think I was just being overly dramatic," she said. "I had just had a near-death experience, after all."

"I'll never forget it," he said. His blue gaze met hers in a look of such angst that Lindsey felt her breath catch.

It occurred to her that maybe Sully hadn't dumped her because he felt she needed time to consider whether she wanted to be with her ex or not, but rather because he had come so close to losing her that it scared the snot out of him and he had done what any same person would do: cut and run.

She stared at him and he asked, "What?"

"There you are!" Violet came racing into the restaurant. Her caftan floated around her and she looked harried as if she'd been running all day. Nancy was right behind her, looking equally stressed but wearing her favorite blue track suit.

"What are you people doing here?" Violet continued. "Don't you know that tonight is dress rehearsal? We have to go!"

Sully glanced at his watch. "Violet, breathe. We have a half hour until we have to be at the theater."

"Really?" Violet asked as she sank into a nearby stool. "Oh, bother."

Nancy slapped the bar to get Ian's attention. "Two cosmopolitans, Ian, and make them doubles."

"Is that wise?" Lindsey asked.

"You're right," Nancy said. "I probably should have ordered triples."

Sully and Lindsey exchanged a grin and dug into their food. For a few brief moments, Lindsey felt as if everything in her world was okay. She was with Sully and they were surrounded by their friends. Then the door to the Blue Anchor banged open and in strode Sterling Buchanan.

CHAPTER 23

Definitely should have ordered a triple," Nancy said. She took the drink Ian handed her and downed half of it in one swallow.

"Oh, for heaven's sake!" Violet snapped. "What the hell are you doing here, Buck?"

The entire restaurant went quiet as everyone glanced from Violet to the man in the suit.

Lindsey leaned close to Sully and said, "An old boyfriend of Violet's."

"What is it with old boyfriends coming to Briar

Creek?" Sully muttered. "Violet, do you want me to show him the door?"

"And me," Ian chimed in. "It's my restaurant. If someone needs tossing, I've got dibs."

"Spoilsport," Sully said.

"Enough you two," Violet said. "Answer me, Buck."

"It's good to see you, Vi," he said. His gaze seemed to drink in the sight of her.

Violet La Rue was a beautiful woman. Her dark complexion was rich and exotic. She had large brown eyes and a gently sculpted face with high cheekbones, a square jaw and a generous mouth that gave her cheeks deep dimples when it curved into a smile. She was wearing her usual flowing caftan, but it clung to her curves and managed to look sexy instead of matronly.

"Really?" she asked. "You are not the type to get sentimental, so what is it that you want?"

"You know what I want," he said. "Another chance for us."

"Uh-huh, so you've said," Violet replied. "How does your wife feel about that?"

"She understands that a man has—"

"Oh, shut up!" Violet interrupted him. "I know exactly what you're doing, what you've been doing with your fancy bouquets of flowers and all that garbage. You're trying to woo me back in hopes that Charlene will give you a chance. Well, forget it. I'm not buying the long-lost-love bit."

"So cold, Vi," he said. His voice was reproving, and Violet arched an eyebrow as if to say she so wasn't going to play games with him.

"Spill it," she said.

"As the father of your child—" he began.

"Oh, no, you don't," Violet interrupted amidst a chorus of gasps. "That child is a grown woman with children of her own. You chose not to be her father when she needed one, so don't be thinking you can be one to her now."

"I think I want to punch him," Sully muttered to Ian.

"Get in line," Ian said.

"I've tried repeatedly over the years to be in her life and in yours," Sterling said. He looked annoyed. "But the two of you have been very insulated by your little actor friends. You always shut me out, Violet, and Charlene followed your example."

"Oh, please," Violet snapped. "I am not interested in your revisionist history. You didn't show up in her life until she was eighteen. And yes, she has had a lot of surrogate fathers, and they have been wonderful to her. Robbie Vine, in particular, was more of a father to her than you've ever been."

"Well, given that Robbie is dead now, don't you think it's time for her to get to know her real father?" Sterling asked. He looked so angry that Lindsey felt a chill creep down her spine.

"The choice is hers," Violet said. "But I'm pretty sure you know that, just like you know what her answer is."

"But that's unacceptable," he said. He yanked on the cuffs of his shirt. "Violet, you have to undo the damage you've done. Time is slipping by."

"You narcissistic jackass. You walked out of her life before she was even born and now you're aware of the time going by?" Violet said. "Man up and live with the consequences of your choice and stop trying to blame it on everyone else."

"That is—" Sterling looked nonplussed to be spoken to in such a manner, and Lindsey had to keep herself from cheering out loud.

"What? The truth? You can't buy a child's love, Sterling. You have to invest yourself, not your checkbook, into your offspring. Now, I'm sorry that high-pedigree wife of yours couldn't provide an heir for you, but Charlene has no interest in you or your fortune. So, respect her wishes and leave her be."

"This isn't over," Sterling said. His jaw was clenching and unclenching as he tried to keep his temper. "I sent Harvey Wargus here to write about the show. He'll write whatever I tell him to. He can make or break you, Vi."

"So that's why that toad is here," she said. "So, when romancing me back into your life didn't work, you decided to send Wargus after me and the show. This isn't Broadway. Who cares if

Wargus trashes the show? Or did you have a different plan? Were you hoping to discover something damaging about me that you could use to cause a rift between me and *my* daughter?"

Sterling's lack of an answer was telling.

"News flash—there isn't anything she doesn't know about me, because that's how we roll. It's called honesty. You should try it sometime," Violet said.

"Vi, you have to give me a chance or I'll—" Sterling threatened but Violet interrupted.

"Or you'll what?" she said. "Murder me like you did Robbie?"

Sterling looked shocked, and Lindsey didn't think he was a good enough actor to be faking.

"You can't believe—" he began but she interrupted again.

"Oh, yes, I can," she said. Her voice dripped contempt like it was acid. "I believe you're capable of doing anything to get what you want. Sully, Ian, I think you need to take out the trash."

Ian vaulted over the bar as if he had a springboard back there. He and Sully stood shoulder to shoulder and moved forward with the formidable stance of a brick wall.

"Gentlemen, you would be ill advised to touch me," Buchanan said, looking decidedly nervous.

Ian looked at Sully. "I can live with that."

"Me, too," Sully agreed.

They moved forward. Buchanan moved back.

"In fact," Sully continued, "I was thinking Mr. Buchanan here looked thirsty for a little taste of the sea. Maybe we can see if that suit of his is drip-dry."

As one, Sully and Ian each stomped a foot forward. Buchanan bolted through the door, moving faster than Lindsey had thought possible. Ian and Sully laughed and knuckle bumped one another. Lindsey turned to find Violet lifting her glass to them.

"Well done," Violet said, and then she downed her drink. She handed the glass to Nancy and clapped her hands. "Okay, people, we have a show to put on. Roll out."

As the others prepared to leave, Lindsey turned back to her plate and hastily tried to shovel in the rest of her dinner. Sully returned to his seat and did the same.

"You all go on ahead," Sully said. "We'll meet you over there."

Lindsey noted the hopeful glances that they got from the others, but refused to acknowledge them. She had no doubt they were all hoping for reconciliation between her and Sully. Whatever.

When they finished eating, she refused to let him pay for her dinner, and he gave her an exasperated look, but she held her ground.

Together they made their way to the theater. It was dark now and the wind whipping in off the water had a definite nip as it yanked and tugged at the hems of their jackets, trying to sneak up their sleeves and scratch them with its chilly fingers.

Lindsey shivered and realized it was time to upgrade to a thicker coat and possibly time to pull out the wool scarf as well. She hunched lower into her jacket.

"Lindsey!" a voice called from across the street. She turned and glanced over her shoulder. Emma Plewicki was jogging toward them.

Lindsey stopped walking, and Sully, beside her, paused as well.

"I got your message," Emma said. She wasn't even winded from her jog. "What's up?"

Lindsey glanced at Sully. She would have preferred not to talk in front of him because she didn't want him to know that she'd been looking into Robbie's background. Then again, if she told Emma what she knew, there was no way in a town this small that Sully wasn't going to find out the information had come from her, so she might as well deal with it now.

"Did you know that Robbie Vine had a child?" Lindsey asked.

Emma frowned. "Yes, why?"

"What if that child was here?" Lindsey asked.

She could feel Sully's gaze on the side of her face. She ignored him and focused instead on Emma's frown instead.

"What are you saying, Lindsey?"

"I think Dylan Peet is Robbie's son," Lindsey said. "I think he may have figured out who his father was and he might have been angry enough at being abandoned as a child that he killed him."

Emma tossed her dark hair out of the collar of her coat. She chewed her lower lip while she pondered Lindsey's statement. "What makes you so sure it's Dylan? Doesn't that seem awfully coincidental to you?"

"It would, but Robbie has . . . er . . . had a tattoo of a stylized sun with a date on it," Lindsey said. Out of the corner of her eye, she saw Sully stiffen. She ignored him. "The date is the same as Dylan's birthday."

Emma raised her eyebrows. "Oh, definitely worth checking into then."

"I thought so," Lindsey said.

Emma looked at her face and then reached out and squeezed her arm. "It's all right. I'll tread lightly."

"Thanks," she said. "Oh, and in case you haven't heard, Sterling Buchanan is in town."

"Isn't he Charlene's father?" Emma asked.

"Yes. He was just at the Anchor talking to Violet, and he made it very clear that he was not happy about Charlene's close relationship with Violet's acting friends."

"Did he threaten her?" Emma asked.

"Not directly," Sully said. "But I got the feeling that he definitely has an agenda."

"Got it," Emma said. "And thanks."

She and Sully watched as Emma hurried off toward the theater.

"So, Vine had a tattoo, huh?" Sully asked.

"It was on his arm," she said. "I saw it when I was fixing that nasty cut that he got."

Sully nodded. But even under the streetlight's bluish glow, she noted that he looked relieved.

"I suppose we should go," she said. Suddenly, she felt as if the bottom of her shoes were made of lead.

"Hey, you did the right thing," Sully said.

"Then why do I feel like such a heel?" Lindsey asked. "Dylan's just a kid, and what if he's innocent? What if he doesn't even know that Robbie's his father?"

"Given how famous Vine was, it was going to come out one way or another," Sully said. "Look on the bright side: maybe it's just a coincidence and Dylan isn't his son and someone else murdered Robbie."

"Great; then who killed him?" Lindsey asked.

"Seems to me a lot of people had reason," Sully said. "Frankly, Sterling Buchanan would be at the top of my list."

"True," Lindsey said. "And boy, I would be so much happier to see him incarcerated than Dylan."

"Come on," Sully said. "Dress rehearsal awaits."

Together they entered the theater and stepped

into complete chaos. Emma was in front of the stage with Violet and Dylan. The rest of the cast and crew were running around the theater, looking stressed and fretful.

"How mad do you think Violet is going to be at me?" she asked.

Sully looked at Violet. She had her hands on her hips and she was obviously giving Emma a piece of her mind.

"You can't take Dylan," Violet was sputtering. "It's dress rehearsal! I need him."

"Sorry," Emma said. "I need to talk to him."

"Now?" Violet asked. "You have to talk to him *now?*"

Dylan looked confused and alarmed as he glanced between them.

"Yes, now," Emma said. "I'm sorry. I just have a few questions."

"But it's dress rehearsal," Dylan protested. "I can't miss it. Why do you need to talk to me?"

"It's about Robbie Vine's death," Emma said.

"But I don't know anything about that," Dylan protested.

"It's just a few questions," Emma said. True to her word, her voice was gentle and her manner kind.

Dylan looked alarmed and then he looked at Violet. She studied Emma, and then she put her hand on Dylan's shoulder.

"She says it won't take long," Violet said. "We

have to do whatever we can to help find Robbie's killer."

Lindsey studied Dylan's face. He looked nervous, but she couldn't tell if it was guilt making him look that way. Again, it felt like a punch to the gut to realize she had ratted out a seventeen-year-old boy.

"Steady," Sully said.

"I'm going to go see what Nancy needs me to do," Lindsey said.

"I'll be backstage if you need me," Sully said.

"Thanks," Lindsey said.

She watched Emma take Dylan out the theater's side door. His shoulders were hunched over and his hands were shoved deep into his pockets. He was the picture of misery, and Lindsey couldn't help but wonder if she had just ruined his life.

CHAPTER 24

"What are we going to do without a Puck?" Lola asked.

She was wearing her Hermia costume, looking perfectly vulnerable, and again Lindsey wondered if that was what Robbie had seen in her. It gave her a tiny spurt of jealousy, which made her feel silly and stupid given all that was happening around them.

"We'll have a Puck," Violet said. "Don't you worry. Emma just has some questions but Dylan will be back. In the meantime, I'll read his part."

Lindsey wondered if she should go and tell Violet what she knew about the tattoo and Dylan's birthday. She hated that Violet might get blindsided by having another actor of hers arrested. Oh, god, the entire show could go under and it would be all her fault.

"Lindsey, there you are!" Nancy cried as she came dashing up the aisle toward her. She had a bunch of costumes draped over her shoulder and her normally sparkling blue eyes looked the teensiest bit deranged.

"What's wrong?" Lindsey asked.

"Ms. Cole lost her floral headpiece," Nancy said. "Personally, I think she lost it on purpose. She's being a bit of a prima donna, you know, and she made a real stink when I put yellow buttercups in it. I thought they would pick up the yellow in her gown, but she said I did it to make her look sallow."

Lindsey pressed her lips together, and tried not to smile. At least she could count on some things not to change.

"Anyway, she said that she and Milton were reading lines up in the balcony and she thinks she might have left it up there," Nancy said. "Would you mind going to look for it?"

"No, not at all," Lindsey said. "I'll meet you backstage for the costume changes as soon as I can."

"Thanks," Nancy said, and she disappeared down the aisle and trotted up the side steps onto the stage.

Lindsey turned and headed into the lobby. The ticket takers and the ushers were all in the lobby, prepping for their assigned positions during the show. The women wore pretty, black or navy-blue dresses while the men wore black suits with bow ties. She glanced at the group, searching for Dylan's mother, Joanie. Did she know he had left with Emma? Lindsey didn't see her and she was relieved. She felt guilty enough without having to look the boy's mother in the face.

She slipped around the lot of them and headed up the staircase that led up to the balcony.

The stairs were carpeted in red and gold, and wall sconces lit the way. The balcony was a modest size, ten rows deep with a fairly steep pitch. The bottom two rows gave a wonderful view of the stage, but the rest were definitely cheaper seating.

Lindsey stepped out into the balcony and wished she had a flashlight. The lights were lowered, as dress rehearsal had begun. She supposed there was no way she was going to find Ms. Cole's headpiece unless she went up and down each row, checking each seat and the floor. Now she understood why Nancy had been so annoyed.

She decided to start with the front row and work her way to the back. Aisles ran down the side of the balcony, so she started with the right side since it was closer. The seats were the sort where the bottom part flipped up. She checked each seat and under it as she went. About ten seats in she spied something on the floor, but it was someone's sweatshirt, not Ms. Cole's rejected headpiece.

She was almost done with the first row when she heard a shout from the stage. She turned and glanced down to see what the commotion was about. One of the actors had missed his mark and collided with another one who was coming out of the make-believe forest that consisted of four fake trees and a wonderfully rendered backdrop.

"Watch where you're going," the actor who played Lysander snapped.

"Me?" the actor who was Demetrius retorted. "You're the one who's off your mark."

"Stop it, both of you," Violet chastised them. "I know nerves are running high, but we don't have time for this. Take the scene from the top."

The two actors exchanged a glare and went back to their spots. Lindsey was about to turn back around when a hard shove hit her square in the back.

The force of the hit sent her pitching forward.

Her hips banged into the balcony rail while her upper body dipped over the edge. Someone screamed from below, but she was so busy trying to grab the rail of the balcony to catch herself that she didn't see who it was.

She gripped the rail with her left hand and managed to hook one foot under an armrest, but someone knocked her foot free and she slipped forward over the edge. She caught her left foot on the rail at the last second, stopping her fall to the floor.

Every muscle in her body was clenched tight, and she was panting for breath as she tried to hold on to the rail with one foot and one hand. Gravity was not helping.

She could hear shouts and cries coming from below but with her body pressed up against the front of the balcony, she couldn't turn her head to see if anyone was coming to help her.

She tried to tighten her grip but her muscles were straining. Her entire body was covered in a sheen of sweat and her fingers began to lose their grip on the rail.

She glanced down. A twenty-foot fall onto metal and thinly upholstered theater chairs did not seem like something she would survive without a lot of broken bones.

A banging noise sounded and someone yelled, "The balcony door is locked! We can't get to her."

"A ladder! Where's the ladder?"

"Can we catch her?"

"Oh, my god, she's going to die!"

Lindsey wasn't positive but she thought that last voice was Ms. Cole and she didn't sound nearly as upset as Lindsey thought she should.

The muscles she'd been clenching so tightly began to shake from exertion. Lindsey knew that she wasn't going to be able to hang on much longer.

"Lindsey, let go!" a voice ordered over the shouts of the others.

She knew that voice. It was Sully, standing right below her.

Let go? Was he planning to catch her? He'd be squashed and they'd both be impaled on the furniture. She really didn't like that outcome.

She felt her grip slipping. Her hand was covered in sweat and her sneaker was losing traction. She was going to fall either way. She had to trust that Sully had a plan that would work.

"All right," she said.

"On the count of three," he cried. "One. Two. Three."

Lindsey let go. She fell, clenching her body tight for impact. When it came, it was unexpected. Another body hit hers, wrapping around her as it did. The other body, Sully, changed her trajectory, sending them over the backs of the chairs. Together the two of them tumbled onto a thin mattress, which had been dropped onto the hard floor behind the seats.

The impact was a double crunch of Sully twisting and hitting the floor and Lindsey landing on top of him. The wind was effectively knocked out of her, but it was a much better landing than slamming into metal chairs and breaking an arm, a leg or her neck.

She rolled off of him and lay on the ground sucking in huge gulps of air and coughing. Sully was beside her doing the same. He rolled toward her and their faces were just inches apart. He pushed a long blonde strand of hair from her face and looked her over.

"Are you all right?" he wheezed.

"Yeah," she gasped. "You?"

"Never better." He groaned.

He pressed his forehead to hers and Lindsey closed her eyes, thanking her lucky stars that Sully was as quick-thinking as he was.

The cast and crew surrounded them. Beth was the first to ask, "Are you all right? Lindsey? Sully?"

Sully pulled away from Lindsey and gave her a small smile. She got the feeling he would have preferred to stay in their cocoon for a while longer and she realized she would, too.

"We're okay," he said.

He sat up and helped Lindsey to sit up, too. Together they got to their feet and made sure that all of their parts were in fact still working.

The cast and crew broke into applause and Violet came up to them, looking pale with her hand clutched over her chest.

"You scared the life out of me, Lindsey Norris," she said. "What the heck happened up there?"

The crowd went silent and Lindsey felt all eyes on her. She realized that whoever had pushed her was probably in this crowd now, so there really was no use in lying.

"Someone pushed me," she said.

CHAPTER 25

The crowd emitted a collective gasp. Sully immediately put his arm around Lindsey's shoulders and pulled her close as if he could protect her from further harm.

Lindsey appreciated the gesture but knew that whoever had pushed her wasn't going to be put off by Sully's presence.

"But who would do such a thing?" Nancy asked.

"Why Lindsey?" Mary echoed.

"It's obvious, isn't it?" Violet asked. "Someone wants to stop this show."

Murmurs rippled through the crowd like the wind warning of a bad storm on the way.

"First, they murdered Robbie," she said. Violet's

voice shook with outrage. “But we refused to let our fallen thespian down and we persevered.”

She paced around the mattress where Sully and Lindsey stood, still holding one another close, as the adrenaline rush of the near-death experience hadn’t diminished quite yet.

“But this evil person will not rest until they have destroyed our show. Now they are attacking our crew. You must each ask yourself if you are willing to put yourself at risk for our show. I cannot tell you what to do, and I will respect your decision whatever you choose. For my part, I will not be bullied or terrorized into quitting even if I have to play all the parts myself.”

There was a beat of silence.

“I’m in,” Ian said with a raised fist. He was wearing his donkey head mask, so it took a little away from the moment, but it was heartfelt nonetheless.

“Oberon stands with you,” Milton said. He looked at Ms. Cole and she gave him a regal nod. “As does my queen.”

Sully gave Lindsey a bemused look and she shrugged.

One by one, the cast and crew vowed to give the show their all. Not one of them bowed out. Lindsey thought it spoke well of Violet and her considerable talent that they were all willing to risk bodily harm and possible death to put on the show.

"Excellent. Shall we all resume our places, then?" Violet asked. Everyone started to move away when Violet turned to Sully. "Except you two. I want you to take her to the police station and file a report with Emma."

Sully nodded as if he'd been thinking the same thing. Lindsey blew out a breath. She knew they were right, but oh, she couldn't help but feel as if somehow she was responsible.

"I'm so sorry, Violet," she said.

"Whatever for?" Violet asked.

"I'm the one who told Emma that Dylan could be Robbie's son," she said. "And now, I was pushed off of the balcony and I just feel like I'm messing up your show."

"You listen to me," Violet said. She cupped Lindsey's face with her hands. "Dylan is going to be fine. Whoever pushed you, it is probably the same person who poisoned Robbie, which makes it quite clear that it wasn't Dylan. So, see? You did him a favor by having him go with Emma and not be on the premises."

"Violet, who do you think is doing this?" Sully asked. His voice was gruff, and Lindsey knew that meant he was fighting to keep his temper in check.

"I wish I knew," Violet said. "But whoever it is, they have no reason that I can think of to go after Lindsey, unless she just happened to be in the wrong place at the wrong time. Another death would shut the show down for sure, so I have to think that's the motive. Unfortunately, I know several people who would be oh so happy to see the show close before it even opens."

"Buchanan?" Sully asked.

Lindsey studied his face. His jaw was set. His blue eyes were snapping with anger. She was surprised he didn't start cracking his knuckles.

"Now, you listen to me, Michael Sullivan," Violet said as she wagged her finger at him. "Don't you even think about approaching that man in anger. You can't fight him. He is protected by layers of lawyers and weaselly minions, whom you will never get through. He is one of the most powerful men in the country and he's not afraid to use that power. If he decides to make your life a misery, he will. Believe me, I know."

Lindsey looked at her friend and noticed the worry lines that creased the corners of her eyes seemed deeper than they had a few weeks ago. She wondered how many of those wrinkles had been put there by Buchanan, and she suddenly had to fight the urge to crack her own knuckles.

"Do you think he murdered Robbie?" Lindsey asked. The thought that they were all just targets because some billionaire was mad made her a little queasy.

"I hate to think that the father of my baby is a killer," Violet said. "But I can't think of anyone else who would try to cause trouble just because he can."

"You know, if I just happened to run into him, say, on the pier, it could be a total coincidence that he falls into the water," Sully said.

"And he will sue you and you will lose your business," Violet said. "You'll be lucky if they leave you with an oar to a rowboat when his lawyers are through with you."

Sully glowered, and Violet patted his arm.

"Go," she said. "Emma needs to know what happened."

Not waiting for their answer, Violet turned back to the stage, where the cast and crew were doing a mad scramble to begin the dress rehearsal again.

"You ready?" Sully asked her.

"As I'll ever be."

They cut through the lobby and out the front doors. The ticket takers and ushers stared as they passed and Lindsey felt her face get warm. She felt like an idiot, like she was some sort of bad-juju magnet.

How could she not have known someone was up there with her? And who was it? Was it one of these people? They had all been in the lobby when she went into the balcony to look for the headpiece. The thought sent a shiver of fear down her back.

Sully pushed open the door for her and she stepped back out into the brisk evening air. They crossed the courtyard to the sidewalk and then turned left toward the police station.

"Didn't we just get here?" she asked. "It feels like we just arrived and now we're leaving."

"I disagree," Sully said. "In fact, I think I've aged five years since I saw you clinging to the edge of the balcony."

"There is that," she said. They passed under a streetlight. "I really thought I was going to go splat."

He leaned close so that his mouth was near her ear and he said, "I would never let that happen."

Lindsey glanced at him and gave him a small smile. "You saved my life—again."

They were both silent. The last time Sully had saved her life, he had also saved her ex-fiancé. It had caused the end of their brief relationship because Sully believed there was unfinished business between Lindsey and her ex. There wasn't, but he had refused to believe her when she told him that.

"It is becoming a habit," he said. His tone was light but there was so much unsaid between them that Lindsey felt as if each of his words was weighted with the heft of their unspoken expectations.

She pressed her arm against his as they walked. There was so much she wished she could say, but she didn't know how.

" 'Thank you' seems awfully unsubstantial," she said.

They were in front of the police station now

and she paused. She turned to face him. The desire to throw herself at him and plant a kiss of gratitude on him that would make his knees buckle was almost more temptation than she could resist.

"Well, what did you have in mind?" he asked. As if he was reading her thoughts, Sully raised his eyebrows at her.

Lindsey was pretty sure he was offering up a dare. The only question now was whether she was brave enough to take it. She took a half step toward him and he hit her with his patent-worthy grin. Oh, how she had missed this man!

She took another half step toward him and was just about to grab him by the front of his jacket and pull him close when the front door to the police station banged open and out stormed Dylan Peet. He looked furious.

Lindsey took a hasty step back. She had no doubt that Dylan had a few harsh words for her, and she knew she had to accept responsibility for talking to Emma about him.

She felt Sully step up behind her as if to give her backup and she appreciated the gesture but knew that this was her problem.

To her surprise, Dylan didn't even slow down and appeared to be planning to blast right past her.

"Hey, Dylan." Lindsey reached out and grabbed his arm. "Are you all right?"

Dylan glanced up as if seeing them for the first time. He looked as if he was visibly trying to get himself under control.

"Hi, Ms. Norris, Captain Sully," he said. "Sorry, I didn't see you."

"So I gathered. Are you all right?" she asked him again.

Before he could answer, the door to the station opened and his mother came out. Her cheeks were flushed and she looked just as angry as Dylan.

"Dylan Thomas Peet, you will not walk out on me when I am talking to you. Am I clear?" Joanie asked—although it was pretty obvious that there was only one acceptable answer to her question.

Joanie's eyes widened as she noticed Lindsey and Sully standing there, and then her gaze went to where Lindsey's hand was still on Dylan's arm. Lindsey removed her hand, knowing that it looked awkward as she did so.

"Why should I stay and listen to you when you don't care what I want, Mom?" Dylan asked.

Joanie walked toward them. She put a fake smile on as if she wasn't having a scorching fight with her son.

"That's enough," she said in a clipped tone. "We'll finish this discussion in the car."

"What's to discuss?" Dylan snapped. "You told me I have to quit the play. What more do you want to take from me?"

"Dylan, I said we'd discuss it in the car," Joanie

said. Her cheeks were bright red and her mouth was clamped in a thin, tight line.

"There's nothing to discuss!" Dylan exploded. His arms went flying up into the air in a gesture of perturbed exasperation that Lindsey had never before seen from the usually low-key teen. "And do you want to know why?"

Joanie looked as if her eyes were about to pop out of her head. Lindsey was sure Dylan had never spoken to his mother like that—ever.

"Because I'm not going to quit!" Dylan yelled. "I'm doing this for Robbie Vine, and nothing you can say or do is going to stop me!"

CHAPTER 26

Dylan spun on his heel and took off running. Joanie looked as if she'd just been slapped. Clearly embarrassed, she cleared her throat.

"You probably think I'm too harsh, but I had to draw the line. It is just too dangerous at the theater. Look what happened to you. As his mother, it's my job to protect him even if he doesn't like it," Joanie said.

"It's okay, Joanie," Lindsey said. "Of course you just want him to be safe."

"He's my baby," Joanie said. Her voice sounded

strained. She sniffed and then seemed to pull herself together. She gave them a brisk nod and strode toward the parking lot.

"Wow," Lindsey said. "That was tense."

"Dylan is seventeen, almost eighteen," Sully said. "She's going to need to loosen her grip or lose him forever."

"Do you think Emma told him?" Lindsey asked. "Do you think he knows that Robbie might be his father? For that matter, do you think Joanie knows?"

Sully shrugged. "There's only one way to find out."

Together they made their way into the police station.

Emma was pacing in the front lobby when they entered. She didn't look happy.

"Hi, Emma," Lindsey said. "Is everything all right?"

Emma looked at her, and Lindsey could tell she was still deep in thought. It was almost as if she didn't recognize them. She shook her head as if to clear it.

"Yeah," she said. "Things are coming together."

"How did it go with Dylan?" she asked.

"Well, his mother arrived and she clarified a few things. Dylan isn't Robbie's son. She said there is no father listed on his birth certificate."

"So, then it could still be Robbie?" Lindsey asked.

"No," Emma said. "Apparently the mother did not list the father's name on the adoption papers, but she did put down his nationality. He was an American from California."

The phone on the counter started to ring and an officer hurried from the back to answer it.

He spoke a few sentences and then put the receiver to his chest. "It's that same reporter from the London *Times*. Do you want to talk to him?"

"Aw, hell no," Emma said. "Tell him the same thing I said yesterday: no comment."

The officer nodded and went back to the phone.

"If I could just get the press off of my back, I might be able to do some real investigating," Emma said. "I have new appreciation for what Chief Daniels went through when he was in charge."

Lindsey had seen the hordes of reporters swarming the town since Robbie's death. Violet had years of experience dealing with the media, but for Emma it had to be overwhelming to have the mayor breathing down her neck as well as the international media, all wanting to know who had poisoned Robbie Vine.

"I'm sorry," Lindsey said.

"No, it's all right," Emma said. "It comes with the job. So, what brings you two here other than an update on Dylan?"

She glanced between them, and Lindsey felt the same speculation that had been in the eyes of the cast and crew when she and Sully had landed on the mattress.

"There was an accident at the theater," she began.

"It wasn't an accident," Sully corrected her. "Someone pushed Lindsey off of the balcony."

"What?" Emma cried. "Are you all right? Did you see the person? When did this happen, exactly?"

"I'm fine," Lindsey said. "Sully's quick thinking saved me. I didn't see the person. I was hit from behind and I went sailing over the rail but managed to catch myself with a hand and a leg on the edge. I'd say it happened about ten to fifteen minutes after you left with Dylan."

"So, whoever did it knew that I wasn't there," Emma said. She looked at Lindsey and frowned. "Why you?"

"I don't know," Lindsey said. "Violet seems to think it was someone who wants to shut the show down. That whoever it is went after Robbie first and then when that didn't work, he looked for an opportunity to cause another accident that would stop the show."

"She's thinking it might be Buchanan," Sully said.

Emma nodded as if she'd already been thinking the same thing.

"Billionaire CEOs don't take the word *no* very well," Emma said. "And I gather that Violet and

Charlene have shut him out of their lives pretty effectively."

"Would he be that vicious because he didn't get his way?" Lindsey asked. "It seems counter-productive if he really wants a relationship with them."

"It does, but you're talking about a guy who moved his manufacturing business to a third world country where the average age of his workers is eleven," Emma said. "I think he pays them a whopping twenty-five cents a day. From what I gather, he's not exactly a touchy-feely kind of guy."

"No wonder Charlene wants nothing to do with him," Lindsey said. "Still, he must realize that if he wants his daughter in his life, this is the wrong way to go about getting her attention."

"Some people respond very badly to rejection," Sully said. "If he's a bully, he might think that this is the way to get her to respond to him."

"Through fear?" Lindsey asked. "Obviously he doesn't realize that Violet and Charlene are made of tougher stuff."

"*If* it's him," Emma said. "And I can see why Violet suspects him, but there are a lot of people who had it in for Robbie. Despite his brilliance as an actor, his personal life was a train wreck. And as for you being a target, he does have a wife and an ex-girlfriend who might not have been thrilled with his interest in you."

"Maybe," Lindsey said. She refused to look at Sully to see what he thought of this statement.

"I'm going to have you fill out a report," Emma said. "I want it on file in case anything else comes up. I have to be honest: I'm going to be really happy when this play is over."

Lindsey and Sully exchanged a look. Neither said anything but both felt the same.

When she finished her report, Lindsey and Sully went back to the theater. The dress rehearsal ran late and no one left until after midnight. Lindsey was so tired she could barely keep her eyes open.

The sounds of a guitar strumming and a dog howling greeted Lindsey and Nancy as they entered the house. Heathcliff liked to sing along while Charlie played his acoustic guitar. They were all quite sure that Heathcliff fancied himself a rock star. As soon as Nancy turned the key in the lock, however, a black bundle of fur broke off in mid-howl and launched himself at the door. Lindsey knelt down in the foyer and hugged her puppy close. Nothing made the world quite so right as puppy kisses.

Charlie strode out of Nancy's downstairs apartment, carrying his guitar by the neck.

"He's getting pretty good," he said. "He's definitely better than my last lead singer."

"Thanks for watching him, Charlie," Lindsey said.

“No worries,” Charlie said. He held up crossed fingers. “Me and the Heathster are like this.”

“Heathster?” Nancy asked with a frown.

“Yeah, check this.” Charlie knelt down in front of the dog and held up one hand. “Give me five, Heathster, my man.”

Heathcliff patted Charlie’s hand with his paw and they both looked at Lindsey for praise.

“You taught him to high-five?” she asked. “I love it.”

Both she and Nancy tried it and Heathcliff patted their hands with his paw.

“That dog is a genius,” Nancy declared. “Now, I am going to pass out. Good grief, I am done in.”

“Good night,” Lindsey said.

“Good night, Naners,” Charlie said.

He led the way up the stairs, and Lindsey and Heathcliff followed. Charlie went into his apartment on the second-floor landing while Lindsey kept going to her place on the third. As she entered her apartment, she felt the tension in her shoulders ease. She was exhausted but the activity of the night, well, that and her near-death experience had her brain in high gear.

Someone had tried to kill her, or at the very least, cause her some serious bodily harm. Why? To stop the show? Because she had angered someone? She thought about Kitty and Lola. Was Emma right? Could it have been one of them because they didn't like the attention Robbie had been paying to Lindsey?

Her theory that it was Dylan who killed Robbie was shot full of holes and, frankly, she was relieved. She'd hated thinking that Dylan might have had something to do with it.

Then again, was Violet right? Was Sterling exacting revenge on her and the show to destroy her because he knew it would hurt her and Charlene?

And, of course, there was always Harvey Wargus. Lindsey knew he hated both Violet and Robbie. After all, they had ruined him. But if he had murdered Robbie, wouldn't he do the same to Violet? Why would he have tried to harm Lindsey? That made no sense unless he was working for Sterling and Sterling was calling the shots. If it was Sterling, he was apparently more interested in hurting Violet than he was in killing her.

Heathcliff sat on the couch and watched while Lindsey made a cup of decaffeinated tea. She couldn't shake the feeling that she was missing something.

She curled up on the couch, snuggled Heathcliff and sipped her tea. It wasn't long before he rolled onto his side with his head hanging over the edge of the couch and began softly snoring.

Lindsey rubbed his soft fur while she pondered the events of the past few days. She'd missed her little fur baby while she'd been busy with the play, and she made a mental promise that she would take him for a nice long walk tomorrow morning to make it up to him. She was so grateful to have Nancy and Charlie to help her raise her boy.

This made her thoughts shift to Violet. It must have been a huge relief to her to have people like Robbie fill in the father gap while she was raising Charlene on her own. She thought about her visit to Charlene on the island and realized that for her to walk away from work and hole up on her island, she must be taking Robbie's loss pretty hard. She'd certainly seemed awfully grief struck when Lindsey had visited her.

The whole thing made Lindsey want to call her own father and thank him for being there, always, no matter what. Her mother, too, for that matter. They were her foundation. They were academics at a small university in New Hampshire. They had fostered her love of books and learning. Without them, she couldn't even imagine what her life would be like.

She drained her tea and rinsed her cup out in the kitchen sink. She heard her cell phone chime from the holder she'd put it in to recharge.

She glanced at the clock. It was well past midnight. Who would be calling her this late? The hopeful flutter that it might be Sully launched inside of her before she could squash it.

Probably, it was a wrong number. A drunk dialer

making a booty call seemed likely given that the bars were just closing. She glanced at the display, but didn't recognize the number. She figured it was better to answer it than to have them keep calling all night.

"Hello?" she asked.

"Lindsey?" the voice asked. She didn't recognize the male voice.

"Yes," she said. "Who is this?"

"A friend," the voice said.

"I don't recognize your voice," she said. She kept her tone frosty. "Who are you?"

"Someone who cares about what happened to you tonight," the voice said.

Lindsey listened very closely. She thought maybe the voice was familiar, but why wasn't he identifying himself? He had to have something to hide. Was it a reporter who'd heard about her fall? Or worse, was it Sterling Buchanan or one of his minions?

"I'm fine," she said. Her voice dropped from frosty to subzero. "Unless you tell me who you are, this conversation is over."

"I'm glad you're okay," the man said. "Sleep well."

The caller hung up, and Lindsey felt a chill sweep over her body from head to toe as she stared at the phone. She didn't like feeling as if she was being watched, especially when there was a killer out there.

What if the caller had been the same person who shoved her and they were just calling to let her know in a very sick and twisted way that they knew she was fine and that they would be coming for her again?

Okay, that's just stupid, she told herself. Whoever had pushed her was out to stop the show, not harm her personally. It could just as easily have been someone else who got pushed. But then, who was her caller and why had he called?

She went into her recent calls and looked at the number again. She decided to call it. Even if no one answered, if it rolled over to voice mail, she would know who it was. After eight rings, an automated voice repeated the number and asked her to leave a message. She ended the call, feeling even more creeped out than before.

She put the phone back in the charger and then checked all of the locks on her windows and doors. No one was after her. No one was watching her or so she kept telling herself.

She had just happened to be in the wrong place at the wrong time. It could have been anyone who had been up in the balcony. The caller probably was a reporter. When she had told him she was going to hang up, he had probably thought better of pursuing his line of questioning.

Now she knew why Emma had been so annoyed with the media. They really were a ruthless bunch.

She got ready for bed and climbed in between

her flannel sheets. She switched out the light, and a few minutes later she felt the telltale dip on the foot of the bed. Heathcliff made a few circles and then collapsed onto the fleece blanket she kept on the end of the bed just for him.

She had thought she'd drop right off to sleep but no. Every time she felt the woozy, fuzzy lull of oblivion begin to overtake her, a creak or a groan from the house would cause her eyes to snap open and stare into the darkness.

The phone call had put her more on edge than she'd expected. She could hear Heathcliff's even breathing. She tried to mimic him but it was no use. Finally, she reached down and pulled his fleece blanket up the bed until Heathcliff was beside her. She absorbed his dog warmth through her heavy covers and finally, she fell asleep.

It was opening day for the show, and the library was abuzz with nervous jitters. Beth had brought coffee and doughnuts from the bakery in the general store, so all of the staff members were overcaffeinated and oversugared. Lindsey would have loved it if it sped up shelving and check-in, but instead, it seemed to make everyone hyper and unable to stay on task.

"Beth, what are you doing?" Lindsey asked.

Beth had dragged a ladder out of the supply cupboard and was dusting off the tops of the bookshelves.

"Cleaning," Beth said.

"I can see that," Lindsey said. "Let me be more clear: Why are you cleaning up there right now?"

Beth bit her lip and looked down at Lindsey. "I'm nervous. You know I always clean when I'm nervous."

It was true. When they had roomed together during graduate school, Lindsey had found Beth scouring their oven in the middle of the night in an attempt to manage her nerves over final exams.

"I appreciate your anxiety," Lindsey said. "But do you think you could clean something closer to the ground? It won't help the play if you fall and break something."

"Oh, good point," Beth said. She carefully climbed down the ladder. "Speaking of falling, how are you feeling?"

"I'm fi—" Lindsey had been about to say fine, but she thought better of it. "I'm okay."

"Just okay?" Beth asked.

Lindsey studied her friend. Her big eyes were sparkling with bright-eyed optimism. "What are you talking about? What's going on in that brain of yours?"

CHAPTER 27

Nothing. Well, I just thought maybe you and Sully . . ." Beth trailed off. "No?"

Lindsey thought about the moment last night in front of the police station when she had almost kissed him. She felt her face grow warm, but she refused to acknowledge it.

"Why would Sully and I . . . ?" she began but Beth interrupted her.

"Because it was such a daring rescue," Beth cried. "There you were dangling off the balcony. Everyone was yelling and panicking and then Sully came dashing up the aisle with the mattress. He threw it down and then told you to let go and you did. And just like that, he scooped you up and carried you out of harm's way."

Beth clasped her hands together over her chest. She looked like a character right out of a Marion Chesney Regency novel.

"More like he shoved me and then fell after me," Lindsey said. "Not to quibble."

Beth gave her an exasperated look. "That man saved your life."

"I know," Lindsey said. "But that doesn't mean—"

“Oh, come on,” Beth said. She looked like she wanted to strangle Lindsey. “How can it not mean that he still has feelings for you?”

Lindsey stared at her friend. Did it mean that? She was afraid to hope.

“So, are you really nervous for the performance tonight?” Lindsey asked in an abrupt change of subject. “How nervous? Throw-up nervous?”

“Okay, that’s mean,” Beth said. “You know I’m nervous.”

“I’m sorry.” Lindsey sighed. “I just don’t want to talk about Sully and me and whatever is or isn’t happening, which I have no idea about anyway.”

Beth considered her for a moment. “All right, I forgive you. And yes, I’m throw-up nervous.”

“Oh, I’m sorry,” Lindsey said and gave her friend a sympathetic hug. “You’re going to be fabulous. No worries.”

“I don’t know,” Beth said. “Everyone is really wigged out. We don’t even know if Dylan will show up and play Puck or if his parents will forbid it. Poor Violet; if I were her, I’d have had a stroke by now.”

“Violet is a pro,” Lindsey said. “She’ll be okay, and the play will be great. You’ll see.”

“Hey, you two, have you noticed that Milton is always here?” Ann Marie, one of their part-time employees, stopped beside them. She was pushing a truck full of new titles to be shelved.

"Well, he does teach chess club and he's on the board," Lindsey said.

"Oh, I know he's always been a regular," Ann Marie said. "But now, it's the two of them all the time." She jerked her thumb in the direction of the circulation desk.

Ms. Cole and Milton were standing across the desk from each other speaking in low voices, but Lindsey recognized the cadence as being the particular iambic pentameter verse of Shakespeare.

"I imagine once opening night is behind them, they'll settle down," Lindsey said.

"I don't know," Ann Marie said. "Performing in the theater brings people together." She gave Lindsey a meaningful look. "For that matter, working behind the scenes brings people together, too."

"Oh, no." Lindsey shook her head. "Don't you start."

"Start what?" Jessica Gallo, their other part-timer, asked as she joined them.

"Nothing," Lindsey said. She gave Beth and Ann Marie a look. "And I do mean nothing."

Jessica glanced at the three of them and shrugged. Then she turned to Lindsey and asked, "So, as to the rumor about you and Sully getting back together, would you care to confirm or deny?"

"Oh, good grief!" Lindsey rolled her eyes. " 'Upon my tongue continual slanders ride . . .

something, something, I forget . . . Stuffing the ears of man with false reports.' "

"*King Henry IV*," Jessica said. "Nicely played, even though you forgot the middle."

"So, no confirmation then?" Ann Marie asked.

"No," Lindsey said.

Jessica and Ann Marie exchanged a look before they went back to their stations.

"But if there was something to report, you'd tell me, right?" Beth asked. "I mean, I'm your best friend."

"Yes, I'd tell you—maybe," Lindsey said.

"Nice." Beth gave her a withering look.

Lindsey said nothing. Did she still care about Sully? No doubt. But she couldn't deny that she had been surprised to find that her feelings for Robbie had been deeper than she realized.

The thought that she would never see his charming grin or the twinkle in his eye when he teased her made her chest feel heavy and tight. She completely understood why Charlene and Violet had cared so much for him. He was an unstoppable force, much like the character Puck that he had played so well.

"Hello?" Beth waved her hand in front of Lindsey's face. "Are you in there?"

Lindsey shook her head. "Sorry. What were you saying?"

"That Jessica is looking swamped at the reference desk," Beth said. She gave Lindsey a curious look, and Lindsey knew it was because she was usually much more on top of what was happening in the library around her.

"On it," Lindsey said.

She left Beth with a wave and made her way across the large room to the reference area. She was relieved to have something to do to keep her mind off of Robbie's death and Sully and whatever had happened between them last night, which she feared had been a reaction to a near-death experience and not a sign that they were reconciling. Then again, Sully never said how he was feeling, so how could she possibly tell?

"May I help who's next?" she asked as she stepped in behind the desk with Jessica, who gave her a relieved smile.

Mrs. Duncan, who ran the local garden center, stepped up to Lindsey's side of the desk while Jessica helped a man trying to find repair schematics for his car.

"Lindsey, I've got a problem," Mrs. Duncan said.

She was dressed in her usual jeans and a flannel shirt over a long-sleeved T-shirt. She had no makeup on, and her brown hair was shoved up under its usual khaki, wide-brimmed hat. Stray wisps had managed to escape, and she had a smear of dirt on her cheek.

"What's the problem?" Lindsey asked.

"I found this in my compost pile at the garden

center, and I don't know what it is," Mrs. Duncan said. She dug into her large purse and pulled out a glass jar, which she plunked down on the counter.

"Ah!" The man looking for car repair information let loose a high-pitched shriek and he and Jessica jumped back from the desk.

Lindsey looked at the jar. Inside was a snake, a very large, coiled-up black snake.

"Is it dead?" She looked hopefully at Mrs. Duncan.

"Oh, no, it's fine," Mrs. Duncan said. "I snatched him up behind the head and threw him in my pickle jar before he even knew he tumbled out of the bin."

"Is that lid on tight?" Jessica asked.

"Oh yeah," Mrs. Duncan said. "Not to worry. See?" She picked up the jar and gave the lid another good squeeze to show that it had gone as far as it could go.

Both the man and Jessica backed away from the desk, or more accurately, away from the snake.

"I think I have some manuals over here," Jessica said.

"Lead the way," the man said, sounding relieved.

Lindsey suppressed a smile, and turned to Mrs. Duncan. "Do you have a camera on your phone?"

"Yes, why?"

"Next time, you might want to just take a picture and bring that in."

Mrs. Duncan watched Jessica and the man zip around the corner of the stacks away from them, and she nodded.

"Got it," she said. "So, how do we find out what it is and if it's poisonous?"

"It didn't bite you, did it?" Lindsey asked.

She hoped the obvious answer was no and that if it had bitten her, Mrs. Duncan would have gone straight to an emergency room, but sometimes patrons surprised her. A few months back, they'd had a woman in who was obviously in labor, but she refused to go to the hospital until she checked out several baby name books.

"No, I'm quicker than any old snake," Mrs. Duncan said with a laugh. "I just want to know if it's safe to release it at the garden center or if I should set it free out in the woods."

"All right," Lindsey said. "Let's see what I have."

Lindsey did a quick catalog search. "How does a pamphlet called *Snakes in Connecticut* sound?"

"Perfect," Mrs. Duncan said.

The computer indicated that it was in the library's vertical file, which was a large, steel file cabinet full of all sorts of publications just like this one, all filed alphabetically by subject.

"If you'll stay with the snake, I'll be right back."

Lindsey stepped out from behind the desk and crossed over to the expanded reference shelves where they kept the vertical file. She pulled out the *S* drawer and worked her way to Snakes. Sure enough, this pamphlet and two others were nestled in the manila envelope.

She took it out of its file and thumbed through it as she wandered back to the desk. She scanned the introduction and said, "Well, there are only fourteen species of snake in Connecticut and only two are venomous, the timber rattlesnake and the copperhead, so your odds are looking good." She handed the pamphlet to Mrs. Duncan. "The authors, Jenny Dickson and Julie Victoria, included pictures of each."

Mrs. Duncan flipped through the pages. "Aha! That's him." She slapped the pamphlet open on the counter and pointed to a black snake. "What do you think?"

Lindsey read the caption. "Eastern rat snake." She continued reading. "But it says here that it would have a white chin. Yours is solid black."

"Oh." Mrs. Duncan turned the pamphlet back around and scanned more pictures. "Aha! Now I have it." She lifted up the jar and stared at the underbelly of the snake. "Yup, that's it for sure."

Lindsey looked at the picture. It was another black snake but this one was called an Eastern racer. "Bluish belly?"

"See for yourself," Mrs. Duncan said and she held the jar over Lindsey's head so she could see.

"Yes, I think you have it," Lindsey said. "What are you going to do?"

"I think I'll release it in the field behind my house. I don't want it scaring customers out of the garden center."

"Sounds like a plan," Lindsey said. She jotted down on a piece of paper the number for the Connecticut wildlife office. "Here's a number for you to call if you want more advice, and I'd recommend calling them before you release it just in case there is something else you need to know about this type of snake."

"Thanks, Lindsey," Mrs. Duncan said. "You were a big help."

"Anytime," Lindsey said. "But remember, next time a photo will do."

Mrs. Duncan grinned. She put her jar back in her big bag and left the library.

"Is it gone?" Lindsey glanced behind her to see Jessica peering around the corner of the shelves.

"Yes, both the snake and Mrs. Duncan are gone," Lindsey said. "It wasn't poisonous."

Lindsey held up the pamphlet to show Jessica, but she put her hand up and waved her off.

"I don't even like pictures of snakes," Jessica said.

"Oh, sorry," Lindsey said. She went and re-filed the pamphlet. She stopped by the desk on her way back to her office. "Let me know if you need backup again."

"Thanks," Jessica said.

Lindsey took a few minutes to walk around the

library and make sure everything was as it should be. The Internet-accessible computers were full. The cushy chairs in front of the newspaper and magazine racks were also full. There was a chess match going on in the corner, and several families occupied the children's area.

She watched as two kids put on an impromptu show in the puppet theater while several toddlers were using the alphabet area rug to stack up the large oversized foam blocks. When a younger toddler came over and smacked down the towers, the cries of outrage were fierce but the mom of the offending toddler was right there, and she got him to apologize and help repair the damage he'd caused. Lindsey wished that all conflicts could be resolved so simply.

There was no sign of Milton when she passed the circulation desk and went into the workroom, where her office was located. Ms. Cole was assisting a patron with a fine, and if she had any opening-night jitters about the play, they didn't show. Lindsey found herself speculating about Milton and Ms. Cole, but then she shook her head. Curious as she was, it was none of her business.

She went into her office and decided to try and work on her presentation to the Friends of the Library. She wanted them to consider broadening the summer reading program to include prizes for whole families; after all, having parents and grandparents model good reading behavior for kids was probably the most effective way to up the community's involvement, especially if prizes were involved.

She was just going over her proposal when Heather poked her head into the office. "Hi, Ms. Norris. I was just wondering—did Dylan call out?"

Lindsey glanced at her phone. The flashing light that indicated a waiting voice mail was solid, so no messages.

"No, not to my phone, at any rate," she said. "Did you check with Ms. Stanley?"

"Yeah, she said she didn't hear from him, either. He wasn't at school today," Heather said. She hesitated and then added, "His mom called my house last night around midnight, looking for him. She called Perry's house, too. As far as I know, he never went home. I'm worried about him."

"He's not in trouble," Lindsey said. "I mean, Chief Plewicki let him go last night, if that's what's worrying you."

"You know he gets sick a lot," Heather said. "What if the stress of all of this is making him ill?"

"I'll call his mother," Lindsey said, "and make sure he's okay."

"Thank you," Heather said. She looked relieved.

Lindsey took a key out of her top drawer and used it to open the locked file cabinet in the corner. The cabinet contained the library's personnel files, and she flipped through it until she came to Dylan's folder. His phone number and personal information were in it, and she carried it back to her desk.

The very first sheet had his phone number, but she took a second to flip through the file. The form was generic, but she noted that Joanie had stapled a handwritten note to the file. It listed all of the ailments that Dylan was known to suffer from and as Lindsey read through the list, she found herself getting more and more alarmed.

Joanie's list of things that Dylan suffered from included dizziness, nausea and sweats. Lindsey couldn't help but flash on the last few minutes of Robbie's life. He had exhibited all of those symptoms.

Maybe she was crazy, but her hand was reaching for the phone to call Emma before she could stop herself. She reached the front desk. Emma was out. She left a message for Emma to call her. At the very least, she wanted to show Emma the file and see if it struck her the same way it had Lindsey.

She had heard stories of mothers who intentionally harmed their children because the mother was mentally ill; could Joanie be doing that to Dylan? Was his illness real or was his mother causing it? The thought made a cold shiver run down Lindsey's spine. Dylan was missing. She did not have a good feeling about this.

• • •

She was just putting Dylan's file away when Beth stuck her head in the office.

"Lindsey, we're supposed to report to the theater early tonight," she said. "Come on!"

Lindsey glanced at the clock. Where had her afternoon gone?

"I'm coming," she said.

She shut down her computer. Then she grabbed her purse out of the lower drawer of her desk and hopped up from her seat. Maybe she could catch Emma at the theater. Beth was dancing from foot to foot in the doorway.

"Did you want to grab something to eat first?" Lindsey asked.

"No." Beth shook her head, looking pale and ill.

"You're going to be fine," Lindsey said.

"I don't know," Beth said. "Perry and Heather both said that they haven't seen Dylan all day. What if his mother is holding him out? What if there is no Puck?"

"There will be," Lindsey said. "Worst-case scenario, Violet plays Puck. You know she knows all of the blocking and the lines."

"A sixty-something black woman playing Puck," Beth said as they walked out of the workroom. "That doesn't seem odd to you?"

"When you consider that in Shakespeare's time all of the actors were men and they played the female characters? No, it doesn't seem that odd.

Besides, Violet would be great. She can do anything."

"Agreed," Beth said. "But still . . ."

"You'd prefer Dylan," Lindsey said.

"Well, yeah," Beth said.

"Break a leg," Ann Marie called from behind the circulation desk.

"Thanks." Beth grinned.

"Good luck," Jessie called from the reference desk.

"Wow, I feel like a celebrity," Beth said. "Where'd the lemon go? I figured we could walk over together."

"I'm guessing she already left," Lindsey said. "You know how she is about being prompt."

They stepped outside the library. The sky was just beginning to get dark, and Lindsey could smell the distinct scent of woodstove smoke in the air. It was early in the year to be firing up the woodstove, but then, the weatherman on television had said that tonight would be the coldest one yet.

Beth huddled in her jacket. She was mumbling to herself and Lindsey wondered if it was a personal conversation or her lines that she was going over. Either way, she decided not to interrupt her friend and instead took a moment to relish the sight of the leaves on the trees in the park taking on the last of the sun's rays in bursts of orange, red and yellow. Breathtaking.

They continued down the sidewalk to the theater. The closer they got, the more Beth started to hum with anxiety.

The ushers and ticket takers were all in the lobby and they turned when Lindsey opened the door as if they were expecting their first guests.

"Cast and crew," Lindsey said.

Kim Berger, who was in charge of the ushers, nodded at them and waved them through.

"Oh, my god, this is really happening," Beth said. "That's it. I can't do it. I can't go on stage."

CHAPTER 28

"What?" Lindsey grabbed her arm before she bolted.

"I can't do it," Beth said.

Lindsey pulled her through the doors that led into the theater. The lights were down. Crew members were scrambling to make sure the set was just right for the opening act, and cast members were in various states of costume, huddled in dark corners while they went over their lines.

"Stop it," Lindsey said. "You just have a touch of stage fright. Shake it off."

"Shake it off?" Beth repeated. "How?"

"Violet will set you right," Lindsey said. "Come on."

Violet was in front of the stage with a crowd around her. From the looks of it, Beth wasn't the only one panicking. The lighting man was holding up colored gels, the stage director kept testing his headset as if he just couldn't believe it actually worked and two of the cast members were wringing their hands and looking as ill at ease as Beth.

Lindsey would have felt sorry for Violet, but she looked energized in a way Lindsey had never seen before. Her eyes sparkled, her skin glowed and her smile was positively luminescent.

"Cast and crew," Violet called everyone forward. "Gather 'round."

As if they had all been tucked into the woodwork, the players and crew came forward, gathering en masse in front of the stage. Violet's gaze moved over all of them with the affection of a mother.

Lindsey felt someone join the group on her other side, and she glanced over to see Sully, Ian and Mary move in beside her.

"Tonight, we perform for our friend Robbie Vine," Violet said. "Fear not that you aren't ready. His spirit will carry you through your scenes."

Lindsey saw Beth visibly relax beside her. Leave it to Violet to remind them that this was about more than the individual cast and crew members. It was a living memorial to Robbie Vine, and if anyone could elevate their abilities, it was him.

"Now remember," Violet continued, "this is theater. It is a living organism that lives and breathes as you live and breathe, and it will live whether you flub your entrance or forget your lines. Be flexible, help each other and adjust, but most important, live."

An air of calm descended over the group. The doors at the back of the theater opened and in stepped Dylan Peet. A collective sigh of relief swept through the assembled cast, and Lindsey saw Violet smile at the young man.

"Dylan, you're just in time," Violet said. Her voice was kind and she lifted her right hand and waved him into the group. The others parted so that he could stand beside her.

Violet took his hand in hers and gave him what Lindsey thought was a searching look. He answered with a slight nod and she turned back to the group. Lindsey noted that Dylan appeared a little pale but otherwise fine. Maybe she was crazy to think there was a connection to his lifelong illness and Robbie's death. Still, she scanned the theater for Joanie but didn't see her.

"Join hands, please," Violet instructed. "I'm going to lead you through a centering exercise."

Lindsey held out one hand to Beth and one to Sully. She felt the spark she always felt when

Sully's callused hand enfolded hers. She tried to ignore it, but she couldn't deny that her heart rate had picked up considerably.

"Close your eyes," Violet said. "Try to clear your mind of all thought and of all emotion. Just be."

Lindsey had her mind clear for about a nanosecond, but then she felt Sully's thumb running ever so slightly back and forth over the pulse point in her wrist, which felt as if she was being repeatedly hit with gentle zaps of electricity.

Did he know what he was doing? She lowered her head and opened her left eye to sneak a peek at him. Even in the dim lighting, she could see that his eyes were shut and his face was perfectly composed as if he were taking a nap. Ugh!

She resisted the urge to kick him. After their near kiss yesterday, her immunity to him was nil. Even the faint scent of his aftershave was slowly making her crazy.

While Violet spoke of the deep, dark quiet of a forest at night, Lindsey tried to block out the impact Sully was having on her senses. She closed her eyes and shook her head as if she could shake him off just as easily. It was a battle.

So many memories of her months dating Sully filled her mind; lazy Sundays spent sleeping in followed by working on the crossword together, late-night strolls on the beach with Heathcliff running between them while he chased the waves, and days spent sailing in the Sound while he taught her how to harness the wind. The memories filled her mind like his touch on her skin and the scent of him in her nose.

"Now slowly open your eyes," Violet instructed them.

Lindsey heard Violet's voice, but it took her a moment to process the instruction. She really didn't want to leave the happy memories she had spent the past few months squashing down deep.

A chuckle forced her to blink her eyes open and when she did, she was mortified to find that she had pressed her body flush up against Sully's. His face was just inches from hers and he was smiling at her as if he'd been reliving the same memories she had and that he'd been happy to do so.

Lindsey dropped his hand as if it burned and stepped away from him. She saw Ian and Mary exchange a knowing look and she felt her face get hot.

She cleared her throat and fanned herself with her free hand. She turned to Beth and asked, "Is it hot in here?"

Beth released her hand and glanced at her, looking amazingly calm compared to the nervous wreck she had been just moments before.

"No; in fact, I think it's chilly," she said. She narrowed her gaze at Lindsey. "Are you all right? You look flushed."

"I'm fi—" Lindsey cleared her throat again. "I'm good."

"Oh, okay." Beth looked at her suspiciously. Then she glanced across Lindsey and said, "Oh, hi, Sully. When did you get here?"

"A few minutes ago," he said.

Lindsey could hear the amusement in his voice but she refused to turn around and face him.

"Now, if you'll all spread out," Violet instructed. "Let's get centered."

They all took a few steps away from each other. Lindsey made sure she was out of range from pressing herself up against Sully again. Honestly, she didn't think she was ever going to live that down.

"Everyone stand with your feet apart and parallel with your shoulders. Relax your shoulders and drop your head to your chest," Violet instructed. "Let the weight of your head pull your body to the floor, and bend over at the waist."

Lindsey saw Milton across the crowd. As the resident yogi, he was doing the proper breathing and could press his upper body flat against the front of his legs. He'd been coaching Lindsey on this move, but she still had to bend her knees a bit.

With a sigh, she followed Violet's instructions. She inhaled and then slowly released it as she lowered her body forward. Her long, blonde hair covered her face and she could feel the blood rush to her head. At least now everyone would look red in the face. The thought made her laugh, which came out funny given that she was upside down.

"You okay over there?" Sully asked.

She turned and saw that he was bent over, looking red in the face, which only made her laugh again.

"Yep, and you?" she asked.

"I think I might be stuck," he said.

She could tell by the gleam in his eye that he was kidding.

"Now rise slowly from the base of your spine," Violet instructed. "Go slowly, vertebra by vertebra. Raise your head at the very end."

Lindsey rose slowly back up. She could feel everyone rising around her as if they were plugged into a collective energy socket. When they lifted their heads, eyes were bright and smiles were eager.

She looked at Beth and asked, "How are you?"

"Never better," Beth said.

"All right, everyone, we have a half hour to curtain," Violet said. "Let's give them a show they'll never forget."

The group let out a cheer, and everyone made for their various stations. Lindsey glanced at Sully as he headed for the backstage area. As if sensing her gaze on him, he turned around and smiled at her before disappearing behind the curtain.

"What has gotten into that man?" she muttered to herself.

"Lindsey! Mary!" Nancy called them over. "I've got the cast arriving for final costume checks, and we need to make sure we have everything we'll need backstage."

"I'll check the back," Lindsey volunteered.

She left the seating area and went backstage. The curtained area they were using for costume changes was stocked with racks and the necessities for emergency repairs.

Nancy had tacked a list to the wall of costume changes, and Lindsey checked it against the items on the racks to make sure they had everything. Even Ian's donkey head mask was ready to go.

The cast had all disappeared to the green room while the crew scurried to make sure everything was in its place. Violet was on the stage going over the last-minute instructions with the stage manager. They both wore high-tech headsets and would be communicating throughout the show.

Violet left to give the cast a final, quick pep talk before she headed up to the light booth, where she would stay for the remainder of the show. Lindsey knew that Emma had posted an officer up there as well as one backstage, while she planned to patrol the audience. It was hard to believe that a small community theater show was requiring so much security but given that just about everyone in town was going to be here for opening night, it seemed the rest of town could get by with the two remaining part-time officers on duty.

Nancy and Mary joined Lindsey backstage just as the stage manager announced that the audience was being let in. Lindsey felt a nervous flutter start in her belly. She wanted the show to go well for so many reasons: to remember Robbie, to make Violet's directorial debut a success and because so many people had worked so long and so hard on the show.

"Let's peek," Mary said. "Come on."

She led Lindsey and Nancy over to the edge of the curtain, where they watched the ushers seating people. The bottom level was packed and the balcony was filling up fast.

"Good grief," Nancy whispered. "It's a full house."

Lindsey scouted the crowd looking for familiar faces. She glanced up a few rows and saw Charlene sitting with her husband, Martin. Lindsey was glad she had put aside her grief over Robbie's death to see her mother's directorial debut.

Lindsey saw Harvey Wargus sitting a few rows over from Charlene. He looked positively aglow, undoubtedly already writing his scathing review in his mind before the curtain even rose.

She saw many of the library's regulars as her gaze moved over the crowd. Carrie Rushton was there with Dale Wilcox, and they seemed pretty cozy. Also, she was pleased to see Mayor Hensen in the crowd, sitting with his wife on one side and

Herb Gunderson, his right-hand man, on the other.

Lindsey recognized Joanie Peet, wearing a black dress, escorting late arrivals to their seats near the front. She paused and glanced at the stage as if looking for someone. Lindsey suspected she was searching for Dylan. If what Heather had said was true and Dylan hadn't gone home last night, then Joanie hadn't seen him since their argument on the front steps of the police station.

Lindsey felt the world shift under her feet. In her mind, she saw Joanie standing on the front steps declaring that she would do anything to protect her son. She had even said, "Look what happened to you!" to Lindsey after her fall.

But how had she known? If she had left to go to the police station when Dylan was taken for questioning, she would have been gone before Lindsey was pushed and there was no way she could have known that Lindsey almost fell to her death—unless she was the one who pushed her.

Lindsey felt all of the blood drain from her face and her heart beat hard in her chest. As she watched the stout woman move through the crowd, all she could think was that this woman was Robbie's killer. She was sure of it. It all made sense.

She was crazy overprotective of her only child. "Crazy" being the operative word, if she was indeed making Dylan sick to keep him dependent upon her. And if Lindsey was right and Robbie was

Dylan's father then how far would Joanie go to keep her son to herself? Would she have murdered Robbie? But why would she try to harm Lindsey? Then Lindsey remembered complimenting Dylan on his resemblance to Robbie on the stage. Had Joanie pushed Lindsey because she was getting too close to the truth?

Lindsey scanned the crowd, looking for the chief of police. Damn it! Where was Emma?

"Why am I so nervous?" Mary whispered, distracting Lindsey from her search. "It's not like I'm on stage."

"I don't know, but I have to go to the bathroom," Nancy said.

"Now?" Lindsey asked.

"It's okay, we don't have a costume change until Act III," she said. "I'll be right back."

"Places, places everyone," the stage manager hissed. "We're two minutes until curtain."

Nancy slipped out the door to the green room, while Lindsey and Mary moved back to their makeshift wardrobe area. Through a gap in the curtain, they could just see Violet as she strode out onto the stage.

Lindsey wished she could run out and find Emma but she just couldn't do it to Violet. Everyone was here. The show was starting. She'd keep an eye on Joanie and Dylan and tell Emma everything she suspected the first chance she got.

Violet had changed her outfit. She was wearing

her usual long, flowing caftan, but this one was a deep ruby red and shimmered when she moved. Her hair was pulled back and twisted into a topknot, which was held in place by a wreath of pearls. Lindsey thought she looked like theater royalty.

"Welcome," Violet said. Her strong voice rang out across the theater.

Lindsey wondered if Sterling Buchanan was in the crowd and if so, was he wracked with regret that he had let this amazing woman and his equally stunning daughter go? She hoped so.

"Please sit back and enjoy the Briar Creek Community Theater's production of William Shakespeare's *A Midsummer Night's Dream*."

Violet left the stage to thunderous applause. Lindsey felt her entire body tense up and she knew she was waiting for something to go wrong, but nothing did.

The applause dwindled, and the stage manager gave the signal. The curtain drew back and the actors in Scene I, Theseus, Hippolyta and Philostrate, walked onto the stage with the extras who played their attendants. The play had begun.

Nancy rejoined them during Scene I and while they could only see bits of the stage through the curtains that had been drawn back, they could hear the actors delivering their lines. So far, so good.

Scene II introduced Mary's husband, Ian, playing Nick Bottom. Lindsey could tell Mary was nervous: she sat on a stool with her right fist pressed to her lips as if to keep from cheering out loud or calling out instructions. It was hard to say which.

Nancy fussed with the costumes, while Lindsey paced in a small circle with her arms wrapped tightly around her chest. How did people do this for a living? Gah, she was so nervous!

Finally, they heard Ian's character say, " 'Enough; hold or cut bow-strings.' "

The curtain closed. It was the end of Act I. Ian came rushing backstage and grabbed Mary close. He planted a kiss on her before disappearing out the door that led to the green room.

Mary turned to Nancy and Lindsey and grinned. "He was fantastic!"

"Yes, he was," they agreed wholeheartedly.

Intermission wasn't until after Act II, so the stage manager was quickly issuing instructions to the set crew, who were doing a mad scramble to change the set. Lindsey saw Sully pull the ropes that dropped a background of green, woodsy trees over the outline of the previous scene's city of Athens while the other crew members turned the interior of the house into the woods. They had only seconds to get it switched. Sully gave a thumbs-up to the stage manager.

"Places, everyone. Curtain in twenty seconds," the stage manager whispered.

In the dim lighting, Lindsey saw Dylan pacing

back and forth. He looked pale and nervous and she couldn't blame him. She'd rather have fiery torches held to her feet than go out on stage.

Beth appeared. She looked ethereal and lovely in her faerie costume. She gave Dylan's arm a quick squeeze and he gave her a distracted smile in return.

Beth hurried across the stage, as she would enter from the other side at the same time as Dylan when the stage manager gave the signal.

Lindsey heard the stage manager begin the countdown, signaling one of the stagehands to grab the ropes to open the curtain. Dylan stepped back from his position behind the curtain. He removed his tunic and took the wreath of ivy off of his head.

"Dylan," Nancy cried. "What are you doing?"

The stage manager looked at him in shock. Dylan's scene was about to start; he couldn't walk off the stage now. They didn't have anyone else to play Puck.

Lindsey stepped forward; if it was a case of nerves, maybe she could help him. But he hurried around her over to the door that led to the emergency exit. He yanked it open and said, "Now!"

Out of the secret-keeping shadows stepped Robbie Vine.

CHAPTER 29

Lindsey heard the collective gasp sound all around her even as her knees buckled and she staggered, but she managed to catch herself on the clothing rack.

"Robbie?" She called his name with the last bit of breath she had in her lungs.

"Lindsey!" His face lit up at the sight of her, and his grin felt as if it was just for her. He made to stride toward her but Dylan grabbed his arm, stopping him.

"There's no time," Dylan said. He shoved the tunic and wreath at Robbie, who quickly pulled them on.

The stage manager was fiercely whispering into his headset as he stared, wide-eyed at Robbie. Then he gave a nod and cued the curtain to rise.

Dylan pulled Robbie into position. Behind the curtain, waiting for it to finish rising, Robbie glanced over his shoulder at Lindsey and whispered, "We'll talk later."

Then he narrowed his gaze at her. She must have looked a fright, because he muttered a curse and strode forward, shaking off Dylan and the stage manager and ignoring the curtain that was almost all the way up.

Robbie reached out and grabbed her shoulders. His gaze met hers with an intensity that made her heart pound. He hugged her close.

"I'm sorry," he whispered. His voice was a low, gruff growl in her ear.

Lindsey could tell from the emotion in his voice that he meant it and she nodded, not trusting herself to speak. He released her and pushed her hair back from her face.

"I promise I can explain," he said.

"You don't have to," she whispered. "I know. It's Joanie, isn't it? She's your 'killer' and she's been making Dylan ill, hasn't she?"

Robbie nodded.

"And she's the one who pushed me over the balcony because I figured out that Dylan is your son," Lindsey said.

His eyes widened in surprise. Then he smiled and shook his head. "I might have known *you'd* figure it out."

"Robbie, come on," the stage manager demanded.

Robbie gave him a curt wave and then turned back to Lindsey. He planted a swift kiss on her lips. It was electric, shocking her all the way down to her toes. Lindsey didn't know what to say or think or believe but the relief that he was here standing in front of her, alive, made her jump forward and throw her arms around him in a tight hug. Just as quickly, she released him.

"Go!" she said.

Her throat was tight and it was hard to swallow around the lump in it. Robbie grinned at her and turned back around. The stage manager was waving frantically for him to go, so Robbie gave him a mischievous grin and strode out onto the stage.

" 'How now, spirit! Whither wander you,' " Robbie greeted Beth as she came across the stage to meet him.

Beth's jaw dropped and she blinked at him as if seeing a ghost. She wasn't the only one to catch the change in the casting. A low murmur started in the audience and rumbled to a grumbling pitch as Violet's voice came over the intercom to announce, "In tonight's performance, the role of Puck will be played by Robbie Vine."

The crowd noise was deafening. Lindsey looked across the stage at Beth. She seemed frozen, transfixed on Robbie as if uncertain of what to do or say.

Robbie stepped toward Beth and looped his arm through hers as if they were old friends strolling together. He lowered his head and whispered in her ear, and Lindsey saw Beth visibly relax and give him the slightest nod.

" 'Over hill, over dale, Thorough bush, thorough brier,' " Beth began quietly at first, but her voice took on the cadence of the bard's words, growing stronger with each syllable.

"'Over park, over pale, Thorough flood, thorough fire, I do wander everywhere—'"

A screech sounded from the front of the theater, and Lindsey looked out to see Dylan's mother striding down the aisle. A man followed—Joanie's husband, Lindsey assumed—and grabbed her hand trying to stop her, but she smacked him hard, forcing him to let her go. In three large strides, she launched herself onto the stage.

Robbie turned and gave Beth a hearty shove back into the wings, where Sully caught her. Then Robbie turned and caught Joanie by the forearms, stopping her from clawing out his eyes.

"I killed you!" she screeched. She was fighting Robbie's hold with everything she had. "You are supposed to be dead."

"Well, faeries are immortal, you know," Robbie said. His humor sent her into a frenzy, and she began to kick while trying to yank her arms out of his grip.

"He's *my* son!" Joanie screamed. "*Mine.* You can't have him!"

Robbie opened his mouth to say something but Emma and her officers leapt onto the stage. In seconds, they pulled Joanie off of Robbie. She was bucking and kicking, spitting and cursing. Finally, they had no choice but to pin her to the stage floor while they cuffed her.

Lindsey listened in shock as Emma hauled Joanie out of the theater, reciting her Miranda rights as they went. Judging by the silence, the audience was just as stunned.

It had all happened so fast. Robbie was alone on the stage. He took a deep breath and then said, "Faerie, dost thou hide from the creatures of the night?"

Lindsey knew this wasn't in the play. She glanced across the stage where Beth still stood beside Sully. This was her do or die moment. Lindsey saw Beth shudder from her head to her feet. Then she skipped, yes skipped, back out onto the stage. She looked at Robbie and said her next line perfectly. And the play continued straight through until the end of Act II.

Intermission, however, was utter chaos. The noise in the green room was deafening. Lola and Kitty had pounced on Robbie as soon as he entered the room.

"I might have known," Kitty said with a smile while Lola wept all over Robbie's shirtfront.

Violet clapped her hands and the noise dimmed to a low rumble. "As you all can see, the reports of Robbie's death were a bit inaccurate," she said. "I imagine many of you are angry with me for not telling you the truth. I apologize, but the police felt this would be our best way to flush out the person who was in fact trying to kill Robbie."

Lindsey glanced around the room. Several

people did look angry. She wondered if she'd be one of them if she weren't so relieved that Robbie was alive. She searched the crowd for him. He had shaken off Lola and Kitty and was standing in the corner of the room with his arm around Dylan's shoulders.

Seeing them next to each other, Lindsey couldn't believe she hadn't realized sooner that they were related. And she really didn't care what the birth certificate said: there was no question that Dylan was Robbie's son.

"But why?" Lola asked. "Why did that crazy woman want to kill him?"

Violet looked at Robbie. He gave her a small nod.

"We don't know for sure, but judging by what she said on the stage tonight, she was feeling very threatened by Robbie because—" Violet paused.

"Because Robbie Vine is my biological father," Dylan said. "And she was afraid he would take me away from her."

Lindsey saw Dylan's friends Heather and Perry staring at him with their mouths hanging open. He gave them a sheepish smile, and Lindsey realized that Dylan must have known before tonight that Robbie was his father.

"Now, we have five minutes until curtain, and I believe that the show must go on," Violet said. "Are you all with me?"

The cast and crew glanced at one another and

then Ian, with his usual overabundance of enthusiasm, jumped to his feet and raised a fist in the air.

"I'm in!" he shouted. The others joined him, and soon it was a cacophony of shouts and cheers as they all scrambled to take their places for Act III.

"Wait!" Robbie cried out and everyone froze.

Lindsey wondered if he and Dylan had to go to the police station. Maybe the show couldn't go on after all.

Robbie took the ivy wreath off of his head and put it on Dylan's. "I think this Puck should finish the show."

Dylan's eyes went wide. He swallowed hard and said, "But I . . . won't the crowd want to see you?"

"Are you kidding?" Robbie asked. "They're getting to see the debut performance of my son."

Dylan beamed at him. Violet glanced between them and said, "Dylan, are you sure you're up to it? I mean, with your mother being—"

"Crazy?" Dylan asked. "Actually, I've known for a long time."

Lindsey saw a flash of pain cross over his face, and Robbie put his hand on Dylan's shoulder and gave it a reassuring squeeze.

"Well, if you want the role, it's yours," Violet said. "You've earned it."

Dylan grinned at Violet and it was so like his father that Lindsey felt herself smile, too. Charm. The Vine men had it by the bucketful.

"Well, don't just stand here people, let's go!" the stage manager yelled.

The cast and crew filed out of the green room. Violet hooked her arm through Dylan's and was giving him a pep talk while pulling him out of the room. Nancy trailed behind, fussing over the tunic Robbie had just handed over.

When the room was empty, Lindsey found herself alone with Robbie. He lowered his head and looked at her from beneath his long lashes.

"On a scale of one to ten, how mad at me are you?" he asked.

Lindsey crossed her arms over her chest and tried to scowl. She could tell it wasn't her best effort.

"I have some questions," she said. "And then we'll see."

"All right," he agreed. He looked nervous.

"How long have you and Dylan known you were father and son?"

He blew out a breath. "About a year."

Lindsey felt her eyes go wide.

"Dylan got in touch with me through my agent," he said. "I'd been trying to find him for years. One look at the picture he sent and I knew he was for real."

"Why didn't you go public?"

"It was too risky," Robbie said. "You see, when Dylan got in touch with me and begged me to keep it quiet and not let his mother know that we'd found each other, I knew that something wasn't right in his house. I quickly discovered she kept a tight hold on him and if he even hinted that he wanted to find his birth parents or, hell, even go away to college, she would have a hissy fit and then he'd be mysteriously ill. Soon I suspected what you did—that she was making him ill—and I was afraid if I showed up claiming to be his father that she'd do something drastic."

"Oh, my god," Lindsey gasped. She uncrossed her arms and Robbie stepped over to her and put his arm around her shoulders. He pulled her close and rested his cheek against her hair.

"Yeah, it's pretty horrible," he said. "She's a sick woman. I got in touch with Violet, and we rigged the whole thing. I suspect Joanie knew I was Dylan's father. I believe the adoption papers she told Emma about with an American listed as the father are a forgery. I hoped that if I showed up in town, I'd draw Joanie's attention away from Dylan. I was right."

"How did you know to fake your death by poisoning?" Lindsey asked.

"Dylan suspected his mother was poisoning him, and he started sending me samples of his food and drink to be tested," Robbie explained. "At first there was nothing, but then, we found trace amounts of anti-freeze."

"Oh, my god, she could have killed him."

"Apparently, she had it down to a science, just

enough to make him sick and keep him dependent upon her. I took up drinking coconut water, because I knew it would make it easy for her to go for me as the coconut would disguise the sweet taste," he said. "On the night I performed my Oscarworthy death scene, I noticed that the cap on my bottle had been tampered with and one taste, which I spit out, and I knew it was showtime."

Lindsey closed her eyes. She would never forget that horrible night.

"So Dylan knew all along?" she asked.

"Yes, Dylan, me, Violet, Charlene and Emma," he said. "That was it. Oh, and the EMTs who carted me off were actually actors. They didn't know the whole story but they knew enough to give the performance of their lives."

"Wait. Charlene knew?" Lindsey asked.

"Yes, I was hiding out with her on her isl—" Robbie cut off his words and gave her a sheepish grin.

If there was a flashpoint for mortification, Lindsey was pretty sure she would have combusted right on the spot. If he had been on the island, then he had heard her talking to Charlene about her feelings for him.

"You—You—!" Lindsey was so mad she couldn't even think of anything bad enough to say. There was no help for it, she was going to have to turn to the bard for assistance, " 'You peasant swain! You whoreson malt-horse drudge!' "

"Oh! *The Taming of the Shrew*," Robbie said. "Well done."

"Argh!" Lindsey growled.

"Now in all fairness," Robbie said, "there was no way I could have known you'd come out to Charlene's island. And I was so happy to see you that I couldn't tear myself away from the window."

"The *open* window, which means you heard everything!" Lindsey shouted.

"Yes," he said. Then he gave her his most brilliant smile. "And just so you know, I feel the exact same way about you, which is why I called you the night you were almost killed. I just had to hear your voice and know you were okay."

"That was you?" Lindsey asked. "I thought you were a reporter."

"No, it was just me. I hated that I wasn't there to protect you," Robbie said.

He went to pull her into his arms, but Lindsey was having none of it. She shrugged him off and stepped back. She leveled her best glare at him.

"You would do well to remember that when I said those things to Charlene, I thought you were dead!"

She turned on her heel and stomped toward the door.

"Lindsey!" Robbie called after her.

The door swung open and Sully had time enough to step back before Lindsey smacked right into him.

He glanced between the two of them, looked irritated, and then looked more closely at Lindsey. "Problem here?" he asked.

Lindsey glared back at him. "Don't you start."

"What?" He raised his hands. "Nancy sent me to find you. Are you all right?"

"I'm—" She paused, turned back to Robbie and snapped, "I'm fine!"

She pushed past Sully and stomped down the hall to the door that led to the stage. Men! Stupid, stupid men! She was so over them! All of them!

CHAPTER 30

Lindsey watched the rest of the play, huddled in the wings with Nancy and Mary. Dylan was amazing. He owned the stage just as surely as his father had.

The applause of the crowd was thunderous, and when Dylan came in from his last monologue, his face shone with triumph. He had nailed it.

The cast went out for their bows; Robbie joined them for the last one, and the audience, which had already seemed to be whipped into a frenzy, went even nuttier. Lindsey couldn't help but be pleased at the success of the show.

"I am exhausted," Nancy said. "I am going

home and putting my feet up with a nice cup of tea and a book."

"No, you can't," Mary said. "We're all going over to the Anchor to toast the success of the show."

"Raise a glass for me," Nancy said. "I'm going home."

"Tell you what," Lindsey said. "I'll stay and get the costumes sorted for tomorrow's show if you'll let Heathcliff snuggle you while you enjoy your tea."

"Oh, a puppy snuggle," Nancy said with a sigh. "How could I refuse?"

"You, too," Lindsey said to Mary. "Go get your café ready for the party. I'll finish up here."

"Are you sure?" Mary asked her.

Lindsey felt both of the women watching her. "I wouldn't offer if I didn't mean it. It won't take very long, and I'll meet you over there, as I'm sure Beth will want to celebrate. She was brilliant tonight. Now shoo."

Nancy and Mary exchanged a glance. Nancy looked like she wanted to say something, but Lindsey shook her head.

"I'm fine," she insisted. Then she laughed when she remembered barking that same word at Sully and Robbie.

Her laughter must have convinced them. With quick hugs, they both departed along with most of the rest of the cast and crew.

Lindsey had the actors dump their costumes on the bench beside her. She inspected them for dirt, makeup or any tears before she hung them back up on the rolling racks. Dylan was one of the last to stop by.

"Are you off to the party at the Anchor?" she asked.

"No," he said. "Robbie and I are off to the police station. The state investigator has arrived and we're going to give our statements."

"I'm sorry," Lindsey said.

"It's not as bad as you think," he said. "My mother has been very difficult to live with for quite a while now. Maybe now she can get the help that she needs."

"No, I meant I'm sorry that I thought you were the murderer," Lindsey said.

"Um, what?" Dylan asked, his eyes going wide.

"Oh, no one told you?" Lindsey hung his tunic on a hanger. "I figured out that you were Robbie's son and I thought maybe you were angry that he'd put you up for adoption."

"You figured it out?" Dylan sounded impressed. "You are clever. No wonder my dad has such a thing for you."

Lindsey felt her face get hot. "Yes, well," she cleared her throat. "I am sorry I thought that."

"No, it makes sense," he said. "I might have hated him if he hadn't been looking for me and if he hadn't stepped up and helped me when I needed him most."

"I'm really glad you're okay," Lindsey said. She gave him a quick hug. "If you need anything, just ask."

"Thanks, Ms. Norris," he said. Now his face was red.

"Oy, hands off my girl." Robbie's voice broke the awkward moment and Dylan turned with his hands in the air in a gesture of innocence.

Lindsey frowned. "I'm not your girl."

"Not yet," Robbie returned. "You underestimate my tenacity."

Lindsey rolled her eyes. "Go on, both of you. I'll see you tomorrow."

"Is that an offer of a date?" Robbie asked hopefully. Dylan glanced between them and grinned.

"I will see you at the show," Lindsey clarified.

"And then a date?" Robbie persisted.

Lindsey turned her back on him to keep from letting him see her laugh. "Good night."

" 'Good night, good night, parting is such sweet sorrow,' " Robbie said.

"Good night, Romeo," Lindsey said. She didn't turn around but stayed busy shaking out one of the faerie's sparkling tunics.

She heard Dylan's and Robbie's footsteps move across the stage. When she turned back to the final costume on her pile, there was a single yellow rose with red-tipped petals lying on the pile. How had he managed that?

She let out a sigh of exasperation and then lifted it up by its long stem and inhaled. It smelled more citrusy than sweet. She ran her finger over the petals. She knew the yellow rose signified something specific. She thought it might be friendship. She could live with that.

"Lindsey, are you almost finished?" Sully appeared behind her.

Lindsey jumped and let out a yelp. She held the rose in one hand and put the other over her chest.

"Gah! You scared me!" she said. "Yes, just one more costume to go."

"Sorry," he said. He glanced at the rose in her hand. "From an admirer?"

Lindsey shrugged. She really did not want to have this conversation.

"It seems like both of the Vine men have a crush on our fair librarian," Sully said.

"Oh, I doubt that," Lindsey said.

Sully stepped close and looked at the flower. "You know what that rose means, don't you?"

"Friendship?"

"Just yellow, yes, but this one has red on the tips," he said. His gaze met hers when he said, "That means falling in love."

His voice was low, almost gruff, and Lindsey felt as drawn to him as she had the very first day she'd seen him. But then, she remembered that he'd dumped her and according to his sister, there were issues in his past that he hadn't shared. She took a self-conscious step back. She just wasn't willing to get squashed again.

She put the rose aside and picked up the last costume to be hung. She inspected it more thoroughly than most in an effort to appear casual.

"How does a boat captain know so much about roses?" she asked. She was pleased that her voice came out light and teasing and not as knotted up as she was feeling inside.

"Simple. He looked it up before he chose it for you," he said.

Lindsey whirled around to face him, but he had turned away and was walking out in the same direction Robbie and Dylan had taken.

"Lindsey, come on!" Beth cried as she hurried in from the side door. "Everyone is gone. We have to get going or there won't be a seat left at the Anchor."

Lindsey glanced from the rose to the stage where Sully had disappeared to the door where Beth was dancing from foot to foot. She had a feeling her life was about to get very complicated.

CHAPTER 31

"Who chose *Pride and Prejudice* for this week's crafternoon?" Lindsey asked. Although she had read the novel a million times, it had never struck her quite as poignantly as it had this time.

"I did," Mary said. "What's the matter? Didn't you like it?"

"No, it was fine," Lindsey said. "I suppose it was a good transition from Shakespeare."

"It certainly was," Violet La Rue agreed. "Although you must have noticed how they both used the classic love triangle to move their plots forward."

"Yes, I noticed," Lindsey said. Her tone was dry and she watched both Mary and Violet duck their heads back over the cards they were making so as to hide their laughter. The shaking of their shoulders gave them away, but Lindsey opted not to call them on it.

"What's the matter, dear?" Nancy asked. "Is art reflecting life a little bit too closely for you?"

Lindsey could tell by the sparkle in Nancy's blue eyes that she was teasing. Still, she didn't have to enjoy it so much.

"I have no idea what you're talking about," Lindsey lied.

"Oh, come on," Beth said. "Everyone knows your life has become an isosceles."

She entered the room, wearing different bright-colored sneakers on her hands and feet, cat ears and a long tail, and she had whiskers drawn on her cheeks.

"*I Love My White Shoes* for story time?" Lindsey asked.

"You just can't beat Pete the Cat," Beth said.

She shook the sneakers off of her hands and took off her ears and tail. She had a canvas tote with her card-making supplies, and she sat down next to Mary at the end of the table.

"So, what did I miss?" she asked. "Have we gotten to the part where we all agree that Colin Firth was the best Darcy ever?"

"We just started, and I thought we were discussing the book, not the film," Lindsey said.

She reached over the card she was working on and took a finger sandwich off of the tray Nancy had brought. She had run with the tea idea, so it was finger sandwiches, hot tea and raspberry petit fours.

"Who do you think would make a better Darcy," Charlene asked, "Sully or Robbie?"

Lindsey, in the middle of an inhale, began to

hack and choke. Violet pounded her on the back while the others watched anxiously.

"Neither," Lindsey said. "If one is Darcy then the other would be Wickham, and I don't think that either of them could be— Ugh, did you know that Mark Twain is said to have felt an 'animal repugnance' toward Austen's writing?"

They all looked at her.

"What?" she asked.

"That wasn't even an attempt at a smooth transition," Mary said with a sad shake of her head. "It was pathetic."

"Do you think we'll ever have a book club meeting where my personal life is not a part of the discussion?" Lindsey asked.

The others all exchanged a look and as one they turned back and said, "No."

Lindsey sighed.

"Oh, look," Beth said. She was pointing at the window.

They all glanced out. A floral delivery truck had just arrived, and the driver was carrying a gorgeous bouquet of flowers into the building.

"I wonder who they're for," Mary said.

"My money is on Lindsey," Charlene said.

"Yes, but is it from Sully or Robbie?" Nancy asked.

"I'm betting on Sully," Violet said. "Robbie's flowers are always huge; not necessarily pretty, but definitely huge."

"Other people work here, you know," Lindsey said. "Those could be for anyone."

"Uh-huh," Beth said. "Come on, let's go see."

En masse, they hurried from the crafternoon room, down the hall to the main part of the library.

Ms. Cole was working the checkout desk and she glanced over her glasses at the deliveryman. She was wearing shades of green today, from her vibrant green blouse to her dark-green slacks. As far as her usual color schemes went, this one was actually not too bad.

The crafternoon group peeked around the door frame. Lindsey hung in back. She wasn't sure she was up for the embarrassment of flowers being sent to her at work. She loved her friends, but they would overanalyze and pick apart any note that came with the flowers and probably the meaning of the flowers themselves.

"May I help you?" Ms. Cole asked the deliveryman.

"I hope so," he said. He put the vase on the counter and checked his clipboard. He pushed back his baseball cap and scratched his head. "It says here that these flowers are for a person called Titania?"

Ms. Cole straightened up and blinked at him. "Excuse me?"

"It reads, 'For my Titania. Ever yours, Oberon.' See?"

He turned the clipboard so that she could see it, and Lindsey saw a tiny smile curve the corners of her mouth up.

"I'll sign for those," Ms. Cole said. "I know who they belong to."

"Well, thank goodness one of us does," the man said. He took the clipboard back when she finished and turned and strode out of the building with a wave.

The crafternooners all tiptoed back from the doorway and then hurried back to their room. Lindsey sank into her chair while the others dished about this stunning turn of events. Milton and Ms. Cole; who could have seen that coming?

Lindsey stared down at the card paper in front of her. She felt a smile tip her lips, not only because the group was not talking about her love life for a change but because seeing Ms. Cole get flowers from an admirer gave her hope.

" 'Do not be in a hurry; depend upon it, the right Man will come at last . . .' " Nancy said.

Lindsey raised her head and noted that Nancy was reading from a slender volume that did not look like *Pride and Prejudice*.

"What was that?" Beth asked.

"A letter from Jane Austen to her niece Fanny Knight," Nancy said. "It's sound advice, if you ask me."

As the two single members of the crafternoon group, Lindsey and Beth exchanged a glance.

"Works for me," Beth said.

"Me, too," Lindsey agreed. "After all, if you can't trust Jane Austen in matters of the heart, who can you trust?"

The Briar Creek Library Guide to Crafternoons

A crafternoon is simply a book club that does a craft while enjoying some good food and discussing the latest book of their choosing. To give you a starting point for your own crafternoon, here is a reader's guide to Jane Austen's *Pride and Prejudice*, a sample card-making project and a recipe for petit fours, which go nicely with Jane Austen and a hot cup of tea.

Readers Guide for *Pride and Prejudice* by Jane Austen

1. Despite being published two hundred years ago, in 1813, *Pride and Prejudice* continues to captivate readers. Why do you suppose this is? Because Austen captures a specific place and time so well? Or because her characters are still accessible?

2. Pride and prejudice are the flaws that the lead characters exemplify. Who is proud in this story and how does it manifest? Which character demonstrates prejudice? How does it impact the story?

3. The appeal of the heroine Elizabeth Bennet is frequently considered to be her strong personality, demonstrated by her sharp intelligence and fierce loyalty. Even though her sister Jane Bennet is described as being more beautiful and of an easier disposition than Elizabeth, it is Elizabeth that Mr.

Darcy loves. If this were a modern novel, given that society is more obsessed by appearances these days, would it be Jane that Mr. Darcy fell for? Why or why not?

4. Mr. Darcy attempts to break up the romance between his friend Mr. Bingley and Jane Bennet. Was he right to interfere if he genuinely believed that Jane did not love Bingley? Why or why not?

5. At the initial meeting of Elizabeth Bennet and Mr. Darcy, they take an immediate dislike to one another but naturally end up falling in love. What modern-day books, novels and television shows use this same story arc? Why does it work so well? What is it that makes it so appealing?

Bonus (could be used for a door prize): Mr. Darcy's first name is only mentioned twice in the novel. What is it? (Fitzwilliam)

Card-Making Idea

A simple but pretty collage card to make for the holidays.

Supplies:

- Card stock or pre-folded blank cards in the color of your choice and envelopes
- A variety of decorative papers from wrapping papers to magazine clippings or photographs
- Acid-free glue stick or hot glue gun or adhesive spray
- Scissors
- Any embellishments you want to add—raffia, ribbons, stamps, buttons—be creative

How to:

Lindsey is not a natural-born crafter, so she does a lot of trial and error on her cards. In making a card for her parents, she printed several copies of the most recent family photograph that included her parents, her brother Jack and herself. She decided to use a red card for the base then she chose a piece of green paper that she crumpled up into a tight ball and then smoothed out to give it texture. She trimmed the green paper so that it was a quarter of an inch smaller than the red card and then centered it on the cover of the card and used the glue stick to fasten it in place. Next she took her photograph and glued it to a red piece of card stock. She then trimmed the red card stock so that it framed the photograph by a quarter of an inch. Then she glued the photo on top of the green paper on the front of the card, making it just a little off center. In the extra space on the cover she made a bow of natural-colored raffia and used a glue gun to fasten it in place. To finish it, she put a shiny green button in the center of the raffia bow. Once dried, the card was ready to send to her parents.

Recipe

Publisher's Note: The recipe contained in this book is to be followed exactly as written. The publisher is not responsible for your specific health or allergy needs that may require medical supervision. The publisher is not responsible for any adverse reactions to the recipe contained in this book.

NANCY'S RASPBERRY PETIT FOURS

½ cup butter, softened
1 cup sugar
1 teaspoon vanilla extract
1⅓ cups all-purpose flour
2 teaspoons baking powder
½ teaspoon salt
⅔ cup of milk
3 egg whites
Seedless raspberry jam

Glaze:

32 ounces confectioner's sugar
⅔ cup of water
2 teaspoons orange extract
Garnish with candy beads or frosting rosebuds

Preheat oven to 350 degrees. Grease a 9-inch square baking dish and set aside. In a large bowl, mix together the butter, sugar, and extract until fluffy. In a medium bowl, whisk together the flour, baking powder, and salt; slowly add to the wet mixture, alternately adding with the milk until well blended. In a small bowl, beat the egg whites until they form soft peaks then gently fold into the batter. Pour batter into the baking dish and bake for 20–25 minutes until a toothpick inserted near the center comes out clean. Once cake is completely cooled, cut the cake into 1½-inch squares. Remove the squares from the baking dish and set on a large cookie sheet about two inches apart. Once on the cookie sheet, slice each square into two layers and put a teaspoon of raspberry jam between the two layers.

In a large bowl, combine the glaze ingredients. Beat until glaze is a smooth consistency. Now pour the glaze evenly over the tops and sides of each cake square. Make sure they are coated completely. Garnish the top with candy beads or frosting rosebuds or the garnish of your choice. Allow to dry. Makes 3 dozen.

Center Point Large Print
600 Brooks Road / PO Box 1
Thorndike ME 04986-0001 USA

(207) 568-3717

US & Canada:
1 800 929-9108
www.centerpointlargeprint.com